GROUND LEVEL:
NEVER GIVE UP HOPE

Rufus Young Jr.

Gotham Books

30 N Gould St.
Ste. 20820, Sheridan, WY 82801
https://gothambooksinc.com/

Phone: 1 (307) 464-7800

© 2024 *Rufus Young Jr*. All rights reserved.

No part of this book may be reproduced, stored in a retrieval system, or transmitted by any means without the written permission of the author.

Published by Gotham Books (December 6, 2024)

ISBN: 979-8-3303-3845-0 (P)
ISBN: 979-8-3303-3846-7 (E)

Because of the dynamic nature of the Internet, any web addresses or links contained in this book may have changed since publication and may no longer be valid.

The views expressed in this work are solely those of the author and do not necessarily reflect the views of the publisher, and the publisher hereby disclaims any responsibility for them.

DEDICATION

This book is dedicated to Rufus and Lura Young.

CHAPTER 1 "THE RED"

Ty (Tie) woke with a start; his senses alerted him just minutes earlier to wake up.

But at that time, he was once again stuck in that pesky dream.

And knowing today, that dream would turn into reality…. today he was going to catch "The Red".

Although he was not bread for hunting, his senses were keen and sharp. We'll just say, sharper than any Black Labrador Retriever that was raised in the inner City.

Ty walked to the street in front of the house, checked his hunting techniques to ensure he knew exactly where his Master was headed, and started after him.

It was still dark out, the morning sun hadn't come up yet, the temperature was a perfect 76 degrees in Tampa, Florida…All plant life seemed to be in bloom, the crisp morning air carried the scents of the oaks, the Spruce, the Ferns, the Fruit trees, and over thirty different varieties of flowers, the slightest breeze can bring forth the earths finest perfumes, as only the early mornings can produce.

Ty was three years old now, and had made this trip many times, but seldom had he made it without his master, on those rare occasions that he over-slept, it was always the same dream at fault, catching "THE RED'.

Now Ty was at the farthest point that he'd ever made it alone.

He was standing in front of Busch Blvd., an eight lane Highway of never-ending traffic, getting across had been proven Impossible in the past, and now it seems as if nothing has changed.

He knew his Master was in that building directly across the highway, with no hope of making it to the other side, he began barking as loud as possible.

Rudy Clayton worked as both full and short order cook at the "Two Cronies Restaurant" on Busch Blvd.

This morning he's also doing all the prep work, he's usually the first one to arrive.

Rudy is a 29-year-old high school grad, with three Children and an ex-wife, all four seem to hate him, for reasons not known to him.

For the last few years, he had been forced into a downward spiral by the child support system, he was 22 years old the last time he had received an income tax return, the only landlord that would except the meager wages he made at the Two Cronies restaurant, were his parents.

This morning, he arrived at 3:30 am, picked up his to-do list, put on an apron and went to work.

The list really left no time for slacking, it required 4 different Salads, 200 Cookies, 8 dozen boiled eggs, and 2 cases of fresh, hand cracked eggs... that's 60-dozen hand cracked eggs.

Rudy decided to start with the sixty dozen... He set the radio to 95.7. The Steve Harvey morning show was on, Steve Harvey was going on about the sad state the American job market had fallen to.

He touched on the cause of the recession,

Rudy stopped cracking eggs when Steve asked for a moment of silence, for a squad of American Soldiers who were killed by a roadside bomb, the eldest was 23 years old.

As he adhered to the moment of silence, a familiar sound caught his ear.

I'd know that bark anywhere, he said, while heading to the door, he maneuvered his way across the 8 lane Highway to get Ty, then led him back across.

Rudy cooked up a bowl of eggs, scrambled with bacon and sausage, then he mashed in some buttermilk biscuits, and a bowl of milk.

It smelled so good; Ty could hardly contain himself.

Rudy put the bowl down in front of him, he went and sat on a milk crate by the door.

Instead of going straight for the food, Ty went over to Rudy.

"I know you're hungry, "said Rudy, go eat.

Ty went for the bowls, ... before Rudy went back inside, he said, ...I have a hard time crossing that Highway myself.

Ty was escorted back across Busch Blvd, after he finished his meal.

Go straight home Ty, said Rudy, get some rest... We're going hunting today, we may even see that Red Fox you've been chasing lately.

All Ty heard was "THE RED", he bolted out, making a circle around his master, frantically looking around, checking nearby brush and nosing the air.

GO HOME Ty, yelled Rudy.

Ty took off toward home, but instead, he stopped by the house that he stopped at every morning.

Chantell saw Ty coming up the front walkway, she yelled, Tootsie, you got company.

With that, a short ball of fur came scampering to the door, all that could be seen through all the fur, were those big eyes, and a tongue.

Chantell opened the screen door so Ty could come in, Tootsie wasn't allowed outside, so Ty and Tootsie played on the screened in porch, while Chantell got ready for school.

No one ever saw much of Chatell's mother, there was no in- house Father.

Chantell was casually pretty, with a beautiful brown complexion, she was very feminine, and she wore a micro- braided hairstyle that fell beautifully around her shoulders.

Her thin frame had just begun rounding out the shape of womanhood.

She was eighteen years old, and although she didn't have a boyfriend, she was no longer a virgin.

Hers was yet another family, feeling the pinch from the recession... As she walked out the door, she turned and said... Hey, you coming?

Ty jumped across Tootsie and headed for the door.

He walks Chantell to the bus stop every morning, after she gets on the bus, he waits at the convenience store across the street, where Miss Louise runs Blimpie Sandwich shop, he walks her home also, she loves Ty's company, she talks to him nonstop, from the store, and all the way home, and being that she lives next door, also made it a nice walk for him.

When Rudy finally showed up, it was in the afternoon, he was accompanied by a co-worker named Cole Manning.

Working together had also brought them together as friends, Cole's pickup truck was always reliable, and he was also Rudy's main source of transportation.

As soon as they came to a stop in front of the house, Ty came running, he was hyped up and raring to go.

As Rudy got out of the truck, Ty jumped in the front seat and sat close to Cole.

Rudy went into the house, he returned with a Pellet rifle and a shoulder bag.

Within an hour, they were rolling into a wooded area, just north of Lutz Fl. A stone's throw away from the Pasco County line.

They only used pellet rifles for hunting, because they only hunted small game, Rudy carried a .38 revolver, just for the unexpected.

They began walking down a trail, due to the heavy rainy season the path had begun to grow over, the woods were lavishly green and alive.

Cole stood 5 foot 10 inches tall, 170 pounds, brown hair and eyes, with an all-Florida tan, he was handsome enough to juggle women around the 7 or 8 range rather constantly, and if he put his mind to it, he can hold onto a 9 for a matter of months.

At age 26 he was a country boy who was laid back and sure about life, his ancestors were more than likely abolitionists, you know, the ones who helped with the underground Railroad, he knew how to have a good time too.

They followed Ty in single file for a while. But it wasn't long before Ty was more than 25 yards ahead of them.

I heard the conversation you had with Tony before you left work today, said Cole, I don't know why you take that shit from him.... I know I wouldn't.

I have to man, said Rudy...the job market is all but shut down for some of us, and he seems like he's trying me, he's looking for an excuse to either, cut my hours, or fire me.

You're a better man than me, said Cole, I've heard some of the things that he says behind your back, and I've seen some of the things that he does behind your back, I'm not gonna tell you, because you wouldn't be able to let it slide.

He almost called me the N word right in my face, so I can imagine what goes on behind my back.

Rudy is 5 foot 7 inches tall, 175 pounds, dark skin, wears a bald fade, built for outdoors, a very agile Georgia boy.

"Look, said Cole...they're all full of shit, I'll prove it to you when we get back to the truck.

An hour later they were deep in the woods, they walked along in the cool shadows of the trees.

The sun managed to break through the trees here and there, the air, crisp and soothing.

Rudy spotted Ty about 30 yards to their left, as he stepped into the sunlight, on the crest of a mound.

Rudy squinted his eyes to make sure that it was him.

Ty was in a semi-crouch, slowly creeping up on something on the other side of the mound.

At that moment, someone else might have mistaken Ty for a black Panther, his coat was glossy black, he had grown muscular, and Ty looked, and actually put you in the mind of, a very dangerous animal.

Then he crouched all the way down and laid quietly, Cole and Rudy got the hint, and made their way quietly over to either side of the mound.

In a low growth clearing, Rudy counted 12 Rabbits grazing, the females always stay close to each other, while the males spread out to sense danger, the males were the targets, the females were needed to make more rabbits.

Almost immediately, he heard Cole's air rifle go off, Rudy took aim and fired, all the rabbits scattered, two lay behind fighting for life, Ty ran out in front of them forcing them in a direction that crossed in front of Cole and Rudy.

They fired again and again... when the smoke cleared, they had three males, Ty brought them in one by one.

How many are we taking out of here today? asked Cole.

"These will have to do, said Rudy...that's about all the time we have for hunting, we need to go check on the stash NOW!

They headed back in the direction of the truck, they came upon an area dense with tall foliage.

They squeezed through, being careful not to leave anything that resembled a path.

In the center of this thicket, a crop of Cense-Mia was being grown.

Now at chest level, there were 30 standing plants, 10 had been washed down by rainwater, lying with roots exposed.

Rudy went to work replanting and pruning, Cole went back to the truck to get the rabbits prepared, and on ice.

When he returned, he had a blue booklet. Rudy recognized the book on site.

This is the proof, a recipe book, that's the book from the kitchen manager's desk drawer, said Rudy.

Yea, said Cole, I take it you've never read this book before.

I can read it when I become the day manager, he replied. Check this out, said Cole.

KITCHEN CREW

Kitchen Managers	2
Head Chefs	1
Chefs	2
Short order Cooks	2
Prep-Cooks	2
Dishwashers	3
Bus boys	2
Waitresses	4

1. The Kitchen Manager must ensure a full staff daily.
2. The Kitchen Manager position is— "White only"
3. The Head Chef position is------------ "White only"
4. Short Order Cook position can carry 1 Negro, if qualified.
5. "No Negros allowed in the dining area"
6. All other positions open to Kitchen Managers approval.
7. All alternate's phone numbers must be posted.

Rudy began to read what looked like a regular work staff list, but as he went on, he saw.... what Cole saw, and it shook him.

He dropped the book, it lay on the ground before him, still open, and on the same page.

He looked Cole in the eye, and at the same time, pointed at the book.

What the.... what.......What the "Fuck" is that, he yelled.

Cole heard the slight tremor in his voice, as Rudy struggled to push back the unclean emotion that was washing over him.

I thought you should know who you're working for, said Cole, I know for the last couple of years, you've been striving, full force, toward that Kitchen Manager position...... it's not gonna happen Rudy, not there.

Tony told me today, that big Mike was going to start training "Me", for the Kitchen Manager position, I was like… what about Rudy, and this asshole says, Rudy's not Managing anything in this kitchen, and he showed me what he called "The Law Book"

I took this book to Fuckin burn it, I just wanted to make sure you saw it first.

Rudy's expression was blank as he looked at the backside of his hands, the color of his skin.

The same shit, over and over again, he said, as he sat on the ground, pulled his arms around his legs, and lay his head on his knees to calm himself… incident after incident passed through his mind, from the way the police react to him, the way he's followed in stores, the way employers only see him in cheap labor positions, everything that has been his experience, told him that this was a calculated attempt to keep him at that place he liked to call "GROUND LEVEL".

To outsiders those who live at ground level, will never own anything, and the things you rent, will be meager, the area you live in will be required to have broken bottles in the street, at uncertain intervals', more drunkards than what one would call normal for any given area.

Another requirement is a steady flow of drugs that are piped into our communities for destabilization purposes, this automatically attracts dealers, thieves, prostitutes, and confusion, also for your enjoyment, you'll have several liquor stores and cutthroat bars, pawn shops, and lived in abandoned houses.

To others, Ground Level is nothing more than a state of mind.

A place where no one's above you, no one's below you, usually at Ground Level, "one has nothing to lose"

I gotta fight back somehow, said Rudy.

I'll go finish the plants, said Cole, you can stand guard. Rudy came to his feet, with renewed vitality, everything was a little more serious now.

He was going to be just like them, this was looking like a united Caucasian system, and he was one of their main targets.

From here, every move will be a calculated step.

He stood watch while Cole replanted and pruned the rest of the plants.

The harvest was only 40 days away.

The Marijuana harvest was the only bright spot left' that he could see, and he didn't want anything to go wrong here.

The hunting was only a cover for anyone who might happen upon them while they were working their secret nursery.

Rudy scanned the area thoroughly, a slight movement caught his attention, and his eye's focused in on that little red fox.

The fox was sitting in a low grass clearing, only a stones throw away, he wasn't under the cover of trees, he was out in the open' looking right at them.

"Ty", come here boy, said Rudy softly.

Ty was stretched out, soaking up some sun over closer to where Cole was working.

Ty came quickly' as Rudy got down on one knee and put his arm around Ty's neck, he cupped his chin and pointed his head directly at the fox.

It took Ty a few seconds to see him, but when he did, his tongue snapped back into his mouth and his whole body tensed........ "THE RED"

Go, said Rudy, and Ty was off like a shot, the fox turned and dashed into the woods, they ran until Ty's bark could barely be heard.

Sounds like a mile away, said Cole.

"Yea", said Rudy, he just might catch him today.

"Yea right", said Cole, hey I'm all finished here, and how bout a product check.

Cole pulled out a blunt, which was bigger than any blunt should be, he pulled it sideways under his nose' as he sniffed it's pungent aroma.... a big smile came across his face.

This is gonna be good.

Ty was closing in on "THE RED", he'd surely catch him today.

The fox ran into some thick brush, Ty didn't go through, being in was just a small thicket, Ty ran around to cut him off, knowing "THE RED", would run right though, Ty waited, "THE RED", stayed inside the thicket.

Ty ran all the way around to make sure he hadn't come out, .. he hadn't, Ty couldn't wait any longer, he jumped over into the center of the thicket, hoping to land right on top of him, now inside, he couldn't find "THE RED", anywhere.

"THE RED", was gone, "but where", Ty sniffed around until he found a hole, he sniffed again.

Fresh air was coming through, THE RED's scent was in the hole but he wasn't.

Obviously, the fox hole went in and out, that means there's another exit.

Ty ran out of the thicket and looked around, THE RED was lying on his belly, with his front paws crossed, waiting.

Ty was infuriated!

THE RED jumped up and ran again, Ty took up the chase once more.

They came to a small creek that ran through the woods; it was only six feet across.

It was easy to jump because the other side was four feet lower than the side they were jumping from.

THE RED made the jump, so did Ty.

THE RED ran along the bank of the creek, he was headed for a tree branch that had fallen, the broke limb went down from the tree, all the way to the ground, it wasn't a steeply sloped limb, but it was only about 8 inches in diameter, he ran up the limb until he was just above the opposite, high side bank, and jumped back across the creek, he ran back along the bank of the creek to where they first jumped from, and waited.

Ty mocked THE RED, did everything he did, the small tree limb let him know of a balance problem that all at once had come up.

None the less, he made the jump and dashed after him.

THE RED jumped the creek again and headed for the same branch, and repeated what he'd done the first time, so did Ty.

As Ty stood wobbly on the branch, he looked and saw THE RED, sitting and waiting.

He realized that as soon as he makes this jump, THE RED will once again jump back across and head for the same limb, and this will go on all day.

Ty turned and went back down the branch and along the bank to where THE RED was sitting, directly across the creek from him.

THE RED was smiling, Ty was pissed.

The jump was easy from where THE RED was. But from where Ty was, the jump would be impossible.

The only way to get back across in this area is that tree limb.

He figured the only way he would be able to catch THE RED in this vicious circle, would be with sheer speed.

Out run him, and catch him at some point in the circle.

Now empowered with a new plan, Ty took off, he ran full out: up the tree limb, he turned and jumped.

This is when he remembered the balance problem, yes.... he was off balance.

The jump was short, he hit the side of the bank, clawing for something to hold on to, on top' there was nothing.

Ty fell backward into the water; he was being pulled down stream by the current.

He was trying to reach the lower bank, but it was a constant battle just to keep his head above water, with no ground underneath, he was at the mercy of the current.

He felt himself getting weaker and wearier, he was exhausted, he'd just concentrate on using as little power as possible to keep from going under.

Thats when he heard the frantic yapping' coming from the bank, it was THE RED, he was jumping around and yapping like crazy, when Ty saw this, panic gripped him, he recognized this as a danger warning, now he could feel it, he sensed danger close by.

He pulled out all his reserve strength and headed in the reds direction.

He fought the current to where the yapping was louder.

Underwater, his foot hit ground; he clawed at it and found there was a bank shelf, beneath the water there.

He pulled himself up and out of the water with the quickness of a man on fire.

He ran up the bank and hunkered down low, laying his body flat on the ground.

He looked over to his right, and spotted the red, he was hunkered down also. Ty relaxed a little, because he knew he hadn't been seen, if he had been, for one, the red wouldn't still be here, and secondly, he'd be running for his life right now.

Ty peeped over the edge of the bank, and there they were, swimming slowly upstream, in stealth mode, no sound, nothing visible but their eyes.

Alligators' a dog's worst nightmare, a dog can send a group of alligators into a feeding frenzy, being it's their favorite meal, they will go out of their way, and as far as taking them off the leash right before your eyes.

These gators were hunting slowly up-stream waiting for an anything that may be riding the current, toward the lake.

It's been a proven feeding ground, and Ty barely escaped certain doom.

"THE RED had saved his life"

He was still trembling inside when he got back to the truck where Rudy and Cole waited. When they saw Ty coming up, the jumped up and ran to mess with him.

They skipped in a circle around Ty, laughing like children, and chanting, Ty couldn't catch "THE RED"

Ty couldn't catch "THE RED"

Ty nipped at their ankles, at the fun they were having at his expense.

Rudy and Cole had smoked that oversized blunt, and were high as a kite.

The product they were growing had been proven to be, top of the line.

They piled in the truck for the ride home; Cole looked in the rear-view mirror as they were leaving, partially because Ty was looking out the back window.

The little red fox was walking down the truck path toward them, he watched the truck leave.

Cole thought to himself...maybe he did catch "THE RED" after all.

I estimate each one of our plants is yielding at least 3 and a half pounds of product right now, said Rudy.

In 40 days, we can expect that to increase to 4 and a half to 5 pounds each.

Out of the plants we started with, we only have 40 healthy survivors.

At 4 and a half pounds per tree, we're looking at 180 pounds.

We already know the product is good, but we still have to price it to move.

At $900.00 a pound, it should move fast.

This quality of herb runs for $1200.00 per pound, once they check it out, they will jump at the chance to save

$300.00 per pound, and we'll still come home with a little over $160,000.

Coles face produced a smile that stretched from ear to ear.

Now that'll work, he said.

I'll start calling all of our contacts next week; they can start setting their money aside.

Yea, good idea, said Rudy.

Cole turned off 41 and headed down Skipper road, he turned again when he reached the railroad tracks, he turned off the road and continued alongside the tracks.

Rudy knew where he was going, Ty did also, the sun had gone down now, Cole stopped and they exited the truck.

A curvy foot path led them to another small wooded area, just off the rear property line of a convenience store, they came upon a fire burning inside a foot high, stoned circle, a rack was placed across the stones, that held a pot of beans, there were four tents in the clearing.

The tents were fairly large, 6 feet by 8 feet, and shoulder height.

There was no grass in the clearing, and the ground was solid enough to sweep clean with a broom.

Cole has a tent here, although he lives with his mother and step father.

There were occasions' when their small place seemed too crowded, or whenever he got thrown out, this is where he'd go.

The other tent dwellers would watch his personal effects for him while he was away.

Theirs a friendly bunch, they look out for each other, and share everything.

Dino, Sam and Rob, occupied the other tents, Sam and Rob, share their tents with the two females of the group, Sherry and Tina.

They put a woman's touch on their little habitat that was visible, and could make a meal of almost anything.

When Rudy and Cole came in, they were holding the rabbits up, as to say "Dinner Time",

They were all sitting around the fire, Tina and Sherry jumped up, grabbed the rabbits by their hind legs, holding them up just as Rudy and Cole had, "Dinner Time", said Sherry, as they went down a path, leading away from the group, Ty right on their heels.

The guys remained seated around the fire, they seemed to know a little bit about everything, they talked a little politics, a little religion, but it was clear that they were pretty much stuck on the Mexican invasion that President Bush, had brought about.

Bringing the American Constructiion & Landscaping crews to its knees, and how that move by government, had led to their present condition.

Rudy sat and listened, but didn't comment, he was thinking about the way his job was treating him, and why?

He only wanted to think positive.

He and Cole left after awhile, they weren't planning on staying for dinner.

Rudy was pretty munchie due to that product check, in the woods earlier.

But what he really needed was some alone time, time to think, things had to change now.

Cole dropped him off at Denny's and was dropping Ty off at the house.

Rudy was being seated, when he saw Jake, an old friend, they had grown up together from first grade.

Jake always had a level head, he was smarter than most, and made staying out of trouble look easy.

He motioned for Rudy to come to his table, he was sitting with a young lady who introduced herself as Linda Filon, Jake had been working at the courthouse as a bailiff since they graduated high school.

Linda also worked at the Courthouse, she's one of the Court stenographers.

Jake, like everybody else had been having woman trouble lately, it was good to see he still had high hopes in the romance department, Linda was gorgeous.

Hey, what's up Jake?

The same ole, same ole, what you been up to?

I've been hanging in there, said Rudy, things made a downward turn today though, you know that piece of shit job I've been working for the last three years, at $9.50 an hour, I just found out, now that I have the proper experience and qualifications to get the position I've been shooting for, that position will "NEVER" be available to "ME".

Why not, asked Jake.

Because the Kitchen manager over there has a staff guidebook to follow, and it states in that book, the position I'm trying for is a "White only", position.

I've been wasting my time, and I'm out of a job, cause I can't go back there, I've already taken too much shit off these people,...man, has this turned out to be a bad day.

Did you say, this was written in the Managers guide, asked Linda?

As plain as day, said Rudy.

Thats Criminal, she replied,...you have a case,it won't be easy, but if you can prove what you just said, you'll have a 70% chance of winning monetary damages from these assholes, if you get the right representation, you'll have a better chance of winning than you will of losing, and I say, that's enough to go for it, I've seen a lot of these type cases, but they very seldom have written evidence, that puts you in the 70% range, I say, go for it, said Linda.

She knows what she's taking about, said Jake.

Lawsuit huh, Rudy thought to himself, I sure would like to fight back, how can I do this, he asked.

The food arrived while Linda was rifling through her purse, she came up with a card.

Emmitt Smith, Attorney at law.

Here, she said, talk to this guy, he'll check this case out for you.

Jake and Linda dropped Rudy off at home.

Ty greeted him like he was the head of the welcoming committee.

His mom was in the living room, watching a movie, THE BODYGUARD, with Whitney Houston.

He wanted to tell her about his job situation, but at the moment, she was into the movie.

Hi Mom, he said

She turned, Ms Harris was looking for you earlier. Ok, said Rudy, as he proceeded to his room.

Chantell wasn't home, Ty's senses were keen enough to detect her presence, so he waited on the sidewalk, he could see her house from here or spot her coming up.

Chantell got out of school, but didn't take the bus home, today she was going to ride with her friend Jeremy.

In a week she'll be celebrating her 19th Birthday, she knew her mom had no money, but Jeremy always seemed to have plenty.

He made it clear, that he wanted to spend time with her, and would be willing to pay for that time.

I'll meet you at your car, after school, said Chantell.

Afterward, she reminded Jeremy that, this was to be kept quiet.

For sure, said Jeremy, this will be our little secret.

She climbed out of the car, her legs were wobbly, but she had $100.00, she got out under the train bridge, to keep all the neighbors out of her business, she bid him a good night, and started walking home,

Chico, Manny, And J.D. saw her getting out, they recognized the car, and called Jeremy over.

Jeremy pulled up to the house, where they all stood outside leaning on a white work van... The sliding door was open J.D. sat there as Jeremy walked up.

They were all watching Chantell walk down the street...that yo girl Jeremy, asked J.D. she look nice.

Yea, you can get caught up in that walk. Said Manny.

Who is she? He asked without turning his head from Chantell.

Oh, that! said Jeremy, that isn't anything, just a trick, that's all.

I gave her a few dollars to keep quiet about it You say she be trickin huh, J.D. asked.

Yea man, she's all-in.

Jeremy was putting on his, bad-act

He wasn't about to stay in the presence of these three for very long, even now, they were feeling him out... Checking for that soft spot, that blank moment in thought, anything.

Hey, I'll get back at you guy's later, I'm out said Jeremy. Where you holding up at now, asked J.D.

I'm in the Villa apartments in Temple Terrace, come holla at yo-boy sometime.

Yea, we'll do that, said J.D.

Jeremy had left the Villa apartments six months ago, you do not let the likes of these three ever know where you live.

Jeremy pulled off and let out a sigh of relief.

Ty was surprised to see Chantell, coming from the direction she was coming from.

He ran to greet her.

"Don't you dare", said Chantell, holding her hands out to make sure Ty didn't jump up and put his dirty paws on her clean blouse, and Ty got the message, and just wagged his tail furiously.

He walked her home, he could smell the scent of the person she'd been with, all over her, this wasn't new... just curious.

After she went inside, Ty put his nose to the ground and headed in the direction that Chantell had come from.

He followed her scent, all the way back to the train bridge, the scent stopped there.

He looked around, he saw the three, Manny, Chico, and J.D., still hanging out in the van drinking, smoking, and talking shyt.

Ty sensed evil in them.

Chantell's mother, Ms Harris, greeted Rudy at the door.

Rudy, I need to ask a favor of you, she said, Chantell's Birthday is coming up, it's her 19th, I have no money and I'd like to get her something, I haven't been able to move around like I used to, my friends have been hard to reach lately, and your actually my best chance at getting a gift of some sort.

I'll see what I can come up with, said Rudy, not wanting to go into his job situation with her.

He thought about something that had already crossed his mind, last year his father bought a very beautiful dress for his mother from a designer in Paris.

The dress turned out to be too small, but mom had never sent it back, the dress and the shoes were still in their original boxes, Rudy checked the box with the dress, it was still a work of art, he didn't know until he picked up the dress, that it had a matching hat also, a simple suede cap with no rim, it came down an inch above the eye brow.

Mom is going to have to forgive me, he took the set to Ms Harris.

I think she'll like this, he said.

Ms Harris was so pleased, she covered her mouth with awe, and went speechless, as tears rolled down her cheeks.

Tell Chantell happy Birthday for me, he said as he left.

Rudy was off to see, Mr. Emmitt Smith, Attorney at Law, he found the address he was looking for, 1100 n Florida Ave.

Henderson Law was printed over the entrance in big brass letters, from outside, you can see the receptionist sitting in her well laid out office, which sat in the center of the lobby.

There was no way of getting around talking to her. Rudy walked in, immediately, she sprang into action. Yes sir, may I help you?

Yes ma'am, I need to see Mr. Emmitt Smith.

I'm sorry, but Mr. Smith stepped out early this morning, I'm not sure when he'll be returning, she added, so you can leave a message with me, or feel free to wait.

Thanks, I'll take you up on your offer to wait a few minutes, to see if he shows up.

Twenty minutes into the wait, a Lawyer strode in, briefcase in hand, a well accomplished looking fellow, he stopped when he saw Rudy.

Is anyone helping you sir, he asked?

I'm waiting to see Mr. Smith, said Rudy. Is he expecting you, he asked?

No, he's not, I'm a walk in.

May be I can get you started till Smitty gets back, step in my office here.

Rudy followed the man down the hall, mainly because this guy looks like he knows his way around a courtroom, and he looks like he's good at what he does.

His office was the fourth door on the left, it was open' so we just walked in, he slid his briefcase under his desk and came back around.

My name is Ron Baines, and you are? I'm Rudolph Clayton.

Well how can I help you, Mr. Clayton?

I have a discrimination Case that I want to move forward with.

Is it work related, he asked. Yes, it is," Rudy replied.

Are they giving you all the shit jobs, did they pass you up for promotion, or did they fire you," asked Ron Baines.

He said this with a very condescending undertone.

This brought Rudy out of his Lawsuit stupor; he was going to have to play offence and defense, simultaneously with this guy.

"Well, I was passed up for a position, because of my nationality," said Rudy.

These kinds of cases are now the hardest kind of case to win, explained Mr. Baines, without a video tape, or documented proof, these cases are getting harder and harder.

I have proof, said Rudy.

What kind of proof asked Baines. Documented, said Rudy.

You have Documented proof? Yes.

A slight smile crept across Baines face, he pulled paperwork from his desk, and began putting little X's on all the places that would require Rudy's signature.

You won't have to worry about Lawyers Fee's, we only get paid if we win your case. I need to see the proof you have as soon as possible, and please, do not dicuss this case with anyone, if you don't mind, I'd very much like to work this case for you.

This guy was going a mile a minute, the smell of money was in his nostrils, like blood to a shark.

I'm going to need the name of the Company in order to check their financial situation, who are these guys?

"The Two Cronies Restaurant".

The paperwork stopped; Mr. Baines gave him an odd look.

Say again! Said Baines.

The Two Cronies restaurant on Busch Boulevard, said Rudy. Baines face went totally grim.

I'll look over your case, and I'll call you in the morning, said Baines.

Have a good day Mr. Clayton.

Rudy was caught off guard by the way' Baines was suddenly rushing him out.

Leave your number with the receptionist, he said. Rudy left the building somewhat confused.

Baines took the paperwork they had just done and trashed it, he went to the front desk, and told the receptionist to alert all the other Lawyers and associates in the firm, to sidestep the case regarding Rudolph Clayton.

He then got the phone and called Orlan Petrini. Hello, Mr. Petrini

Yes, speaking.

This is Ron Baines; I've done some work for you before.

Oh yeah, I remember you Mr. Baines, you're the Lawyer, what do I owe the pleasure.

Well, a young man just left my office, he wanted to go after your restaurant chain; on a discrimination suit, I've shut him down for the moment, I'll have to call him back in the morning and let him know why this Lawsuit is a no-go,.. but just to be safe, get all your ducks in a row.

Thanks for the information, Mr. Baines, I owe you one; have a good night, thanks again.

Word about Chantell had gotten around school, the guys, inner circle, referred to her as "The Trick Ho", her best friend, Alan, from Town & Country was in that inner circle, he and Chantell were getting pretty close; he never knew he could pay her for sex.

He approached her this morning with a new brand-new agenda.

He knew this was going to be awkward, first of all, she was a close friend, second, she was black, and he was white.

Chantell, he yelled down the hall. Hey Al, what's up?

I've got a test coming up in American Lit…and I'm not ready for it, I wanted to know if you would come over after school and help me get prepared.

Chantell looked a little bewildered, what's up today, she asked, guys have been coming to talk to me all morning, I don't even know some those guys, now I got a date with my best friend after school, you go girl.

Allen knew his parents wouldn't be home. Once he got her there, the situation didn't turn out awkward at all. Turned out she really liked him, and was in the market for a relationship, she enjoyed his company, they were good together.

They talked more than usual; they played around and teased each other as they got dressed.

What about the test, she asked.

I'm gonna have to do a make-up test, there was no time for studying.

She laughed.

Alan pulled $100.00 from his wallet and handed it to her; she looked at the money, and then looked him straight in the eye, trying to find any sign, of what was going on.

Alan caught her bewilderment quickly.

I didn't know if you had any money, I want you to take this, just in case you come up a little short somewhere.

She let out a sigh of relief, and gave him a hug, thank you, she said, as she lay her head on his chest.

She didn't want him to drop her off at her house; her mom was way too suspicious for that.

She told him to drop her off at the train bridge; she'd walk home from there.

When she opened the car door the interior light came on; she gave Alan a kiss good night, and started to walk. She almost screamed when she spotted the dog rushing toward her.

Damn Ty, you scared the hell out of me, what are you doing up here anyway?

Ty knew, if she didn't come from the usual bus route, she may come from the train bridge.

His hunting skills were on point, and he couldn't wait to come face to face with "THE RED", again.

The white van sat outside the house, Chico, Manny, and

J.D. watched as she kissed the white boy.

Damn, she trickin with white boys too, said J.D., man she is off the chain.

Let's check this bitch, said Chico.

Chantell saw the three walking toward her. "Hey, what's your name, Ma", said Chico. "Chantell"

Chantell, you can hang out with us, and party for awhile if you want.

Chantell said nothing, she tried to remain calm, as she continued on.

This invitation doesn't go out to just anybody, we make sure we take good care of those ladies who know how to get theirs.

No, that's alright fellas, I'm going home.

Chico jumped in front of Chantell, she stopped.

I know you don't think you're too good' to hang out with us, do you.

Chantell said, "Yeah", and walked around Chico, he went to stop her again, but was stopped short, when he saw every tooth in ty's mouth, and heard a growl that sounded like he sincerely hated all three of them.

Chico stepped back quickly, without making another sound.

Come on Ty, said Chantell, trying to calm her protector.

The three stood there; afraid to move, as Chantell led Ty away from them, all three were pissed, at being turned down b this little whore.

Don't worry, said J.D., we're gonna get that bitch, it's just a matter of time.

The call came early that morning, "Hello",

Hi, this is Ron Baines; I'm trying to contact Rudolph Clayton.

Yeah, speaking.

Mr. Clayton, our firm has received your case, it seems the venue your case falls under, will come before a judge that has no tolerance for these type cases, it would be useless to go forward with this case' at this time, because if he denies the claim, no other judge, anywhere, would overturn his ruling.

If you don't mind, I'd like to keep this on the back burner; for a couple of months, and see what happens at a later date.

And there's no way around this judge, Huh, asked Rudy.

No, he will end up with every case of this type, for at least another month.

Well, if there's nothing more you can do at this point, I'm gonna have to take your expert advise, and hold off for awhile, thanks for trying, Mr. Baines.

I'm sorry we couldn't do more, have a nice day. Yeah, said Rudy.

Faced with another open schedule, Rudy went and jumped back in the sack, the rain came out of nowhere, the raindrops falling on the roof, and coming down through the trees, put Rudy in an ever so deep sleep.

He dreamed he and Cole were out in the woods, harvesting their first crop of Marijuana.

They both had shoulder bags, and limb, after limb filled each bag, they both stopped cutting and chopping, because the heard someone knocking on the door. They looked at each other as they wondered, who the hell could that be, wait' something's wrong with this dream, we're in the woods.... "There's No Door".

As the knocking continued, he realized, someone was actually knocking on the front door.

He rolled out of bed and went to answer the door, still in his shorts.

Through the peep hole, he saw a man outside, huddled under the small awning, in this type of rain, the small awning didn't do much, the man was soaked.

Rudy opened the door quickly, and motioned the man inside, he wore a business suit, and appeared to be in his early fifties, and though lean, he still appeared strong and sturdy.

Hi, my name is Emmitt Smith, I'm from the Law firm you visited, and you're Rudolph Claton, right.

Yeah, right, said Rudy.

I want to talk to you about your case, if you don't mind, the receptionist at the office said you came in and asked for me.

Yeah, I got your card from a friend, Ms. Linda Filon, she thinks pretty highly of you, said I needed to see you, but when I couldn't raise you on the phone, or catch you at the office, another lawyer at your firm, a Mr. Baines, he looked the case over, he called earlier this morning, to let me know, that there's no way that this case can make it through the sitting judge at this time.

That's the song and dance he told everyone at the firm to give you, that's why I'm here.

Your name was signed in to see me, Emmitt Smith, after he intercepted my client, Mr. Baines saw something in your case that he didn't like, I can see it wasn't you he disliked, so it has to be your case.

Between you and me, Mr. Ron Baines has very little respect for the oath he took to uphold the law; the people he's been in cahoots with lately are "ALL", on the wrong side of the law, we can go over your case today, right here' from beginning to end, and see if we can find out what's going on.

Rudy's head was spinning, as he tried to keep his composure intact, it was obvious that treachery was trying to settle in all around him.

He had been shut down and betrayed by someone who was sworn in to act in his best interest, his anger, and "ground level" position, made him take a closer look at Mr. Smith.

"How serious are these allegations I'm throwing around," he thought to himself, are they as serious to me, as they are to them.

What happens when I show him my proof, do the truth and I, get buried somewhere?

Mr. Smith's conversation has the ring of truth to it, I'll stick with him, but caution is the word of the day.

I'm going to get dressed, I'll be right back with you," said Rudy, when he went to his room, he put on a fresh pair of khakis, his white Nikes, and a tee shirt. He grabbed his .38 revolver, and stuck it in his sock,

He went back to the front room, and it was time to lay his cards on the table.

Mr. Smith, I want you to understand something, I'm not going through this to be played, baited, or used, I'm doing it so these people will know, that I'm not black, white, brown, or plaid, I'm American, plain, and simple, and an American can apply for any job in America.

So, if you're here on an agenda that doesn't line up with that, I'd suggest we part ways now, cause I hate being lied to, or misled.

Mr. Clayton, let's get to work, please.

After a couple of hours, they found out they work pretty good together, they threw facts and ideas' back and forth, they found some promising answers, uncovered some lies, and began feeling comfortable about going forward with the case.

There was no judge standing in the way of the case, waiting to stamp it out, like Mr. Baines had told him.

All systems were go.

Mr. Smith was pleased to hear about the Managers guidebook.

If that Guide says what you say it says, our chances of winning this case just skyrocketed.

The only way we could lose, is if we make a mistake, somewhere down the line.

So, we have to check everything we do, and be careful, and quiet about it.

First, we need to find out if this is an isolated incident, said Smith.

The policies you read in that staff Guide, may only apply to that "one" particular restaurant.

We'll have to check the rest of the chain to be sure.

Orlan Petrini, owner of a vast chain of restaurants, called Sam Hubbart, the lease manager of the Busch Blvd.

Restaurant, in Tampa, Florida. Sam, this is Orlan.

Yes sir, what's up?

I want you to be on the lookout for an employee of yours, I've been informed that a discrimination Lawsuit was brought to one of my Lawyers' who nipped it in the bud, but for safe keeping, clean up anything, that you Southern boys do to deter the other factions of life.

You sure it's from here, I haven't heard anything.

Yeah, it's the Busch Blvd. Store; get on it right away, will you.

Sure thing!

My source says, he's holding the guy off for a couple of months, which should give you plenty of time.

I'll get the scoop and find out what we're looking at, I'll call you if there's anything to this.

There was a knock at the door, Rudy and Emmitt just ignored it and kept working.

The knock came again, with a more urgent tone, that knock, he recognized.

Rudy opened the door, the rain had stopped, the air smelled fresh and crisp.

Once again, Ty was playing welcome wagon. Why didn't you bite her, Rudy asked?

Felicia Young stood on the small, front porch, where have you been, I thought you may have fallen off the face of the earth, she said, as she strode past him, bumping him with her shoulder, then giving him a little shove to boot,

Rudy looked out the door again, it was really nice outside, he wanted to get out of the house now.

He turned around just in time to catch a glimpse of the skirt she was wearing, "Damn", just crossed his lips, more like a reflex type thing.

He and Felicia had tried their hand at a relationship a few years back, it didn't work out, however, their friendship had grown stronger than ever as a result.

Felicia went straight to the kitchen; he hadn't noticed the bag she was carrying.

Hey, I got something I want you to taste, she shouted from the kitchen.

Rudy sat back down with Emmitt Smith; this is what we're going to do.

We have a little something to work with' in the way of funds, so what we'll do is, get someone to visit these Restaurants, posing as inspectors of some sort, someone who would automatically have the full run of the house, and see if they can come up with anything resembling that guidebook.

The more restaurants that have it, the better.

So far, we've located 65 of the restaurants in this chain, 22 of them are in the Southeast, we'll check them first.

With my company card, I can pay the person we hire

$400 per store, I don't want to use anyone from the firm, as word travels, and improper connections may show up to work against us.

We should be able to get started in about two days; I should have some authentic looking credentials by then.

See if you can find someone who could pull this off, keep in mind, this will not be easy, and there can't be any mistakes, this can very well' come back to bite us in the ass.

I may know someone that fits the bill; I'll give you a call as soon as possible.

Rudy walked Emmitt outside, he got in his BMW, and pulled off, Rudy sat outside on the front steps, going over the events of the day.

He didn't feel like he was smart enough to keep up, he was being pulled this way and that, by these Law navigations, he knew he had to find a foothold somewhere before these guys intentionally dash him against the rocks.

Felicia stepped outside, balancing two bowls, she handed Rudy a bowl, here, try this, she said.

Rudy took the bowl, it was hot, the seafood aroma was loud, the seasoning' louder.

It's Crab Chilau, she said.

He tasted it, oooohhh, who made this, he asked, without coming up for air.

She popped him upside the head, "I DID", I'm not gonna have you taste something that somebody else made.

Good huh, she said, while digging into her own bowl. Hell yeah, said Rudy.

One thing Felicia did far beyond average, was cooking, breakfast was her specialty.

She baked some biscuits' one morning that were so light and fluffy; they floated right out of the pan.

Felicia sat on the step directly behind him, she hiked up her skirt, and put her legs on either side of him, he leaned back between her legs, thighs in his under arms, head resting in pure warmth.

Who's the guy in the BMW, she asked.

That man don't want you, for one, and two, you're all up in my business.

I can get that man if I wanted him, for one, and two, you want me all up in your business, you'll explode trying to keep a secret from me, just like your little Marijuana project.

Cole pulled up in his pick-up about the same time three schoolgirls were coming down the sidewalk, Michelle, Candy, and Chantell,

Michelle wore a loud blue sun dress, Candy was playing her short shorts, Chantell wore boy shorts.

Cole stood admiring the girls as they approached, kinda like a wolf, looking over a herd of sheep.

Rudy motioned for the girls to come over, Michelle, come here man, said Rudy.

They all came and gathered around the steps.

I just wanted to shake your hand, "Congratulations", they tell me you're gonna be at FAMU next year.

"Next Year", I'm gonna be at FAM next semester, I've already got all my high school credits, I got a full scholarship in music, I've already got my room in the dorm, "I, Am, Ou-ta Here".

Ooh, she's so smart, said Felicia, you go girl.

Yeah, show em how smart you are, and have fun at the same time, make it look easy.

And what have you been up to, Miss Candy. I'm gonna Model when I get out of school. Candy, said Rudy, you look like a man!

Everyone laughed,

"This", she said, as she struck a pose, showing off her feminine assets..... "Speaks for itself".

Chantell let me holla at you for a minute. She followed Rudy into the house.

This ain't no big deal, said Rudy; your Mom has been worrying about how late you've been coming in lately, and...

Chantell cut him off, she always think I'm doing something wrong, I'm just hanging out with friends after school, and I don't be coming in real late.

It's about time you start letting your Mom know what's going on, she'll understand.

That drama queen's understanding is zero; she wants to keep treating me like a child.

I know you love your mom, and don't want to worry her, I'm betting you're gonna do the right thing.

She's gonna be mad with me on Tuesday though, I told her I was going out.... I hope she don't think I'm gonna be coming home early.

That's right; Tuesday's your birthday huh.
"Yep", what you got for me?

Don't worry, I got you.

The girls headed down the sidewalk, singing a song by Alicia Keys, sounded good too.

Your name was mentioned on the job today, said Cole; the manager asked me if I knew, if you thought they were racist or discriminatory, their trying to find out why you left without a word.

They don't know I'm trying to file suit, do they. "Are You"?

Yeah ... do you still have that guidebook from the manager's office.

I've had it gift wrapped, with your name on it.

Good, hold on to it, I'll come get it when everything's in place, I better get moving if I'm gonna get the jump on em.

He called Emmitt Smith.

Mr. Smith, I just got word that management has been asking questions about me.

"Oh yeah", we're gonna have to speed things up a bit, I'll file suit first thing in the morning, I'm going to need that manager's guidebook to file also.

I'll go get it, said Rudy.

Good, then we'll have to put someone on the road tomorrow also.

I know someone that might be willing, I'll give them the low down tonight.

We're ready to get started then, I'll come by first thing in the morning to pick up the book, and I'll be dropping off the directions and addresses of all the Two Cronies Restaurants from here to the state line.

Sounds like a plan, said Rudy.

By the time he got off the phone, it was already getting late; Felicia had found a movie she wanted to watch... De Ja Vu, with Denzel Washington.

She sat on the floor playing Solitaire and watching the movie at the same time.

Rudy lay on the sofa, the 40-inch television screen provided the only light in the living room.

Hey, I need you to help me out with something, said Rudy.

What's up, she replied.

Look at this, he said as he showed her the Managers guide that Cole had dropped off.

He showed her a couple of key pages, she could hardly believe what she was reading, oh boy, now that's fucked up, where'd you get this?

This is the Managers guide book, you're reading store policy for The Two Cronies Restaurant.

Is this what you and Mr. BMW were talking about this morning?

Yeah, said Rudy.

Man, you can't hold water, didn't I tell you' you can't keep nothing from me, and remind me "Never" to work for those assholes.

Me and Mr. BMWs going to put a little heat under their ass and force them to change that shyt, I was thinking, you've worked in enough kitchens to know how to do routine, health, and code checks, tomorrow we're going to have someone pose as an inspector, to see if we can come up with any more of these Managers guide books in their other restaurants.

Mr. BMW asked "Me" to find someone who can pull this off, so far, we're looking at 30 restaurants, he said he will pay the person that does this, $400 per store.

Did you just say, he's paying $400 a store? Yep.

Me, me, pick me, I'll do it, I'm serious, pick me. You think you can pull it off, asked Rudy.

If you give this job to someone else, I will kill you, I ain't playin, I'll kill ya, I've been turned down for so many jobs, it's starting to mess with my self esteem, I stopped searching just to hold on to this little bit of dignity I'm clinging to, and you won't be sorry, if they have this book in their Restaurant, I'll find it.

You start tomorrow morning; you can sleep over if you want.

I ain't going nowhere.... I'm not missing out this time, you're going with me, right, she asked.

No, Mr. BMW is worried about making mistakes, you may have to go at it alone.

If that's the way it has to be done, that's the way I'll do it.

Everything went as planned the next morning, Felicia set out with everything she needed, all of her credentials were in order, rental car, cell phone, travel plans, and

$1500 travel expense money.

Emmitt Smith filed the case.... the heat was on.

Felicia's first stop was the Orlando store' on orange blossom trail, (Sir named the O.B.T.) this part of the city never shuts down, the activity on the trail continues twenty-four seven.

She pulled into the parking lot of the restaurant, and parked as close to the front door as possible.

This restaurant was twice the size of the one in Tampa.

Fear gripped her as the reality of her mission sank in, could she do this.

The gravity of who she would be dealing with' came into play also, she realized how important it is that she convinces the staff, that she is' who she says she is.

"Let's Do This Felicia", she said to herself.

She stepped inside the restaurant and stood there, trying to force herself to stop trembling.

The store was immaculate, Extra-large wooden, maple colored beams ran from one end of the ceiling to the other, the smaller center beam rafters Criss crossed, connecting each of the large beams, the light fixtures came down through the rafters, creating the ambiance of a far more expensive establishment.

The place was only half full, she spotted the only African American couple in the place; seated in a far corner,...why would they be seated way back there, with all these nice window seats, they even had open seats at the Chef's table.

As they were on the black side of town' they should be more integrated, with the exception of the one couple, everyone else was Caucasian.

That did it, the blood pumped through her veins; bringing back clearly, the reason she was here in the first place, she's the person who was "Bringing the Heat".

She stood up straight, this is for you, she said to herself, she was looking at the black couple' who had been tucked away in a far corner, and basically ignored.

Her white blouse with the silver, black rimmed bar, that read, "INSPECTOR", showed clearly, her black skirt fell just above the knee, and her black pumps, gave her that professional aura she needed, she had her hair pulled back, with those plastic rimmed glasses, and a clip board.

She caught the first waitress passing her way.

Hi, you don't seem to be too busy, can you take me to the kitchen please?

The kitchen manager was a little edgy, like he'd been blind-sided.

This is just a routine inspection, from what I've seen so far, this place looks pretty good, she went through the kitchen so professionally' no one doubted who she was.

The kitchen manager stayed close; she saved the manager's office for last.

She walked in the office and looked around... the manager stood at the door.

How was she going to get that book out of there?

She opened a drawer, the book was right there, she closed the drawer, and got a large pamphlet off the shelf above the desk, and walked out of the office.

Immediately, the manager stopped her.

I'm going to have to ask you' not to remove anything from the office, everything in its place, so to speak.

She replaced the pamphlet; it was just as she thought, this guy wasn't going to let her walk out of here with that book.

I've seen enough, you run a first-class kitchen here, I'll be back with your copy of the inspection, she said.

She went back to the car and sat out there, upset because the book was still inside.

As she thought about it, if she would have taken the book, it could be proven as theft in a court of law and could in fact be one of those mistakes that Mr. Smith is trying so hard not to make.

She called Emmitt Smith.

Mr. Smith, have you filed the case yet? Yes, I have, said Smith.

What's the case number, she asked. The case # is 10034.

Thanks, I'll call you later.

She got the digital camera from her purse and went back inside, she went to the manager's office, got the book from the drawer, with her marker she wrote 10034 on page 26 and page 30, she handed the book to the manager, hold this up like this, she said.

We always get a picture of managers whose kitchens come up clean, stand under The Two Cronies logo, "Smile" ... she managed to get two more shots of the book, page 26, and 30, and she was out' with signatures and all.

This will probably be the way she'd have to get what she needed.

Next stop, "Jacksonville".

Amos sat behind Chantell in their third period class, he was an overweight kid, not handsome, low self esteem had gotten the better of him, he had always admired Chantell, he also knew he didn't have a chance in hell, until a rumor he'd heard about, perked him up a bit.

Chantell.

Amos, she said mockingly.

Can you and I work together today; I need to talk to you about something.

I'm working with Anita today, Amos, Well, can we talk after school?

"After School", she asked, turning in her chair, what's up Amos?

I need to talk to you, he said.

Is it important, she replied. "Yeah", he said.

Well, I'll work with "you" today then.

They maneuvered their way to the back of the room.

What I wanted to talk about is personal, so just let me talk, and this is about females.

"Females", Amos I thought you said this was important. What's more important than our relations?

The way he said that made Chantell realize, this was more or less, a heart-to-heart talk,... and always important.

What's bothering you Amos?

What's bothering me, is me, I exercise everyday; and I'm getting fatter and fatter, I can't burn it off...

I'm not a handsome guy, I'm 18 years old now, and have never had a girlfriend' and my future is looking worse.

By the time I get twenty, I'll be 50 pounds heavier than I am now, there are no females attracted to me now, and they will be even harder to attract later. Chantell, I would like very much to lose my virginity before my life is over, he said playfully.

Here, I was saving this.... he put a roll of bills in Chantel's hand, I want to do this with "You".

When Chantell realized he wasn't joking' her intent was to hurt this guy's feelings for even thinking such a thing....but she said nothing, she sat there staring at the wad of cash.

Her 19th birthday that was coming up caused her to remain silent.

She slowly started to count it, $400.

She looked over at Amos, picked up her purse, opened it with one hand, she craned the other hand with the money in it, over the purse, and dropped it in, she closed the purse and placed it back on the floor.

Amos leaned over to say something, but she put a finger to his lips, I don't want to talk about this.

Later that evening she found out that Amos definitely wasn't a virgin, and had a healthy sexual appetite' by the time he was finished' all she wanted to do was sleep.

Amose's cousin didn't wake them up until midnight, they were using his bed' and now he needed it.

Amos also had to borrow his car, He dropped Chantell off at the train bridge, they said their Goodnite's, she wasn't even mad, that he had lied about being a virgin.

Well..... Well..... Well, look what we have here.

J.D., Chico, and Manny were jacked up on Cocaine tonight, they were hyped up, the adrenaline was rushing through their veins' as the spotted Chantell getting dropped off at her usual spot.

This bitch is trickin with everybody... except us. I got a problem with that! Said J.D.

Me too, said Chico.

She keeps blowing us off like we ain't shit.

Well fellas, it's time to show'this ho, the error of her ways.

And let it be known, "Church is out".

They stopped Chantell in the street, come hang out with us for a while, said J.D.

He took her by the hand, and started toward the house, Chantell broke free.

If any of you' take one step toward me, I'm gonna scream my head off, and all of you fuckers will go to jail.

Chico and Manny swung at the same time; Manny hit her on the ear, and Chico's blow landed flush on the jaw, the blows came from opposite sides, and landed at the same time.

Chantell crumbled on the side of the road, unconscious.

They picked her up quickly and put her in the back of the van, they drove across the street, and through the tall grass, it was just a short distance to the river.

They drove across the river in the shallows' where the riverbed was rocky and solid, then up the opposite bank, this had to be done at an angle, still the ride was bumpy, the hit one bump so hard, the back doors flew open; the almost lost Chantell and Chico, Chantell was still unconscious, And Chico was there to make sure she stayed that way.

They brought the van to a stop behind one of the larger pylons of the train bridge, they were completely out of sight, there would be no passersby, and no interruptions, J.D. sprung from the passenger's seat, into the rear of the van, shoving Chico out of the way.

I'm first, he said.

When Chantell came to, she was deep inside her worst nightmare, these guys acted like they hated her guts, she was being beaten, Choked, and passed around, both of her eyes were swollen shut,... she wondered what she had done wrong' the fear for her life was real now.

Ty had already been down to the train bridge earlier, he waited to see if Chantel would show up, she didn't, so he went back home' and waited on the sidewalk; in case she came from the other direction.

Hours had passed, and she still hadn't showed.

Ty decided to go back once more, he enjoyed the walk, he considered it; part of his hunting training.

Sometimes he felt like he could find almost anything, once he puts his nose to the ground, the whole world opens up for him, he could determine what type of animal, reptile, or person had passed, and what direction they were headed.

When he reached the train bridge, he picked up Chantell's trail,.. Then, he picked up the scent of the "three".

Ty became uneasy, he sniffed the air all around, he found a familiar scent to follow, he crossed the river in the shallows, further up, he spotted the van.

Chantell's blood smelled loud; Ty's face contorted into a fist of rage.

He ran full speed toward the van, teeth bared, in a low growl, he appeared completely mad.

He lunged and hit the back of the van so hard, he almost knocked himself out.

The three inside were startled, they grabbed their guns and ran outside to find the intruder.

Just as J.D. stepped out of the passenger door, he'd barely got a shot off, before pure fury engulfed him, J.D. felt his neck being ripped open; he fell to the ground, writhing in pain.

Ty spotted Manny and charged at him, Manny managed to get a shot off just before Ty clamped down on his arm, and bit all the way down to the bone, Manny couldn't stop screaming, Chico just started shooting.

Ty ran back through the thicket, and across the river. The little gang of three was pissed.

Chico told J.D. and Manny to go back to the house and tend to their wounds, and he was going to clean up their trail.

Chico opened the vans sliding door, Chantell lay sprawled out on her back, naked and still unconscious.

J.D. and Manny thinks I'm dropping you off at the park with just a warning about what would happen if you ever told anyone about this, but the reality of this is that you're never gonna let this go, so now that we're alone.... There's something I have always wanted to do.

Chico climbed back into the van; he turned Chantell on her stomach.

He wrapped an extension cord around her neck' twice, put his knee in her back and pulled until it cut off her air supply then tied it in a knot.

She regained consciousness for only a few seconds, as her body fought for life,.. then the pain left completely.

He carried her over a hundred feet into the brush and dumped her; he covered her naked body with the wheat grass and palmetto leaves that grew plentiful in that area.

It had been a week since Rudy had left the job, Cole called and let him know that his last paycheck was there, and to come pick it up.

Rudy told him he'd pick it up at closing time, to make sure that everyone who might want to ask questions would be long gone.

Tim will be closing, said Cole, he'll be there till 2:00 A.M.

Good, said Rudy.

Ty ran across Rudy's trail on the way home, from the direction the trail led, Ty knew where he was going.

He headed for the restaurant, when he reached Busch Blvd. Once again, he knew he would never be able to make it across, he wanted to start barking' in hopes' that once again, Rudy would hear him, but he was feeling much too weak; he stepped up to the curb and looked up the highway and then down, to his surprise, there was no traffic, in either direction, he could hardly believe his luck.

Ty started across; a car swerved to avoid hitting him, the drivers in the next two lanes slammed on brakes and skidded to a stop just in time, as Ty walked by slowly in front them.

The pickup truck in the fourth lane sped past, missing him by an inch.

Ty never saw, or heard, any of this, he made his way to the center Island, his legs were a little wobbly, he checked out the other half of the highway, it was exactly the same, no traffic, he proceeded across, and all four lanes came to a halt; as he made his way across.

He never saw the bright headlights of the cars' less than two feet in front of him.

Rudy came out of the side door of the Two Cronies restaurant; he put his last paycheck in his back pocket, as he told Tim he'd see him around sometime.

Then he turned around and saw Ty, Ty, hey boy, what you doing here?

And how did you get across that highway?

I told you, don't ever try to cross that damn street, it's too dangerous, come on, let's go home and grab something to eat.

Ty tried to get up, but no matter how hard he tried, his body wouldn't budge, the pain forced him to let out a whimper.

Rudy turned around when he noticed Ty wasn't following him.

Come on boy, said Rudy.

Ty tried to pull himself with his front legs, but only moved a few inches.

Rudy ran back to see what was wrong, he noticed the blood around his mouth, the flesh in his teeth, and then he saw the hole in his left side; near his stomach and another under his right front leg, near his chest.

Rudy almost lost it, his best friend was in real trouble, Rudy picked him up and started running.

He had to make it to Sally's place, Sally was an animal lover, who'd picked up an uncanny ability to treat animals medically, she treated all animals, no matter what was wrong with them.

He had only gotten about 5 blocks when he noticed Ty's breathing had stopped.

A second check showed that it was too late.

The walk home didn't provide any answers. He sat with Ty for a long while, before he wrapped his body in a thick quilt, and had a private burial in the back yard, a wooden cross with his name on it was placed at the head of the grave.

The loss of his best friend played heavy on his mind, he couldn't figure who would do such a thing.

He wanted to throw a fit, and stomp' an cry like a kid, but these type losses, proved never to be too far from him, this made him more aware of where he lived.

Felicia wrapped up 16 restaurants successfully, every stop after that, seemed to be onto her, no managers guides were found, and the managers made it almost impossible to view any sensitive documents, she felt she could do no more, and headed home.

She'd only been gone 6 days, and was totally alarmed when she found out all that had transpired in her absence.

Chantell being listed as a runaway, Ty, being shot and killed.

I'm never going to leave here again, she said.

She cried over Ty's death; she knew Ty loved her more than he did Rudy.

At the first meeting of the Lawyers, on the discrimination suit.

Three Lawyers showed up on behalf of the Two Cronies restaurant, they all looked very well paid, clean cut, high profile.

Today the lawyers were only supposed to exchange information, but these guys said that they were authorized to settle, here and now.

Orlan Petrini had profiled the man named in this suit; he was a nobody' who would surely be happy to receive the lump sum that he was going to offer.

He could take this out of his petty cash, and be done with the whole thing, instead of paying his lawyers for months on end, and still end up paying the same amount.

We are authorized to settle at $12,000, the paperwork is all in order.

You are, kidding me' right, said Emmitt Smith, we have a clear-cut case of discrimination on file against you, and a clear case of conspiracy, and we've got the evidence, we can start the negotiations at a quarter mil, give me a call when were headed in the same direction.

Emmit left the three men in the conference room, looking through the new cases that were piled before them.

Orlan Petrini showed no concern at this news, his 100- acre estate was lavish, the home was worth well over 30 million, and every inch of the property was well manicured, he did the majority of his work from home, he hardly ever had to leave.

Today he practiced putting, every time he sinks a putt, an electronic gadget kicks the ball back out at another angle.

Get Ron Baines on the line, he said. Ron Baines speaking.

Mr. Baines, this is Orlan Petrini, that law suit you warned me about, it went through, and I've got to admit, you caught me off guard, you told me, you were going to hold the case up for at least two months, and when you knew I trusted you... you stabbed me in the back and filed the lawsuit before I could clean up.

Mr. Petrini, I didn't file it, I still have the paperwork from my meeting with this guy' right here in my desk.

You expect me to believe that you had nothing to do with this?

No Sir, nothing at all.

Mr. Baines, your name isn't on the lawsuit, but I know you've got something to do with it, you've worked for me before, you know how I operate, if you had nothing to do with this, then it was you who dropped the ball somewhere, you've got to turn this around, fix this, or you will be held accountable.

Ron Baines' world suddenly went spinning off track.

Orlan Petrini had a bad reputation, and even worse temper; he knew he was trapped' he had to cooperate, and he had to think of something fast.

The only thing he could do' was to get the man to withdraw the lawsuit before the state picks it up, And the quickest way to do that, being the man's a nobody, was to use scare tactics.

Baines got in touch with a couple of thugs that he'd represented in the past, they owed him' and now it was time to collect, he put them on the trail of Rudy Clayton, their dept would be cleared and they'd even make a few extra bucks, as soon as either the lawsuit was pulled, or the key player didn't show up for court.

Emmitt Smith insisted on paying Felicia for every store that was checked, and the ones that she tried to check, but came up empty, so all together, she was paid for 20 stores, when he handed over a check for eight thousand dollars, she almost fainted.

She deposited the money in the bank, all but a thousand dollars, and that thousand was burning a hole in her purse, she had the urge to do something' that the lack of funds had prevented for quite some time.

They headed for the beach in Pinellas County; the Clearwater beach jazz festival was in full swing.

They stretched a blanket out on the grass, a bucket of Kentucky fried chicken sat between them, in the small cooler, Hennesey and Coke.

They listened to all the various Jazz Musicians, playing their hearts out.

The Hennessey brought them to the brink of being the perfect couple, the talked, danced, joked around, dishing out little love taps, wrestling, there was even a little smoochin' going on.

They had such a great time, they couldn't leave.

The bands had packed up and were long gone, the closing of the park was the only reason they left at all, they did leave, but went only a short distance down the beach to Johns Pass; they got a motel room and planned a fishing trip for the following morning.

The fresh air was exuberating, the water, calm and peaceful, laid out like glass.

The trip took them five miles out into the Gulf of Mexico; the Charter provided all the gear and bait.

The Marine life in the depths of this particular body of water amazes even the most seasoned fisherman.

Felicia caught an Octopus, her attempt to get it off of her hook, resulted in the eight-legged creature wrapping around her arm and setting its suction cups in with all its might.

Felicia ran screaming, her inability to remove the creature from her arm had begun to scare her, Rudy's loud laughter didn't help a bit.

Rudy grabbed the creature and carefully removed it, before she started panicking, a little Asian woman asked if she could have it' just before Rudy went to throw it back in the water, he handed it to her, and it wrapped around her arm and dug in again, she walked away with it wrapped around her arm as if that was completely natural.

They fished all day, and later that evening Rudy and Felicia took a picture with the second biggest catch of the day, a 29-inch, 15-pound Grouper.

Felicia hugged that thing like she already knew how good it was going to taste.

The guys on the dock cleaned and fillet the fish.

When they got home the next day, they knew something was wrong.

A somber crowd gathered at Ms. Harris's house.

People stood along the roadway; tension was in the air; as they approached the house.

Mr. Rudy, Mr. Rudy, Chantell Dead. "What", said Rudy?

Chantell dead, repeated Kevin, her Mama dead too.

Rudy looked around, all the men up and down the street were pacing back and forth angrily, the women all had tear-stained faces, and helpless; confused looks.

Felicia gathered the victims' relatives together; she knew they weren't going anywhere soon, they were moping around aimlessly, trying to grasp this sad turn of events, so she offered to cook up some food, to tide them over.

Rudy talked with community members who had information about what had happened.

When he heard about the brutal rape and murder, his strength left him, he cried unwillingly and uncontrollably, afterwards only anger was left.

Chantell's body was found Tuesday, September 22nd, Her "Birthday".

Ms. Harris answered a knock at the door; A police officer stood there.

Is this the Harris residence? "Yes, it is," said Ms. Harris.

May I come in please; I have some news that's kind of delicate.

Sure, come on in Officer.

You should probably have a seat Ma'am.

I'm fine Officer, I need to…Ma'am please have a seat. Ms. Harris sat down reluctantly.

Ma'am I'm sorry to inform you, that we found your daughter's body today, we're going to need you to come down to the coroner's office to identify the remains.

Ms. Harris was coming up out of her chair, as he said, it looked like foul play was involved, her body shook violently.

No, she said, No.... No.... No, her eyes went wide' and she reached for the Officer, who recoiled, thinking she was going to attack him.

When he saw her other hand, grasping her chest, he reached forward to catch her, they both went to the floor.

The Officer tried to calm her, but her body continued jerking, only the whites of her eyes showed when she went limp.

The medical examiner called it, traumatic shock, the news she received was more than her system could take, she died instantly.

Rudy somehow felt that he was going to cross paths with those responsible.

He let it be known that he would "Never" stop looking for them' and that they were going to pay dearly, Chantell was under his protection as a community, and we let her down.

The police were coming up empty, very little evidence was found at the crime scene, they had no leads.

A school mate named Amos, came forward, it seems he was the last person to see Chantell alive.

He was taken in for questioning, so was his cousin, the borrowed car was back at twelve thirty, they knew the events of the evening that he described' was the truth, he had a solid alibi and was not charged in any way.

The coroner estimated the time of death at approximately, two O'clock A.M. three days ago, Saturday morning.

Where was I at that time, Rudy asked himself?

I was picking up my last paycheck about that time, that's the same night Ty got shot, and about the same time.

Ty walked Chantell almost everywhere; he may have been there that night.

Rudy called Tony Smalls, a detective at TPD' he was raised in the neighborhood and knew Chantell.

Rudy told him that Ty had been shot and killed the same night that Chantell was raped and murdered.

Chantell and Ty were close, there may be a connection. I'll be right over, said Tony.

Tony brought a whole squad with him; the dug up the grave, exhumed Ty's body, and took it with them.

At the lab, they took samples of the blood around Ty's mouth, the flesh in his teeth, and they were going to trace the bullets that were removed from the body.

Rudy felt they were finally on the right track, if he were right, the identity of the culprits would soon be known.

Once I find out who they are, I can find them from there, he thought to himself.

Felicia came over that following weekend; she just wanted to get out of the house.

Let's go check out the Bulls game today, she asked.

We can do that, said Rudy, sensing she wanted some company today.

It wasn't a bad idea, USF was playing Tennessee, that was sure to be fun to watch, and it was.

Tennessee fell under the South Florida Bulls 28 to 10; it was a Bulls night tonight.

Raymond James Stadium had a capacity crowd, that's unusual for a college game; the USF- Tennessee game always brought a party type atmosphere with it.

Tonight, after the game, everyone headed for Ybor City to celebrate, Felicia and Rudy followed the crowd.

Ybor City is a solid mile of clubs, three blocks wide, both sides of the street on all three blocks, no cars allowed on the center block, people occupied every square foot, and one can very easily "over party" here, every temptation known to man flows rampant throughout this strip.

Rudy and Felicia stopped and got a bite to eat at Carmine's, one of the few Restaurants on Ybor strip that has a full menu, the party atmosphere was carrying itself wildly, up and down the strip.

They walked all the way down to the far end of the strip, to the Broadway Bar, the bar was full of familiar faces tonight, they started greeting people as soon as they stepped inside.

Felicia was corralled to a table where her good friend Naomi and her husband Kirt were sitting.

Rudy went to the pool tables in the back room, it was refreshing to see so many old friends.

He saw Nikki Parks, coming through the crowd, making her way to the pool room.

I thought that was you, she said, when she spotted Rudy, she walked straight up to him, she was wearing the hell out of that little black dress, and high heels, she wore her hair short and curly, the gold sash earrings and lipstick accentuated her high yellow complexion.

Rudy gave her a hug and kissed her on the corner of the mouth.

I have a table up front, come join me, she said.

This game is just about over, save me a seat, I won't be long.

Got cha, said Nikki.

He couldn't help but watch her leave....pure poetry in motion.

Felicia had noticed two unfamiliar faces; they got up from a table on the other side of the jukebox.

They went in the pool room, behind Rudy, she hadn't realized she was paying attention to this, until Rudy emerged from the pool room, and went to Nikki's table.

That's when her intuition kicked in; the same two guys came out also.

They leaned on the far wall, behind Rudy's table.

She eyed them intently, although they tried to act casual, she felt that their presence at this point, had something to do with Rudy, she went over to the table.

"Hi Nikki", she said.

Hi Felicia, have a seat girl.

Maybe later, right now I need to talk to Rudy, if you don't mind.

I'm not stepping on any toes here, am I?

No girl, you're straight, I just need a word is all.

Rudy followed her through the crowd, and out the front door.

Come on, hurry, she said. What's up, asked Rudy.

They crossed the street, and started back up Ybor strip, Felicia looked casually behind them, and sure enough, the same two guys were coming out of the front door;

They continued to walk casually until they made it to the corner, they turned the corner' and ran full speed, trying to find a place to hide.

They found a place, behind a scissor grate' in a store front.

Those guys are up to something, said Felicia.

Rudy pulled out his .45, the day Chantell's body was found, Rudy stirred up so much shit, Felicia thought it was best' that they were strapped at all times, she bought Rudy a snub nosed .45 revolver, and a .380 for herself.

The two guys came running around the corner; they passed the cubby hole, where Felicia and Rudy were hiding.

"See", I told you, I bet you believe me now, don't you!

Rudy didn't answer, he stepped out of hiding, pulling Felicia with him, the two guys were half a block away.

One was combing the area from the sidewalk; the other was in the middle of the deserted street.

They looked a little upset at having lost sight of their prey.

Go back to the club' and get with Naomi and Kirt, said Rudy.

You coming?

No, I talked so much shit about what I was gonna do, to whoever had anything to do with what happened to Chantell, these guys are probably looking for "me", they had something to do with it, I can feel it.... hurry up, "Go".

Felicia headed toward the Club, running.

Rudy crossed the street, headed toward the two guys.

They spotted him and headed toward him.

A row of cars lined that side of the street, and from the angle they were coming, a parked van was about to block their view.

When it did, Rudy cut through from behind the van, catching them both by surprise, he opened fire, hitting both men once, the first' lay between the van and the car parked in front of it, holding a wound to the stomach, just below the rib cage, his breathing suggested' he wasn't going to make it.

The second was hit in the side, he turned and ran, Rudy followed the second, he ran convulsively, not fast at all, he ran around back of the nearest building and sat on the ground beside the dumpster.

Rudy kneeled down in front of him, keeping a close eye on the pistol that lay on his open fingers.

The fingers tried desperately to grasp the pistol, but there was too much nervous system damage.

Please man, don't kill me, he begged.

Don't do that man, said Rudy, don't you dare sit there and beg for your life, after what you did to Chantell, you killed her, an um gonna kill you, plain and simple.

"Chantell", the little girl that was killed? I had nothing to do with that, I'm working for this lawyer, Ron Baines.

"Ron Baines", said Rudy, what the fuck are you doing for..... Rudy recoiled, blood spattered all over the side of the dumpster, Felicia seemed to come out of nowhere.

She stepped up and shot the man twice in the head, what are you talking to this motherfucker for, she snapped at Rudy through tears, as she kicked the man repeatedly, this is one of the no good bitches that killed Chantell,... you fucking die, she yelled, as she shot him again.

Rudy pulled her away, trying to calm her down, she was in a state of madness, they left in a hurry, needing to get away before someone stumbled upon them.

He took her back to his parents' house; she curled up in bed and talked in her sleep for most of the night.

Rudy sat on the floor, and listened.

(at Ground Level, instances will arise, where the law isn't even considered,...it's primal, those at Ground Level, don't ever get far away from the first law of nature,... Self Preservation.)

Over breakfast the next morning, no one spoke for quite some time.

Rudy broke the silence.

I don't think those guys were' who we thought they were. "What", said Felecia, who else could they have been?

That one guy, he said he was working for Ron Baines, a Lawyer, from the same firm as Emmitt Smith,.. so I called Emmitt this morning an told him about it.

Felicia was so startled, she almost choked,.. please say, you didn't tell "Anybody" about what happened last night.

"No", I told him I was "threatened" by a guy that said he worked for Ron Baines, he asked if I was ok, I said yeah.

He said he was going to pull Baines phone records, office, home, and cell, and see who he's been talking to.

Rudy, make a pact with me right now, said Felicia, not to talk to anyone about what happened, "No One", promise me.

I think we're good, no one saw what happened, and no one can trace those soft rounds we were using.

"Say It"!

Okay, I promise.

Good, now that we've got that out of the way,... What were you and Nikki talking about last night.

She was looking pretty good last night, Huh. You trying to get with Nikki, she said playfully.

No cock blockin Felicia, that's out, don't even try it.

I can't stop you Rudy, but please don't make me hurt Nikki,... I like her.

Rudy checked his messages, there was one from Tony Smalls, the detective.

Rudy, this is Tony Smalls, come down to the precinct today when you get a chance, I think we got something.

Tony took him through their findings.

The blood analysis that we took from Ty's mouth' brought up two separate strands of D.N.A. we ran them through the police database.

See, anyone who's been convicted of a capital felony (Violent Crime) must give up a D.N.A. sample.

These two guys were already in the system, the first

D.N.A. strand matched a James Dawson, alias, J.D., the second was a positive match for Emanuel Menendez, alias, Manny, they both have lengthy records,... lets see if they have alibi's.

Rudy stared at the photo of J.D., he had seen him before, he picked up the photos of both men.

Detective Smalls quickly relieved him of the pictures.

I know what you're thinking Rudy, "but we got this", we've already put out an A.P.B., on them, they'll be in custody shortly, we have the caliber and make of two guns' from the bullets we recovered.

They don't match any registered weapons on file, they're probably throw away.

Rudy hadn't noticed the crowd of detectives and police officers that had gathered, one by one, behind, and on either side of him, his body tensed, he'd been lured into a trap, they knew what he'd done the other night.

He felt a panic attack coming on, he was surrounded, there were to many of them to make any kind of move, he looked up and saw a man approaching, he was coming from the front office, by his uniform' he clearly out ranked everyone else there,... it was the Chief of detectives, the man was carrying an Urn.

He handed the Urn to Rudy.

My name is Nathaniel Albright, I'm the Chief of detectives, when the Chantell Harris case opened, we had nothing to go on, couldn't find a place to start, no evidence, nothing,...I sincerely believe, that those murderers would have gotten away, free and clear, if it hadn't been for your Dog.

We have reason to believe that this animal "was" at the scene, and tried to save this young girls life, "alone", and was shot and killed in the process.

Your dog Ty, is a hero,... he was cremated this morning and placed in this Urn, his name is engraved on it.

He's also been presented, the Medal of Honor, that's strapped around the neck of the Urn.

It says in the bible, there's no greater gift' than to lay down your life for another.

Ty gave the greatest gift, that can possibly be given, then to top it off, ... he brought back all the evidence we needed to work this case, Ty simply saved the day.

The detectives began to chant,.. Ty...Ty...Ty, as each person came around to touch the Urn.

The applause started around the room.

Rudy ended up shaking hands with all of the detectives.

Ty really did save the day, he thought to himself, the detectives made him feel how much he missed Ty.

They were still celebrating their new leads as Rudy left, Rudy couldn't get comfortable around them, as they were, real detectives, and he had quite a few, real crimes, floating around him at the moment.

From there he went straight home, Felicia was gone, he sat and thought about the pictures the detective had shown him, and where he'd seen this guy before,.. Then it came to him, he got the .45 and headed to that first house from the train bridge.

The van that's usually parked there around this time of day, was gone.

He walked up and looked in the window, the place was empty, it had the look of someone who'd made a quick move.

He broke the window of the back door to get inside.

He looked for any clue that might say where this guy was headed, a lot of stuff was left behind, can goods, cleaning products, trash was strewn throughout the place.

He spotted something shiny on the floor, it was on a clean section of carpet, where a dresser must have been.

It was an earring; it was still on the velvet covered display that it was purchased on, or stolen on, or whatever, the place where the second earring went was empty.

When Rudy took a good look at the earring, he realized he'd never seen anything quite like it.

It was a diamond stud, beautifully cut,.. and dead center, closer to the base, a tiny fountain like image shown.

The closer you look, you could see a very detailed, blue water spout' moving in super slow motion.

So tiny, it made you wonder how it was possible to create such a thing.

Rudy looked around to see if he could find the other one, no luck there, and no luck on finding any directional addresses lying around either.

He pocketed the earring and continued to search.

He left empty handed, being sure to wipe down any prints he may have left.

The police "will" come up with a last known address for

J.D. and just so there's no misunderstanding, his prints shouldn't be found there.

Rudy stopped off at a pawn shop on Hillsborough Ave, the jeweler said he'd give me $250.00 for the earring.

No thanks, said Rudy.

Well now he knows it's real, not cubic Zirconia, if a jeweler at a pawn shop offers you $250.00 for any item, that item is worth five times that much.

He returned home, in his room, he searched for a place to display Ty's Urn.

He removed the books from the center of the bookshelf, put two bookends up to hold the remaining books on either side,.. he placed the Urn in the middle, with two small ferns on either side of it,.. it was perfect.

The throw rug in front of the bookshelf was Ty's favorite spot, on rainy days or too cold nights, he'd be whining at the door, once inside, he heads for that rug and plops down for the night.

Rudy looked around the room, his bed was centered under the window, his work desk was on one side, the walk-in closet on the other, the bookshelf and dresser were on the wall at the foot of the bed.

This was his sanctuary, it wasn't much, but at this moment, he was grateful to have a place where he could spend some time alone, in peace.

He lay back and tried to relax.

He woke to the smell of someone cooking, his mind pictured Felicia right off the bat, but this aroma went much further than Felicia, it went all the way back to his childhood, that could only be Mom.

He crossed the kitchen on tiptoe, she paid no attention to him as he crept up behind her, he pressed a finger in the center of her back and said.

This is a stick up!

Boy, you robbed me five times in the last week, what you doin, practicing.

Lady, you gonna have to give up some of that seafood dish you got going there.

It's a Tuna Casserole, bring your little finger gun back in about twenty minutes and it'll be ready.

That thing you're doing with that Lawyer, how's it going, she asked, you really got a case?

This Lawyers pretty smart, said Rudy, he thinks were onto something, the lawyers he's up against already made a settlement offer, he turned it down, said it was a joke offer, he's counting on getting four or five times that much.

I think he should go for it too; Felicia told me she checked out quite a few of their businesses, and they were all "Visibly" prejudice, and you've wasted 3 years of your life there,.. did it really take you that long to see it.

Ma, still hadn't seen it, it had to be shown to me, in writing at that.

It's just hard to believe that a man can think he's better, different, or more than another man.

His Mom just looked at him, head slightly tilted. Rudy knew that look; I'm missing something ain't I.

Yeah, ...Money,...countless men only follow instructions, their basically told what to think, like puppets, the ones in control of these puppets, in one way or another, may get the feeling of being more than he actually is, if the man in charge said, treat all Patrons with the utmost respect, and all job opportunities goes to any man or woman that qualifies, ...then that's the way it would be.

So, it's the man in charge that's defiling the laws of the land, said Rudy.

Yes,... Sue his ass off.

Rudy called Emmitt Smith for an update.

Yeah, Rudy we're in luck, our company has phone monitors on all upper level, in house staff, we litigate for superpowers who live with paranoia, any information leaks' can have catastrophic consequences, the monitors are always in place, but very rarely utilized.

Because of the professionalism incased in this firm, so casual is the system now, we hardly pay attention to it anymore.

Ron Baines called a man by the name of Orlan Petrini,.. Petrini called him back, and Baines has two calls back-to-back, to two different guys, the names aren't important, what's important is, they both have lengthy criminal records.

"Who is this Orlan Petrini guy," asked Rudy.

Get this, he's the owner of The Two Cronies Restaurant chain, he also owns a lot of Commercial Real Estate, and the list goes on.

So, he's the man in charge, said Rudy.

Yeah, that's the man, seems Ron Baines has worked for him before, I'm filing the phone tapes as

Exhibit B, just in case Baines was being forced to act against you.

This man Petrini is known as a crude businessman, he hasn't been labeled a gangster or anything, but he is a tough cookie, we can't be too careful.

Orlan Petrini turned page after page of Documented Evidence brought forth by his Lawyers, his grim expression told his feelings about the matter.

No African Americans or Hispanics are allowed to work as Managers.

And I see at least four other positions' per store, that's flagrantly been written into the Managers Guide, openly denying employment for certain Nationalities,.. who could be that grossly incompetent.

What are we looking at in damages?

It'll be best if we settle quickly and quietly, said the lead Lawyer,.. their leaning in the area of a quarter million.

And if we challenge them, what then, asked Petrini?

Well, if they get the judgement, which at the moment is in their favor,.. damages could run up to two million.

I'll settle with them, get the paperwork prepared for a quarter million, but hold on to it until I give you the go ahead.

We have to respond within ten days Sir, however if you need more time, we can manipulate the system and slow things down a bit.

I'll let you know, said Orlan, good night gentlemen.

Orlan wanted more than anything to settle, he was a crude businessman, he moved around the underworld also, he was a lot of things, but prejudice wasn't one of them, he didn't want to wear that label,... he'd settle out of court.

A quarter million wouldn't hurt him, but he'd feel a 2- million-dollar loss.

How and where, did that business killing flaw in the Managers Guide come from, a closer look at the businesses he ran, must be put into effect.

He sent a message to his second in command, insisting they meet as soon as possible, such glitches could not be tolerated.

The message reached Marcus White at a small meeting of the Arian Nation, a splinter cell of the Ku-Klux-Klan, this part of his life he kept secret, not that he was ashamed of it, but because it was a "Secret Society".

Orlan Petrini knew nothing of this, and didn't need to know, by Marcus Whites standards, he drove up and met Orlan at his home.

Our problem seems to have grown a bit, said Orlan, we now have 17 counts of Discrimination filed against us, this came by our own hand, and there's little chance of getting from under it, 17 Managers Guides were reviewed before we could pull them, all of them were Blatantly Discriminatory,...I want you to find out who made this Horrendous mistake, and get rid of them, and have our doors open properly, for "all" patrons.

They turned down my first offer to settle, my next offer will be what they wanted, a quarter million,..if they turn that down, then' they know they've got me by the balls, and this thing can cost us two, maybe three million.

"What", said Marcus.

Yes, ... that's what we're looking at.

Orlan,...let me go down there and do a little damage control, and see if we can put a little water over these flames, ...I'll call you in 48 hours' with a report.

Marcus ran back to his car and put in a call, ordering another meeting of his Arian brothers.

He couldn't hold his head up, from the sting of embarrassment, for he was the one who had revised the Managers Guidebook, and that move may cost Orlan a small fortune.

He couldn't see where he was wrong, why couldn't white people have a place they can go and enjoy a meal, and good company, without the mongrel people of the world sitting among them, he thought of Orlan, who started this business with one rundown Sports Bar, and two commercial rental properties, left to him by his father, and his first wife's father.

He was content with the earnings from his and his wife's inheritance, he merely maintained the buildings, just enough to them running, the change came when his beautiful wife left him for a more ambitious man.

From that point, Orlan poured himself into his work, it wasn't long before he was prospering mightily.

He remarried, but still spent countless hours working, Marcus White was placed in charge of his labor force, he also did some trouble shooting,... he was introduced to Orlan's wife, as Orlans second in command.

He was spending more time with her than Orlan was, inevitably, she introduced him to her bed.

Orlan dosn't know I've been fucking his wife for him for the last 4 years, and as long as everything keeps running smooth, he'll never even question it.

He only called 4 of his most trusted Arian brothers, he brought them up to speed on the situation at hand.

It seems, we've run up on a "Mongrel" that wants to play hard ball, an absolute nobody, challenging the big boys, staring right in our faces, with no back up what-so-ever,...no money, no education, nothing,.. And he's challenging us for a small fortune, one to the likes of which he's never seen, or will ever see, we're going to teach them a very valuable lesson,...playing with the big boys, is "Dangerous", it's safer to watch the big boys play,.. from a distance, this is the message we're sending to our little Mongrel friend.

Stan and I will pay the Lawyer a visit, we've got to find that evidence they've acquired.

Earnest, you and Bubba make sure that little shithead doesn't show up in court, their crying prejudice,.. Let's show them "extreme" prejudice.

Cole showed up at Rudy's Parents' house, right in the middle of dinner, Mrs. Claton set a place for him at the table, not bothering to ask if he was hungry.

He did say' Hi Mama C, before he went to work on that Tuna Casserole.

After the meal, they went outside and sat on the tailgate of Cole's truck.

Cole started in about a girl he'd met, her name was Mira.

I really like this kid, he said, I think she's a keeper, she likes me too, she's already talking about us living together, right now she's living with two roommates',

And I'm living with my parents, or at the campsite.

So, the thought never really presented itself as something do'able,..."until today".

I had a little talk with Mrs. Culpepper today, she was telling me that since her husband's death, bills have been coming from everywhere, when she mentioned she was going to start getting rid of her husband's properties, I asked her about that two story, block house over in Temple Terrace, and,...well, to make a long story short, I just signed a promissory note for $70,000.00, that's all she's asking us to pay for it, but it has to be in cash, and within 90 days, Rudy, the place is great, and huge, I guarantee you, if she puts that place on the market for

$200,000.00,... it wouldn't last a week, we're not ever going to get a deal like this again, not in this lifetime.

I take it, you're planning on financing this with the money we get from our crop, asked Rudy?

Yeah, we can go in 50\50, you can have the second floor, with that Giant sized Master Bedroom, there's a full bath in there, the second bedroom up there has a half bath,...I'll take the bottom two bedrooms, Thirty five Thousand apiece, and we'll have our own home baby boy.

"How many hits do we have so far," asked Rudy. Fifty pounds are as good as sold already, replied Cole.

That's not a bad idea Cole, you may be onto something, count me in,.. I've got a Lawyer who can look over everything for us, I've never bought a house before, I don't know how it's done, if it's worth as much as you say it is, that's a worthwhile investment.

We'd better start the harvest next week then, said Cole, once we get them hung for the dry- out period," the whole crop should be ready within ten to fifteen days, and one month after that, we should have the seventy we need.

Cole, I know you really like this girl, Mira, but we haven't known her that long, so...

I'm not dense, said Cole, she'll never get wind of what we're doing.

Good, said Rudy, and let the house deal be a surprise also.

Rudy felt good about the house deal, it was like Cole was reading his mind, he could finally move into his own spacious lair, he wanted to check the place out as soon as possible.

Getting out of that room would be a blessing, Mom and Dad would be happy too.

You think you can get Felicia to move in with us, she's tight work, said Cole, I like having her around,.. maybe you two can spark that old flame back up again.

I don't know about that flame stuff, but seeing about getting her to move in with us is definitely a positive step.

You know she still likes you! She still tolerates me.

Have you been out to check on the crop lately, asked Cole.

Not since the last time I went out there with you. Let's run out there right quick and check on things. Why, we're cool, said Rudy.

Know what, ...when we first started putting this little crop together, it was just something daring and exiting, something to get the old blood pumping, now it's getting more important, now I'm pretty much counting on this, I don't want anything to go wrong.

What can go wrong, asked Rudy.

Well, the shit we're doing is wrong, and when you do wrong shit, wrong shit happens.

I know, but a lot of people do wrong shit, we're not the first people to grow weed, this whole country was founded on people doing wrong shit.

The Dupont's, the Rockefellers, the Getty's, the Kennedy's, the Two Cronies, they've all done wrong shit, you don't go to jail for what you do,.. you go to jail for getting caught.

Cole smiled at the humorous remark.

Ok partner, let's go see about our cash crop, said Rudy.

They were just about ready to get into the truck' when they both noticed a figure coming up the sidewalk.

Is that Felicia, asked Cole. Yeah, that's her, said Rudy.

They both spoke without taking their eyes off the figure, she wore black spandex, that stopped at the middle of the calf, the sun dress hung from her shoulders by spaghetti straps, the dress was cut so it was longer in the back than the front, it wasn't tight, it just had a flow that caught the eye.

Do you think she's trying to walk like that, asked Cole?

I never could tell, she's always walked like that, act's like she could care less about it,.. it sure doesn't go to her head.

Somewhere in his subconscious, he noticed the black sedan parked at the curb on the block behind her.

It only registered to him as a visitor on the block or something.

Felicia was carrying a plastic bag, the type that comes from the grocer.

Where you guy's going, she yelled, as Cole and Rudy were getting in the truck.

I was gonna cook something for you.

Mom cooked a Tuna Casserole, I'd advise you not to cook, you're welcome to the Casserole.

I like your Moms Tuna Cassarole, I'm going to get a taste, I'll be right back, I'm going to leave this in the refrigerator.

She returned eating from a small bowl, she opened the passenger door and proceeded to climb in.

Where "you" going, asked Rudy?

I'm gonna hang out with you and Cole.

You're not dressed to go where we're going, we have to go out in the woods for awhile, its muddy and nasty, your little white sneaks, and little footies with the balls in the back, won't make it.

Just because I go to a nasty place, don't mean I have to get nasty.

Hmm, is that something like, just because I go to the barbershop, doesn't mean I have to get a haircut.

That's what I said, she replied, I know where you're going, I want to see your little garden.

Rody gave her that, "I don't think so" look. I'm going, she said.

O.K. with you Cole, Rudy asked?

Yeah man, I told you I like having her around, lets ride.

Cole took I-275 north, that's the route he takes when he's a little anxious.

Felicia was settled in, she got the pen and pad from over the sun visor' and was content with her writing.

Hey, Cole and I were planning on getting a place, your name came up, so I figured I should at least ask you if you wanted to move in with us, tell her about the place Cole.

I'll do better than that, I'll take you both over there tomorrow, you and Rudy can have the whole top floor, Mira and I will have the bottom, and believe me' we won't get in each other's way.

She looked as if she was thinking, she showed no expression to a readable point, she was playing with her lip with the pen, looking straight ahead, when she asked,...you want to stay with me?

They drove as far into the woods as possible, then got out and walked, thirty minutes later, they were there, Felicia was amazed by the size of the plants, and how healthy they were.

The man they were looking for, had finally emerged from the house they were watching, he wasn't alone, he was with a white guy, they sat on the tailgate of the truck,.. and now a female has shown up.

They watched as they all climbed into the pick-up truck. Follow them, we may be able to catch him alone.

The four men in the black Sedan, with North Carolina plates, were all focused, they were prepared for the job at hand, they planned on breaking some bones today.

This guy was definitely not making it to court.

When Cole made the turn-off leading into the woods, the black Sedan kept going past the entrance, so as not to alert them to their presence, they doubled back and pulled in, parking off to the side of the road, out of sight.

It was muddy as marsh land in that area, the four Arian

Brothers took off on foot, their nice slacks, and patent leather shoes, were no longer in mint condition, it showed on their faces.

It wasn't long before they found Cole's truck.

They couldn't tell what direction they went, they were nowhere in sight.

The self-appointed leader of the group noticed the tracks, it was obvious who the tracks belonged to, for there were no other tracks anywhere.

This is too good to be true,.... their alone in the woods.

They began following the tracks' that were so graciously left for them.

Rudy and Cole went from plant to plant, checking their progress, the plants weren't grown in neat rows as a garden might look, there were no more than five plants grown in a given area, area's that provide cover from being spotted, from passers by, or from overhead.

Their progress was well above average, especially for this time of year, it was moving into winter season, yet it was still above 80 degrees in Florida.

The tree's still plush and green, maybe the Fall missed us this year,... that's the price you pay for living in the tropics,.. It's great.

This would be the perfect time to harvest, the plants are peaking.

Felicia was surprised there was no obvious Marijuana aroma present, you only smell it when you step up to the plants.

The silence of the woods was suddenly broken, their was a yipping, almost barking sound a little too close to the hideout, they all ran to check it out.

The little Red Fox was yipping frantically, at first, they thought he was just being territorial or something.

The he turned and faced the other direction, yipping at something he knew was coming, he turned back again and yipped at us a few more times, then darted into the woods.

"What the hell was that," asked Felicia?

That was a warning, said Cole, someone or something is coming.

They all ducked down low in the brush and remained still.

That little Red Fox did warn us, didn't he, said Rudy, freaking out over that fact.

Yeah, said Cole, he's been close by ever since we got here, Ty's been chasing "The Red" for the last ten months, they spent a lot of time together, and learned a lot from each other,... he's doing what "Ty" would have done.

One of Ty's friends, looking out for us, ain't that some shit.

Ssssh, Cole whispered, ... look. They all looked.

Someone "was" out there, they were able to make out four figures, they all walked together, stopping frequently, looking over the path as they were trying to figure out which way to go.

All the while, they were pretty much headed in our direction.

That's the way "we" came, Rudy whispered, you think their tracking us.

Silence fell over them as they watched the figures. Yeah, said Felicia, their following our trail.

Fuck, said Cole.

They don't look or act like Cops, said Rudy.

They're not hunters either, said Cole, but believe me, they're tracking us.

Cole, we can't let them follow that trail, it'll lead them here, "no one" can come here, for no reason whatsoever,...look this is what we're gonna do, we're going out this way, and come back around to cut them off, we've got to get them off that trail.

Then what, asked Cole, we didn't bring the air rifles, we can't pretend we're out here hunting.

Cole, there's no more pretending, those people are looking for "us", we need to find out who they are, and stop their forward progress toward our shit,... once they see us, the trail is mute, we'll play the rest of this encounter by ear,.. Any sign of trouble, I'm gonna have to take point.

Felicia, you ready. Yeah!

Here we go, stay close.

They went into action as planned; they came up on the left of the four men, they laughed and talked as if they were on a leisurely walk through the woods.

The four men spotted them, their prey was coming straight to them, the men stopped and waited for them.

"Hi", how you guy's doing, said Cole, seems like everybody wants to take a walk in the woods today.

We were actually looking for you guy's, said one of the men, were here to deliver a message.

The self-appointed leader made his way over in front of Rudy, staring him in the eye.

The message is,... you should be more careful of who you fuck with.

All four men charged at that moment.

Two of the men rushed and grabbed Rudy, Rudy struggled hard to free himself, a blow to the side of the head drove him to the ground, lying on his back, he felt the .38 revolver he'd tucked into the small of his back.

He reached for the gun and rolled at the same time, trying to gain an extra second on his attackers.

The gun came out smoothly, and he fired into the first man's stomach, the man was going to his knees' holding his wound, Rudy quickly trained the gun on the other man, the man simply started to back up, hands in the air.

Rudy looked for Felicia, he caught a glimpse of her' coming out of her shoulder bag, pointing, and firing into the chest of another.

The man was still coming for her when Cole came running and mowed him down, and continued running, Felicia broke out right behind him, Rudy got to his feet and ran through the nearest brush thicket, making sure he was out of sight by the time the other men produced their weapons.

Rudy ran furiously, he could hear someone running behind him, but he felt comfortable with the distance between them, it wasn't likely that someone who didn't know these woods would catch him.

He headed toward the high ground, staying low, the tall wheat grass was providing cover.

Pssst, he heard it loud and clear, it came from the direction of that old left over section of storm drain, it was completely overgrown, if you didn't know it was there, you'd never know.

He headed in that direction, until he saw a hand motioning him over, it was Felicia, Rudy was relieved to get inside the 4 foot high section of cement tubing,

Cole was peeping out the other end, being this hiding spot was on high ground, they could see everything below, the men weren't far behind, now there were only two of them, they searched the grounds below thoroughly, frantically.

The self-proclaimed leader screamed at the top of his lungs,... you may as well come out, you can't hide from me,.. You're a dead man, you hear, a fucking dead man.

They stayed hidden until they were sure those guys were gone, they hurried back to the truck, only to find it had been trashed, tires slashed, windows busted, seats ripped up.

Are you fucking kidding me, said Felicia, look at this, I'm thinking we're lucky to be alive right now.

I think I know who they are, said Rudy,... the Lawyer Emmitt Smith, said the guy's who came at us before, were connected to Ron Baines, the first Lawyer I'd talked to about the lawsuit I'm working on, Ron Baines has been connected to a Mr. Petrini, the owner of the Two Cronies restaurant chain.

That guy said, "be careful of who you fuck with", that can only be Petrini.

That sounds like a long shot, said Cole, but I wouldn't put it past them.

We also may have to take in consideration the fact that someone may have gotten wind of what we're doing out here.

Let's get out of here, said Felicia.

The fear and frustration in her voice' made Rudy and Cole pay closer attention to her.

They both looked her over.

The once white sneakers and footies, were now mud boots, all the way up to her calves, the spandex were ripped in several places, showing flesh, she was dirty from head to foot, she pulled sticker burrs from everywhere.

Rudy and Cole both had to cover their mouths to keep from laughing.

She had already started beating on them before they burst out laughing.

They had to call "Tripple A" to tow Cole's truck, the tow truck driver was kind enough to drop Felicia and Rudy off on the way to the shop.

Rudy took a long hot shower, the fatigue set in soon after, he got to bed and fell into a deep sleep.

Marcus White met up with his Arian brothers in the designated spot, his anger overflowed when it was brought to his attention, the mission was a failure.

He swung before the self-appointed crew leader could react; the hardwood floor broke his fall.

"Get out", yelled Marcus White, do not return with another report of failure.

He only had two men left of that crew, the other two were nursing gunshot wounds' and had to be transported to a doctor who was on their payroll.

Marcus had successfully gotten into the office of Emmitt Smith; he gathered up every piece of evidence against Orlan Petrini, and the restaurant chain.

Let's see how far this case goes now!

"Wake Up", the voice came through a dream he was having,... "Wake Up",

Rudy woke up coughing and gagging, he rolled out of bed and almost collapsed,... why was it so dark.

Light headed and dizzy, he headed for the hallway, the smoke so thick it almost choked him out, that's when he noticed the flames, dancing as they ran up the wall, he heard a window break, and in came a ball of fire, it hit the wall six feet from him, and exploded, the accelerant

Brought the fire down the wall to the carpet.

Rudy turned and fought the smoke and flames all the way to his mother and father's room.

They herded together, all coughing and gagging and running for the back door.

Mom and Dad were completely puzzled, Dad wanted to stop and fight the fire with pots and pans of water, Rudy knew that would be a losing battle, against the barrage of Molotov Cocktails that were coming through window after window, he pushed them through the back door, yelling, Run,... Run,... just Run.

They had barely stepped off the last step' into the back yard, when the gunfire erupted.

Dad was first, he was hit twice, he tried to continue on, but fell a few steps after.

Rudy and Mom tried to get around the corner of the house, Rudy ran directly behind his Mom to ensure she wouldn't be hit, Rudy took the next three bullets, he fell, but watched his Mom make it around the side of the house, he was relieved, then he heard her scream,.. the scream was cut short by more gunfire at the front of the house.

In the darkness, Rudy saw the backyard gunman coming toward him.

Did you actually think you could get away from me?

He pointed the gun' about the same time the flames had reached the gas main... the whole house seemed to jump up off the ground, then "Explode".

He didn't even have time to shoot, he was impaled by a 5-foot section of metal tubing that went straight through his chest, and into a tree behind him.

The debris followed immediately, the man was killed instantly, Rudy himself was covered by the devastating fallout, he heard voices, as the neighbors came running, then he heard nothing.

The self-appointed leader jumped into the black Sedan and sped off, he didn't have time to collect his Arian brother's body, the neighbors were coming from everywhere.

He knew his Arian brother was dead, no sense in them both getting caught.

A young neighbor saw the man with a gun get into the car and sped off.

He grabbed his keys and went out after him, he dialed 911 on his cell phone and told the duty dispatcher he was following a man who just shot someone.

He followed the Sedan clear across town, all the while leading the police to their location.

The self-appointed leader had no idea he was being followed.

The sirens and squad cars came from every direction, making his getaway run short lived.

He was taken in as a suspect, he called Marcus White to bail him out.

Marcus decided to cut his losses, deny any connection or involvement whatsoever.

His Arian brother sensed the separation, panic caused him to yell into the phone.

Marcus, brother, you've got to get me out of here, they've got the guns, and now' eyewitnesses are beginning to show up.

You may have to do some time, said Marcus, I'll get you a good Lawyer and you'll be O.K., as long as you keep quiet,....don't tell them anything.

It wasn't long before the charges against him were filed.

Marcus White put some distance between them, cut all ties, and left him out to dry.

The man was given a public defender, who dropped the heavy file on the table before him, the Lawyer looked about as enthusiastic as a man who was about to attempt to hand feed a hungry lion,... you have no bond, said the Lawyer, you are being charged with "Felony Trespassing",

"Throwing a Missile Into An Occupied Dwelling", "Discharging A Firearm within City Limits",

"First Degree Arson",

"Three counts of Pre-Meditated First-Degree Murder", "One count of Attempted Murder", "Reckless Endangerment", "Disturbing The Peace", And "Resisting Arrest", One of the Murder Charges you're facing is for the death of the guy that came with you.

Sir, we're going to have to fight to have your Execution postponed until tomorrow.

The death penalty is already on the table, unless there's some reason you shouldn't die,... if not, then your pretty much,... dead.

The self-appointed leader sang like a bird.

He gave up Marcus White, the media got hold of the story behind the gruesome attack, and it spread like wildfire.

The destruction at the crime scene, along with Marcus White's face' was plastered on television screens across the nation.

Soon after, investigative reporters discovered that Marcus White was second in command to an Orlan Petrini.

The case immediately turned 'high profile, now the Media people came out of the woodwork, the self-made Millionaire was now the new target, Petrini's face replaced Marcus White's on television screens across the land, he was being labeled a Racist hate Monger.

Hordes of media personnel were being posted at Orient Road Jail, awaiting his arrest' and extradition to Tampa.

Petrini watched as this series of events unfolded before his eye's, the television media showed no mercy, he knew they would be coming for him soon.

The thought of running' flashed through his mind.

What reason do I have for running, he thought to himself, I never ordered anyone killed, Marcus alone is responsible for this, I'll just tell the truth, he's going to have to pay for his own stupidity.

Marcus White pulled up to the Arian Nation's headquarters, and meeting hall' after nine hours of driving, being careful to stay off all major highways.

He ran inside and hid the evidence he'd taken from Emmitt Smith's office.

He left hurriedly, he had to get home and get a few things before he went into hiding.

He quickly pulled onto the street he lived on, it wasn't far from the meeting hall, paying no attention to the two unmarked cars that fell in behind him, he parked in the driveway and got out quickly, the car door barely shut when the darkness was replaced by searing lights from all sides, blinding him, when he was able to see, what he saw left him listless, the entire Police force, completely surrounded the perimeter of the house, guns Zero'd in on him from everywhere he looked.

He was afraid to even breathe.

The Police Chief approached him, "We have to talk", he said, as he led him to the Police Cruiser.

You're being placed under arrest, you'll be extradited to Florida as soon as possible,...you have the right to remain silent,...his Miranda rights being read to him sent chills down his spine, he felt nauseous.

Orlan Petrini was also taken into custody for questioning, he too' would be visiting Florida.

Two days later, Rudy opened his eyes, the darkness overtook him, he couldn't see anything.

His mind raced' trying to figure his situation, his last memory came back, he was lying on the ground, paralyzed with fear, when he realized the gunman was heading in his direction, he was afraid to move, he wanted to play dead, but the thought of the gunman standing over him, was more than he could bear.

He fought to make his eyes focus through the darkness, he saw a light, he wondered why it was so hard to focus in on it, slowly, the fog started to clear.

It was a television mounted from the ceiling.

He was in bed, this is a hospital, he attempted to rise' but his body refused to move, they must have given him something, he thought, there was no pain whatsoever, despite the heavy bandage job that suddenly came to his attention.

He looked over, and Felicia was sitting in a chair beside the bed, it was a hospital sitter's chair, big and comfortable.

She was asleep with her hand in her purse, no doubt she had a good grip on that .380 of hers.

I won't be waking her up suddenly, I definitely don't want to get shot again.

Cole came into the room backward, holding two cups of coffee, he glanced over at Rudy as he headed over to give Felicia her caffeine fix, he and Rudy's eyes met, Cole stopped, never breaking eye contact.

Rudy, he said, not really expecting a response.

Yeah, said Rudy.

The response caught Cole off guard, his body jumped involuntarily, just enough to spill coffee all over his hands, the noise he made woke Felicia.

He's awake, he told her.

She stood over his bed looking into his eyes, a smile crept across her face.

Hi, she said, she held his hand, "Welcome Back". How long have I been here?

In a few hours' you'll be starting your third day. Three days,... what kind of condition am I in?

From what I hear, you're a pretty lucky guy. Is Mom and Dad here too?

Felicia looked at Cole,... Cole turned away.

We'd better let the nurse know he's awake, said Cole. I'll get her, said Felicia.

The nurse entered the room, exited, and full of energy, a prominent looking young woman, her parents were probably well off, no signs of everyday woe's touched her persona.

She looked as if she was delighted to see Rudy.

Hi,... it's good to have you with us, she said, moving around the room' checking monitors, how do you feel, she asked, now she was checking the drip from the bottle over the bed.

There's no pain, so let's say, I feel good.

Good, she replied, as she pumped up the heart rate monitor, she'd wrapped around his upper arm, she repositioned the bedrail so she could sit on the bed.

My name is Miranda, I've been looking after you since you got here, you seem to be healing rather nicely, you've been through quite an ordeal.

We removed a bullet that was lodged in your right shoulder blade, another from your right thigh, and yet another bullet passed cleanly through your right forearm.

With your help, I'm going to nurse you back to one hundred percent.

I asked your friends not to discuss anything further with you, I wanted to be sure you were completely stable when we had this talk, it's a sensitive matter, I'll try to talk you through it.

I'm sorry to have to tell you this, but I won't put it off any longer,...neither your mother or your father made it through this ordeal,...they both died two days ago.

From what I've heard, they were pretty much the center of your life, you have my deepest condolences, an I'm going to be keeping an eye on you' every minute, we couldn't save them,.. but you, I'm not going to lose.

I'd like to be left alone," said Rudy' if you don't mind.

Alone in his room, he tried to remain stable, the news really wasn't a surprise, it was some kind of miracle that he himself had survived, besides, he'd read the "look" on the faces of Cole and Felicia when he mentioned it earlier, he couldn't think of a worse scenario for his situation, they didn't even know why they died, it was all my doing, fucking with rich people was the biggest mistake I could have possibly made.

The feeling of sadness stayed with him for quite a while, the anger stayed longer, the feeling for "Revenge" wouldn't leave.

Once you take a life, you can't put it back! Therefore, you can't be forgiven,

You can ask God for forgiveness, And God will forgive you, but you'll still have to pay for what you did.

I don't care who's responsible, they gotta die!

Cole and Felicia came to check on Rudy every day, Cole hardly ever Left. Felicia did a lot of running; she took care of all the funeral arrangements.

Rudy signed off on a fifty thousand dollar life insurance policy from his father's employer.

And asked Felicia to put together the best going home ceremony possible.

She really put her heart into it, she rented Harmon's funeral parlor for the wake, Mt. Zion Church for the Funeral, along with the big hall for the reception after

The burial, she purchased Giant double Headstones that sat upon double Vaults.

She was able to get a top-of-the-line caterer, with whom she could put in for a steady running order, because of the great number of people who had become involved with this incident, including the media, and a lot of the more Prominent Community leaders who'd love to be caught on camera at such an event.

She hired two singers, the Valet parking crew, and 100 White doves.

Cole kept Rudy informed about what was going on.

The Two Cronies Restaurant had been burned to the ground by the locals, the same day that Cole quit.

Cole was getting more protective, Rudy could barely get rid of him, he also picked up a .357 Magnum, he was sure Rudy was still in danger.

Rudy's injuries were healing rapidly, Nurse Miranda was good at what she does, and was always proud when her patients' progress was well above average.

Her work spoke for itself, Rudy was able to attend the Funeral under his own power, no crutches or anything.

He could hardly believe the number of people that showed up, he looked over the crowd in awe.

Speeches were given by the most Prominent attendees, they spoke of the treacherousness of the Racist hate Monger, then on how precious life is.

The two teenaged singers sang in mirrored movements and passion, tears fell to the floor from the touch of the heartfelt songs.

One hundred Doves flew from the gravesite, circled the site twice, then headed for the horizon, they're supposed to symbolize or even be, Spiritual escorts.

Emmitt Smith was there at the reception, he and Rudy went off to a separate table to talk strategy.

The physical evidence had been taken, it wasn't found in the search of Macus White's or Orlan Petrini's homes.

The Lawsuit filed on The Two Cronies and their constituents now contained close to 40 counts, 22 would be tried in Civil court.

All the dots have been connected, Orlan Petrini, Marcus White, and all their thugs have been identified.

"We Got Em", there's still a chance we can get that evidence back.

How,... we know their responsible, but that evidence is their only chance of getting a reasonable doubt verdict.

We couldn't find any fingerprints or anything, but I know it was them.

Rudy asked Cole to take him by the crime scene.

The scene was disturbing, the front concrete steps were still in place, the house, gone, only black ash, a few strewn boards, and sporadic debris remained.

He stood in the center of the black ash, looking over what was left of his life, he saw several small metal objects that were familiar,...and singed.

He moved the ash around with his foot' from one end to the other, he was about to call it quits when something shiny caught his eye, he moved the ash around until he found it.

When he wiped the ash off, it was that earring he'd found at J.D.'s last known address, he looked at it closely, it still held the same effect as it always did, he'd never seen anything like it, he slipped the stud in his pocket and looked around a little more.

Cole came up beside him, if they try anything like this again, next time they won't catch us slipping.

I don't know, their arsenal seems to get more and more intense, I don't think any of us will survive another attack.

I'll be in the car, said Cole; you're probably trying to find some closure in this place.

Actually, I'm trying to find my guns!

Well, if you left them in the house that night, there's nothing left of them, we haven't seen anything around here yet that hasn't been melted down.

I was thinking the same thing, until I found this. Rudy showed him the Diamond stud.

It didn't burn, Cole looked at it closely....Damn, how'd they do that, there's an image inside, a little fountain.

It may belong to one of the guy's that killed Chantell, the one they call J.D., I found it at his place.

He's going to miss this, said Cole.

If I run up on him.... he won't miss it at all!

"Oh yeah", If I'm not mistaken...you don't have a gun. Not at the moment.

I don't think I've ever seen you without a gun...it's a good thing no one knows you don't have one.

Rudy looked at him a little puzzled.

You remember that guy Stewey...you put the barrel of your gun to his chest and pinned him to the wall...he thought you were going to kill him, he started shaking, then pissed himself...the poor guy didn't leave the house for a month; he was too embarrassed to show his face...and for a small fee, let's say 10 bucks, I won't tell him that you don't have a gun.

Rudy laughed...you got a deal, he said.

Good,.... now we can move on to Cedrick....can I get 10 more for that one.

Damn, said Rudy.... I've got to get a gun. I can go on you know, said Cole.

They were using Cole's Moms car, she let him borrow it for the Funeral, he hadn't put together the money he needed to get the truck out of the shop.

They returned to the reception and started soliciting volunteers for the cleanup.

Felicia was exhausted, but continued on, she had been the perfect host throughout the event.

Rudy walked through the main hall and into the Sanctuary, he stood in front of the Alter, 12 Candles burned on either side of it, Flowers of every type, from over 200 attendees surrounded it, leaving an Isle so one would be able to kneel before the Alter, leaving heavy burdens, and sending out last wishes.

Goodbye Mom, Dad, see you soon.

J.D., Manny and Chico landed a pretty lucrative painting contract, they were painting a 300 unit Apartment complex, in the Liberty City district of Miami.

All three lived together as they always had, it cut down on expenses, sometimes their party habits went way too far, the hookers were in and out regularly.

The painting job they'd gotten was going well, they had to hire four more guys in order to meet their contract deadline.

They all put the past behind them, they could hardly believe how much smarter they were' than everyone else.

The Brutal Rape and Murder of that Child caused them all to drink a little heavier than before...to do just a little more drugs than usual.

You just had to kill the bitch didn't you, said J.D. in a drunken stupor....hope you got your rocks off asshole...we were just supposed to be teaching her a lesson, now everyone's looking for a Murderer.

They have no idea who their looking for, said Chico, were in the clear...and believe me....she learned her lesson, I've got to admit, that was the most intense rush, anyone could ever imagine, if I had the chance to do it all over again....I wouldn't change a thing.

After that night, they never spoke of it again, to each other, or anyone else.

J.D. was the driver this morning, he made the rounds picking up their new employees, they all went out to breakfast then headed to work.

He stopped for a traffic signal' and was rear ended by the car following, everyone in the van was a little shaken, mostly because it caught them by surprise, no one was hurt, so they exited the van to check the damage.

The driver of the other car had made a last minute attempt to avoid the accident, he turned the wheel and slammed on the brakes...the corner of his bumper hit the back of the van' dead center, the van's bumper was now "V" shaped, the back doors were hit dead center also, and jammed shut, the damage would run about a thousand dollars.

The van was over ten years old and had seen it's better days...Manny just wanted to leave, it wasn't much of an accident, they were making good money and could have it fixed in a week or so, besides, the van had side doors, so what if the back doors couldn't be used for a little while.

J.D. and Chico eyed the driver of the car.... he was intoxicated, he was also driving a newer model Bently.

We just struck pay dirt, Chico whispered to J.D.

The man staggered from the vehicle and met them at the bumper, alcohol wreaked from every pore...the bags under his eyes indicated...no sleep.

Now look what you've done, said the man, why in Gods name would you just stop in the middle of the road.

J.D. stepped forward, entering the man's personal space.

We stopped because of this red light here, I can see you've been drinking, if we get the cops involved, you're gonna go to jail today, right after they take your driver's license' and give you a D.U.I., its gonna cost you over ten thousand dollars to get out of this mess...so here's the deal, just give us three thousand for repairs and were out of here, no cops.

Three thousand dollars for that little scratch...hell no.

Well, we'll let the police handle it then, it's your ass on the line.

The man didn't flinch...it was as if he was calling their bluff.

Come on, let's go, said Manny, we're going to be late.

I'm not gonna let this rich fucker get away without paying shit, if he'd rather go to jail than pay us, then so be it, J.D. called the police.

Two patrol cars were there instantly, the driver of the other car was arrested for drunk driving, wreckless endangerment, and cited "At Fault" for the accident.

The patrolman asked J.D. for his identification, insurance paperwork, and registration.

J.D. produced everything the officer needed.

The driver of the other car could be seen sitting in the back of the patrol car, the handcuffs were digging into his wrists, he appeared quite uncomfortable, his facial expression showed just how he felt about his car being towed by a dirty little tobacco spittin redneck, with the Ora of a third grader.

I should have just paid them the money, he thought to himself.

The police report stated that J.D. was not at fault, for insurance purposes, the last thing to do was to run the drivers I.D. through the Data Base.

J.D.'s identification drew a red flag as soon as it was entered, he was wanted for kidnapping, Capital Rape, and first Degree Murder.

The officer glanced up at J.D. to see if the man seemed agitated in some way....he wasn't, he may not even know there was a warrant out for his arrest.

The officer remained calm, he went back to the van and asked to see all of the passengers I.D.'s, they produced them willingly, they knew their records were clean, they had handled their business so professionally, there's no way anything could pop up.

The officer returned to his patrol car and ran Chico's I.D., it was clean, Then Manny's...the kidnapping, Rape, and Murder charges came up on him also.

The officer discreetly called for backup and went into his stalling routine.

Five more patrol cars appeared out of nowhere, no more stalling was needed, the officer pulled his weapon and approached the van.

J.D., Chico, and Manny were all standing outside talking. Get on the ground, "NOW".

They all turned to face a Glock, 9mm.

The whole paint crew lay spread eagle on the ground, as they were hand cuffed and searched, they were all arrested, the van taken into impound.

The authorities kept them separated so they wouldn't be able to put together coinciding Alibis.

The newly hired painters all had Dade County I.D.'s only three were from Hillsborough County; where the crime was committed, those from Dade County had the same Alibis, they were released, the Hillsborough County suspects got a chance to see each other at one point in central booking, they all swore to deny any involvement.

They have nothing on us, said Chico, we're going to walk on this shit, and they know it, they're just fishing.

I wonder how they found us, asked Manny. You sure you cleaned up everything, asked J.D.

I'm sure...they have nothing, trust me guy's "Deny Everything"

Again, they were separated in two-way mirror holding tanks.

Four O'clock the next morning, two bologna sandwiches and a carton of 2% milk appeared before them, and so began the questioning phase.

The officer questioning Chico didn't appear threatening at all, he looked more like the book worm type.

Chico pegged him for a shrink.

The man sat across from him at the table' going over the notes he had.

Chico faced the two-way mirror, where three more officers watched intently, one expert at body language, a behavioral science expert, and a female detective, who was next in line to question the suspect.

I can get a couple more sandwiches here shortly, said the officer; I just need to ask you a few questions.

You've been accused of a very horrific crime, you're being accused because your D.N.A. was pulled from the animal companion of the victim.

Although Chico knew this wasn't true, his heart sank' because J.D. and Manny were still sporting visible bite marks, from the dog that attacked them that night.

They may have gotten D.N.A. from that dog, but if they did, it would be J.D. and Manny's.

Even though "I" was the one that killed her, they may have to take the fall, they know it won't help their situation to say I killed her, in the eyes of the Law' if you were all a part of it, you're all equally guilty.

Sir, said Chico...when you came through that door, you looked to me to be very intelligent...like a pillar of society...like someone who knows right from wrong, and has dedicated his life to doing the right thing, then you sit down across from me, and the first thing out of your mouth....is a bald face lie, I'm going to have to decline answering any more questions until my lawyer arrives.

The interrogator turned to look into the two-way mirror before exiting.

Things didn't go so well for J.D. and Manny, the dog bites matched perfectly with Ty's dental impressions, and both of their D.N.A. were pulled from the animal.

The van was pulled into the forensics lab and gone through for microscopic evidence, it wasn't long before blood was found under a seam in the vans floor board, further testing proved it to be a match with the D.N.A. of the victim, Chantell Harris.

J.D. and Manny's innocent plea's fell on deaf ears, ten days later J.D. and Manny were expedited back to Tampa.

By the time they got there, there was nothing on the table for them' but the death penalty.

Neither one of them actually knew that Chico would kill the girl, and neither one of them was present when he did.

Now, from what they'd heard, Chico's lawyer got him off clean, he claimed he just met J.D. and Manny when he got to Miami, they hired him to help paint an Apartment Complex.

There was nothing to tie him to the others.

He got away clean, J.D. said to himself, he hadn't seen Manny since their arrival.

He wanted desperately to tell him not to talk to anyone here about their case, and to deny any involvement with it, if anyone asked,

Particularly the inmates.

Chantell Harris had a lot of close family contacts throughout the city, and by word of mouth alone, they can make this a real hell hole.

Manny shared a cell with an older gentleman, he didn't talk much, but he seemed like a powerful man, the guards walked on eggshells around him, treated him with kids' gloves, teams of lawyers would come to go over his case.

The man told him' He was innocent of the charges that were being brought up against him, he told of the Hate Monger label that was being attached to his name and told bits and pieces of how it came about.

It seems we're pretty much in the same boat, said Manny, I'm about to be charged with a murder I didn't commit," he told his story in return.

Out in population Manny was anxious to get into one of the Clicks, he'd feel safer with some friends that were committed to each other, the rougher the better.

He told his story to a group of guys he wanted to get in with.

Me and my boys killed this little no good black whore, man we punished that bitch, beat her ass to a fucking pulp,...After we fucked her half the night, that bitch won't be playin them fuckin games no more.

You were one of the guys who killed the girl awhile back, over in Sulphur Springs.

Yeah, that was us, I'm a Gangster with a Capital G. baby, I don't play that shit, said Manny, putting on his bad Mutha, (shut your mouth) attitude.

He'd expected better results from his new friends, but I guess, if you look at it the right way, what they were showing him was "a" kind of respect.

Word traveled behind his back.

There were ten guys in that pod, that knew Chantell personally, two of them had seen her body' where it lay, off from the train bridge.

And had been having nightmares about it ever since.

The following week,.... the time had come.

Manny sat at a shady table in a far corner, the inmates called it the smoker's bench.

Manny's crew sat with him.

When those ten guys approached; Manny's new crew remembered they all had something to do, and left abruptly.

The ten sat with' and around Manny, he welcomed them, they weren't as much upon him, as they were blocking the deputy's view.

There were smiles all around, while they were laughing and joking, Marlon pulled out a long shiev, he began sharpening it on the edge of the concrete table, where they sat.

Manny saw the lengthy blade.

Man, I gotta get me one of them, said Manny, admiring the workmanship of the blade.

This one's for you, said Marlon, I'm just sharpening it up for you.

"Yeah", thanks bro, I'll pay you back as soon as my money gets here.

Andrew pulled out a shiev also, I brought this one for you too, he said.

Manny looked around, all ten had shiev's.

Marlon looked Manny in the eye, but all he could see was Chantell's body lying there, it was puffed up to twice its normal size, she looked as if she'd been beaten with a tire iron.

Tears rolled down Marlons cheeks, he rushed Manny, covering his mouth with his hand and holding him tightly from behind, he sank his shiev in his throat till it came out the other side.

The rest of the men joined in just as quickly, the blades were ripping Manny's body apart, the blood flowed freely.

It was over in record time, the deputy on duty saw nothing, Manny lay twitching over in the far corner, not a square inch of his body was left without a stab wound.

Upon returning to the hospital, Rudy was met by Nurse Miranda, she, a little reluctantly' handed him his medical file.

I've authorized your release, she said, you'll heal faster from this point, away from the Hospital...I know you don't have a place to stay, homeowners' insurance never seem to cover terrorist attacks,...or Alian abductions, their just not that common around here.

So, I hooked you up with an apartment, my Mom has a few places that are unoccupied at the moment, I can cover you till you get on your feet, that way I'll still be able to check up on you.

Me and Cole here, have been working on getting a place, but it won't be ready for another month or so,... I won't be able to pay you back till then.

Don't worry about paying anything, you're welcome to it for as long as you need it.

As she spoke' there was something in her tone, and her eye's; that touched him, he almost responded to what he was feeling from her, then it came to him,...he'd just went through a traumatic experience, hell, everyone was being more sensitive toward him.

And here I am, jumping to conclusions, where she was just being nice, that girls so far out of my league, how could I even think she'd be interested in me,... wishful thinking, I guess.

The place was nice and peaceful, it was out of the way; and just what they needed.

A few days later, a couple of pieces of furniture found their way into the apartment, a little array of cooking utensils also.

Cole had made himself at home, hadn't left since they found the place.

Cole slept on a sleeping bag, and Rudy on the sofa.

There was no television,... the knock on the door didn't wake Rudy or Cole.

The unlocked door swung open, and Felicia walked in, a plastic grocery bag in hand' bearing the name Sweet Bay.

She didn't bother waking them, she went straight to the kitchen, she opened the refrigerator, it was just as she thought...empty.

She cooked as they slept...as the aroma of the food passed under the noses of the two men, they both came to life.

She made sure she cooked more than enough; the guys were acting as if they hadn't eaten for awhile.

They dug in as Felicia lay on the carpet playing solitaire.

Is that all it takes to get you up and moving, Felicia Chuckled.

I don't know if you've noticed, but things aren't looking too good, said Rudy.

Yeah, I know, said Cole, maybe we should go ahead and start on the crop today.

How?, asked Rudy, your truck isn't fixed yet, we have no transportation, and no money, there's no way we can take anyone else with us.

I was thinking we can rent a U-Haul box truck...that way we can get everything in one Wop.

You got money for the truck?

Cole tilted his head toward the figure lying on the carpet playing Solitaire.

Rudy looked over at her.....he was absolutely right, Felicia still had thousands of dollars, one thing Felicia hated, was spending money.

Since she got that check from Emmitt Smith, she only bought three or four outfits, got her hair and nails done, she partied a couple days, and after that' she locked that purse up and put it away.

And talking about a thrifty shopper, I sent her to the grocery store with 20 bucks, when she came out' the grocery cart was running over, and she still had change.

They discussed the situation with her, she agreed to pay the truck rental.

I'll get the truck before they close this evening, I'm going to have to do this alone.

What, said Rudy.

No offence Rudy, but I've seen a couple of your puny attempts at running, you're not ready yet, just in case something jumps off, we will have to leave everything...and run, really run,...cause getting caught is "not" an option, you're going to stay here.

"No", you're gonna need someone out there to watch your back.

I'll go with you, said Felicia.

Rudy and Cole looked at each other, then at Felicia.

They remembered their last bout in the woods,... she held her own the whole time.

Hey, you guys be careful, said Rudy.

The U-Haul was rented, they made it out to the spot undetected.

Cole brought his battery powered saw-Zaw and went to work, it was cutting through the trees with ease....Cole had Mapped out a route through the thickest part of the woods to get back and forth from the site' to the U-Haul totally covert.

God only knew what would happen if they were caught mid-trip, dragging these trees.

Cole had cut down nine trees, he wanted to move them out first, then start the cutting again.

Cole grabbed two trees,... Felicia could only pull one.

Cole caught a movement overhead, a large black billed Hawk landed on a branch just above them.

Cole stopped,... look at that, he said.

Look at what, Felicia asked? Looking around. Right there in the tree.

Damn, what kind of bird is that?

It's a Hawk,... I don't know what kind of Hawk, but it's a Hawk, I've never seen one that big.... it's almost as big as an eagle.

Is it dangerous?

She seems to be ok with us being here, come on let's get going.

Danny Hamilton and his now aging father sat in their pick-up right off the highway, they had been tracking the movements of a large black billed Hawk...and setting traps in places the bird frequented.

Danny followed the bird, trap in hand,... it wasn't long before he spotted the bird through his binoculars.

He climbed a tree 100 feet from the tree the bird was in,... he set the trap...made sure there was adequate food.

The bird was a perfect specimen, he began taking pictures, with his zoom lens he could bring the bird into perfect clarity, he snapped picture after picture.

He was zooming in on the bird, when something else passed in front of the lens...he put the camera down and squinted, he saw two people...trying to get a better look, he got the binoculars, he could see them clearly, a white guy and a black female, both wearing working clothes, boots and gloves.

He watched them for awhile,... they were moving out some trees, probably to plant in their yard,..."Or not"... the trees didn't have the roots on them.

When Cole and Felicia made the next trip to the U-Haul Danny ran over to the location, the trees were very well camouflaged, but Danny; being a weed smoker, spotted them right away.

"Marijuana"..... their hauling a load of Marijuana!

The feeling of not having to pay for weed for a very long time was exhilarating, he began breaking off limb after limb, at around four pounds, leaving quickly' seemed like a good idea.

He stuffed the weed in the toolbox that ran across the bed of the pick-up.

He let his father know that all the traps had been set.

After he took his dad home, he made his way back to the woods, he darted in and out, using the highest trees and binoculars, until he found the U-Haul box truck.

He then made his way back to the original location, the two people were still at it, moving trees with an urgency.

Danny found a place way out of site...and waited.

After twenty four trees had been hauled out using the route Cole had mapped out,...they were both tired as hell, the small box truck was full, as the tree branches weren't tied down, the fullness of the trees filled the truck quicker than expected.

They'd have to come back and get the rest of the trees later;

They headed for Riverview, their good friend Dally, granted them the use of his Barn.

Cole backed the truck up all the way inside the barn to unload their cargo...Dally covered it with a large tarp, and tied it down, it would have to be hung for drying soon.

By the time they got the U-Haul hosed down' removing the weed smell, it was getting late...they decided to get the rest of the trees tomorrow, they were beat.

Felicia didn't even want to cook, she had Cole stop at

K.F.C. and picked up dinner for them all.

Cole turned the radio on for the drive home, he was running through the stations, when a broadcast came across the airwaves.

James Dawson and Emanuel Menendez, alias, J.D. and Manny, the suspects in a world wide man hunt... have been apprehended and taken into custody, in Miami Florida, for the brutal rape and murder of a Tampa Teen Chantell Harris.

They are being Summoned, for extradition to Tampa, as we speak.

"They got them Mothafucka's" yelled Felicia, they got em, they got em..."thank you God", they got em.

"Hell yeah", said Cole, that's what's up.

Felicia and Cole did the Cabage Patch dance in their seats...they couldn't wait to tell Rudy the good news.

They all sat on the floor of the apartment, discussing the recent capture and eating K.F.C.

Rudy only thought about ways he could possibly get to them, they shouldn't be sitting in a comfortable jail cell, eating three meals a day, they should be burning over an open flame,...I know a lot of inmates that would love to get thar fire going.

Calm down Rudy, that's not a healing attitude you're in, everything will work itself out from here, she said.

I can't believe how close they came to getting away Scott free, said Cole.

Rudy lifted his Coke to the sky,,,,, To "Ty", he said. Felicia and Cole followed suit,..... to "Ty".

They were up early the next morning, Felicia felt fresh and ready to go.

Rudy wasn't going with them today either, today would be just as dangerous as yesterday...he protested, he even attempted to show them that he could run.

The attempt only lasted a few seconds, before he was nearly paralyzed with pain.

It seemed as if his right shoulder, his forearm, and right leg, were all shooting lightning bolts through his body, he stood stiffly, balancing himself on the good leg.

I'll see you guys when you get back, he said sadly,

Hey, we'll come back to get you on our way to Dally's place, there won't be any heat out there.

Rudy was easing his way back to the apartment as they left.

A chill was in the air as they made their way to the site, although there was no sign of the cold weather setting in for quite some time.

Cold days would pop up every now and then, but here you could plant the late crops that'll flourish even in December.

This is considered a late crop, the plants would struggle to survive in January, moving them now was great timing.

They stood and looked over the site. Cole ran from one end to the other.

Felicia looked as if she was about to panic,...her hand slipped into her shoulder bag and gripped her .380 as she looked all around.

Cole stood with his hands on top of his head, fingers interlocked, he was confused and near panic himself, what the fuck is going on here, where are the rest of the plants.

Their gone, said Felicia, their all gone....she was shaking...ever since she'd agreed to do this, she had been nervous, the feeling that something could go wrong wouldn't leave her,...now, was the police here in the woods...watching them...or something worse.

Lets go, she said, we've got to get out of here. Cole saw the fear in her eye's

I'll walk you back to the truck, but I want to look around.

I'm not gonna sit out there in that truck by myself, and I'm not gonna leave you out here by yourself.

Cole gave her a hug...she began to regroup, she willed the trembling to stop, and found the peace she needed to go through this situation, whatever it may be.

The sun started to dissipate as rain clouds started to roll in overhead.

Cole looked around frantically, for any sign of the weed's disappearance,...he finally found the direction the tree's were dragged in...they'd followed the trail only a short distance before the rain started, slow at first...then harder.

The trail would be impossible to follow in the rain.

A loud screeching sound startled them, they both looked up at the same time.

A lightly camouflaged bird trap was set up in the tree, that big Hawk that had been hanging around the day before' had been trapped inside, the trap was too small for her to turnaround in, she couldn't stand straight up either, she was in a crouched position, it was impossible for her to even open her wings.

That trap's never been there before,... it wasn't there yesterday.

It may have been, said Felicia, maybe we just didn't notice it.

From where that trap is, one would have a clear view of our comings and goings, whoever set that trap,..."Stole our Weed".

Cole made his way to the tree and retrieved the trap; the rain was really coming down now.

The bird was agitated, and they were all soaked.

They placed the bird in the back of the U-Haul, then picked up Rudy' and headed for Dally's place as they went ever the events of the day.

So you're saying, there's over fifteen whole tree's missing, asked Rudy?

Yeah, the place had been cleaned out by the time we got there, someone has been out there setting traps,... whoever it was, probably spotted us yesterday.

That's fifteen tree's some asshole has beat us for, that's too much man, too fucking much.

I don't think we're going to be able to do what we had planned.

We may still be able to cover everything...the tree's have been growing steady, they should all produce a better than normal yield.

We're talking between eight and nine pounds each, said Cole.

We'll see what's what, when we get to Dally's.

The rain had passed over by the time they got there, Felicia was anxious to see Sandra again (Dally's Wife)

the girls went to the house, while the guys headed for the barn.

Wait a minute, said Cole,...I got something for you Dally.

He opened the back of the U-Haul and brought the bird to Dally.

Would you look at the size of this fella, said Dally, never saw a Hawk this size before.

Well, we're gonna get started in the barn...you coming?

I'll be there, just give me a minute, said Dally, never taking his eye off the bird.

Cole and Rudy cut and hung branches in bunches on hooks over the thin heating plates, the thin layers radiated heat, speeding up the drying out process, they wouldn't

be able to get an actual weight until after everything was dried out.

They were finished in well under seven hours,...Dally never made it in to help, he was putting the finishing touches on a giant bird cage he'd built alont the side of the barn...it was twenty-five by twenty-five square, and fifteen feet high.

He turned the bird loose inside; it flew to the rock perch Dally had set up, along with food and water.

Dally talked to the bird like it was an old friend.

So, this is what you were doing out here, said Rudy, giving the cage the' once over.

That bird needs room to move around, being cooped up in that little trap would have killed it.

He went on and on about the bird, that's all he wanted to talk about. Cole said he was becoming obsessed with it.

Sandra had Hot Dogs and Cokes set up on the back porch for them' when they made it back to the house.

Dally sat the empty bird trap on the porch,... Sandra saw the trap, she gave it a second look, and put her hands on her hips, staring at Dally..... please don't tell me you've been raiding Mr. Hamilton's bird traps, she said.

Dally looked at the trap as if it was his first time seeing it,... Damn, that is one of his traps.

Cole, Felicia, and Rudy looked at each other. Who is this Mr. Hamilton, asked Rudy.

He's been trapping around this area for years now, he provides the bird sanctuary with many different breeds of birds, the sanctuary only holds them for so long, their all released back into the wild,... they give the birds a complete check-up there, making sure the bird population remains healthy,...his job is never done.

How long did you say he's been trapping? he's been doing that for over thirty-five years! thirty five years huh...how old is this guy? he's in his late sixties now.

That doesn't sound like who we need to find, he's a little old, we were thinking that whoever set that trap,... would also be the culprit that took the rest of our cargo, but I don't think the guy you mentioned would be up to the task.

The guys went back out to the bird cage to mess with "Cain".

Dally had named the bird.

The girls continued chatting it up on the porch.

We've got to get this truck back today, said Cole, we'll have to drop it off, its 10:00 pm now, if we get it there before twelve midnight' we won't have to pay for another day.

We'll get back with you in about two weeks, Rudy told Dally.

This stuff will be ready in a week, Dally exclaimed,.. I'm gonna let it hang loose like that for a couple of days, then I'll close the panels and turn up the heat,...pull all the moisture out, leave the leaves and buds nice and green,...it'll weigh up better, the color will fade a little by the time you get it bagged up, there won't be any change in the way it smokes,.. that's good weed, and good weed,... smokes good.

We'll be back in a week then," said Rudy. They dropped Rudy off at the apartment.

You try to take it easy and rest up, we'll take the truck back and drop it off,.. we'll be right back.

The truck rental was on south Dale Mabry, but Felicia told Cole to keep going straight instead of jumping on I- 275, which would have been faster,.. and instead of making the turn onto Dale Mabry, she summoned him to keep straight across.

Where are we going, asked Cole. I want to check on something.

What is it we're checking on.

Turn here, she said,... Sandra gave me directions to the Hamilton's place, we'll just pass by,..see what's up.

Good thinking, said Cole,... I haven't gotten over that shit either.

This is it' right here.

The lights were out in the house, but there was a light on in the storage shed, out back.

There was a pick-up truck parked just outside the shed.

Cole jumped the fence and walked calmly to the pick-up, there were remnants of Marijuana all over the bed of the truck, he turned and went to the door of the shed, it had a sliding door, and was open about two feet,... Cole peeked inside.

The kid inside was only seventeen or eighteen years old, he was busy stuffing Weed into garbage bags.

Cole slid the door open wide...Danny sprang to his feet, shaken at the intrusion.

He recognized the man at the door immediately, his mouth began moving' in an attempt at an explanation, but the words were somewhat stuck in his throat, he looked around as if looking for an exit, there we're none.

Cole held his .357 Magnum straight down beside his leg, as he looked around inside the shed, he saw that the kid had filled twenty two garbage bags with weed.

Looks like you've been pretty busy, said Cole. Danny still couldn't find his voice.

Relax, said Cole,... it looks like today's your lucky day,.. it was only by a stroke of luck that I found you,.. so I'll pass that luck on to you.

This is what we're gonna do.

I'm going to back that U-Haul up,... and you're going to put my shit back where it belongs.

Mr. Hamilton got up to take a leak, he saw the light on in the shed through the blinds.

"What in God's name is that boy doing out there", it's almost midnight,.. I hope he doesn't have any of those knuckle head friends of his out there, by god they'll come back later and steal everything.

About that time, Cole stepped out of the shed,.. Mr. Hamilton saw the gun in his hand.

Cole waved for Felicia to bring the truck,... Mr. Hamilton was freaking out, he too owned a gun, but at his age' he didn't trust his ability to confront a criminal.

He didn't know what to do, he knew his grandson was in grave danger.

Cops,... I'll call the Cops, he dialed 911.

Operator,... I'm being robbed, there's a man in my tool shed, he's armed,... I think he has my Grandson.

We'll send a patrol car right out, stay inside, don't make any attempt to stop him.

Cole made Danny load all the bags into the U-Haul.

Once they got back on the road, Cole, and Felicia had a good laugh,... luckily, they'd gotten every stick of weed back.

Everything was going to go as planned, the hunch had paid off beautifully.

I'll pay the truck rental for one more day, said Felicia.

Its not like we have a choice now, it's after Midnight, we're gonna have to pay it anyway,...I know how you hate spending money, but we couldn't have done any of this without your help, we're not going to be broke too much longer, you're going to get all your money back and hen some,...even though that damn kid just chopped the hell out of this batch, it's all good, we'll just have to find another way to dry it out.

Ahead in the distance, the red and blue twin spinning lights of the Sheriff's cruiser appeared, the cruiser turned sideways across the road ahead, immediately, another Cruiser appeared and blocked off what was left of the road.

He glanced into the side mirror' before attempting to change lanes,... the lights ahead had somewhat camouflaged the lights that were behind them.

There were two Sherrif's on his tail. NO,.... NO,.... NO.

Felicia looked into his face and knew there was trouble, she looked into her side mirror.

Give me your gun, "Hurry". Cole gave her the weapon.

Make this left turn right here, use your blinkers. Cole made the turn.

At the same time, Felicia as able to toss both weapons from the vehicle, the timing was perfect, the Cops hadn't seen a thing.

Two blocks later, they were surrounded, the Police Cruiser lights colored the night sky.

They were arrested for possession of a controlled substance, for distribution,...that charge automatically comes with a Racketeering charge also.

Don't say anything till we get some representation, at least we were able to shed that weapons charge, we'll have to play it by ear from here.

When Rudy woke up the next morning, the apartment was empty, his concern grew as he hadn't heard anything from his best friends.

He called everyone he could think of, it wasn't until he called Felicia's sister that he found out what happened.

Felicia shared an apartment with her sister...she gave him all the details surrounding his friend's arrest.

Rudy called Emmitt Smith, he was more than happy to help, he got his hands on the Police report.

It doesn't look good for your friends, he said,.. I'm not sure what I'll be able to do,...drug cases are not my specialty...I have some people I can talk to, but they're going to want money.

What kind of money, asked Rudy. The more,... the better, he replied.

Talk to them,... I'll see what I can come up with.

When in Police custody, all mail coming in, or going out, is read by detectives.

Conversations that are too delicate to be overheard by detectives are coded in some way' to throw off anyone that may be listening.

Felicia's sister said that I was to go pick up two heaters that she wanted, they were on the side of the road' just west of Mayberry.

Rudy knew this was code, and knew it was important, he had to think hard before he started to pick it up.

They were arrested just west of Dale Mabry, that must be where the Mayberry comes in.

There were no gun charges, the two heaters are the guns,... these are directions to the guns, she dumped them before they were arrested.

Rudy made his way to the location, it took him a couple of hours to find them, they were in the roadside drainage system.

He dropped Felicia's little .380 off at the apartment, and kept Cole's .357 Magnum with him.

Time is of the essence when dealing with this country's legal system.

And money is the key,... he was going to have to raise some money fast.

He made his way to Tampa's West side, one of his associates, Kelly, was always on the market for some good weed, the West Tampa projects holds a lot of connects that are truly in the game.

Rudy knew them socially, but had never done business with them, he knew where money's involved, evil can always be spotted somewhere close by.

Kelly was his best bet; he was about as levelheaded as they come.

Rudy knocked on the door,... a figure stepped out of the shadows at the corner of the house.

Who you looking for?

Tell Kelly, Rudy's out here.

The man was back in no time,... come around this way, he said.

They went in the back way, he walked through the house to the living room,... and stopped.

The whole room was covered in sheets of plastic, the furniture, the television, the floor, everything.

And there was a Mountain of weed in the center of the floor, almost as tall as Rudy.

Hey, what's up baby-boy, said Kelly.

Hell, I wanted to talk to you about some business, but I can see I'm a little late.

Rudy watched Kelly's little operation for awhile, there were four girls, and four guy's bagging weed, one made ounces, one made quarter pounds, one made half pounds, one made full pounds,...the girls worked as levelers, the baggers just put weed in bags, the levelers scaled them to exact measurements.

I've got all the weed I'm gonna need for awhile, said Kelly.

I've got two more loads coming in back to back, I gotta pay these guy's a hundred dollars an hour to get it packaged up before I run out of room.

So, you trying to move some weight too huh.

Yeah,... don't worry, I know not to come out west, it looks like you've got the whole west side "Locked Down".

Rudy headed for Dredd's place next, at the same time he was on the phone with Chis and Courtney, twin Country boys out of Plant City.

Hey, Cole asked me to check with you guys and see if you're gonna be needing some "Hay".

Yep, we're gonna need about six bails, if the price is right.

Yeah, the price is right, holding steady at a "G". When can we come and check it out.

Come down this weekend.

Rudy raised the price to a Grand, trying to make up for some of the losses they'd encountered.

The Dredd man needed four pounds,... Rudy touched base with ten sure fire sales' along with the ones Cole had already gotten,...it was going to be a busy weekend.

Rudy called Dally to come pick him up, Dally was still infatuated with his bird, and talked about it on end.

He'd been able to get the bird to do a few things, and he was anxious for Rudy to see what he'd been able to teach his new companion.

But now was not the time, he could tell Rudy wasn't himself,...I put together a few of the orders that you told me about, said Dally, the weeds ready, all you have to do is start moving it.

Damn,... I'm kind'a scared, said Rudy,...it never crossed my mind that I'd be doing this alone.

Wish I could help, said Dally, but what I've done so far is about all I'm gonna be able to do, Sandra's already on my ass for having a barn full of weed' that belongs to someone that just got busted for weed, she knows, all it takes is one slip of the tongue, and everything we've worked for is gone,...this is you and Cole's little project, cold feet can be tolerated if it were just you two involved, but Felicia didn't have nothing to do with it, she was just trying to help you out,...you; in your condition and all,...don't get scared now, not while she's sitting in jail with the rest of her life in jeopardy,...start putting those orders together, and get em moving.

Rudy didn't speak, he took a deep breath' and focused on doing this job with all the care it entailed, no more mistakes, his friends were counting on him.

Later on, Dally came into the barn hurriedly, a big shit eating grin on his face.

Rudy, have you been listening to the news lately?

No,... not for a couple of days, what happened, asked Rudy.

Those two guys that killed Chantell,... one of them is dead already, they killed his ass in jail.

He was stabbed to death,.. said they counted over three hundred stab wounds.

Was it the one they called J.D.?

No, the other one,...goes by the name "Manny".

The news made Rudy feel better, there was a natural order of things that on most occasions' takes care of a lot of loose ends.

Well,... one down, and one to go, said Rudy.

Marcus White spoke with his new lawyer, he'd separated himself from Orlan Petrini, the charges he was facing were too extreme.

Since Orlan arrived, the Media was focusing all of their attention on him.

Marcus realized that if he put all the blame on him, the Media would eat it up.

He came up with a plan to shed most, if not all' charges against him.

It couldn't be proven that he himself gave the orders, or that it was his plan,...he couldn't be directly tied to the thugs he'd hired to do the job.

He told his lawyer to ask the court for leniency, and in return, he would turn states evidence against Orlan Petrini.

Marcus's trial was pushed forward, for those who were anxious to hear his testimony.

Marcus Whites lawyers portrayed Orlan as a ruthless Mob Boss, a card-carrying member of the Ku-Klux-Klan, and a Communist bully, they were told that the men that wreaked havoc on the Claton family,... were Orlan's men.

This was done to divert a discrimination lawsuit' that was directed at him by a member of that family.

Orlan sent me to a hotel in Tampa, I was to wait for a man to deliver a package, I was to take the package to a specific location.

Detectives rushed to the said location, the meeting house of the Arian Nation.

The package was exactly where Marcus White said it would be, it contained the missing evidence that had been stolen, due to a break-in at Emmitt Smith's office.

All I did, said Marcus, I went to Tampa, picked up a package, and returned.

I had no knowledge of anything else that may have transpired.

The story was so well put together, the prosecutors knew it would stand up to a reasonable doubt, they could care less about Marcus White anyway, Orlan Petrini' was the wealthy one' who was pulling all the strings.

They taped the testimony,.. checked and rechecked it, until they were sure it was waterproof.

The deal was made, Marcus was only sentenced to six months, for his part in the travesty.

It was hard to believe, his plan worked like a charm,.. he was facing something in between fifty years and the death penalty,...he had won his life back.

A newfound energy rushed through him, future plans raced through his mind...the rest of his life was going to be wonderful.

Orlan Petrini however...with the charges that were about to come at him like a landslide, would not "ever", see the light of day again.

A day and a half later, everything was packaged and counted, Sandra had been bringing Rudy's food out to the barn, he didn't want to stop, he did his own cutting, packaging, and leveling,...he ended up with one hundred forty four pounds, just about half of what they would have had originally if everything would have went smoothly.

The money was going to be way short, that didn't matter much now, cause all their other plans would have to be set aside,.. the main goal now was to get Felicia and Cole out of jail.

Chris and Courtney were right on time, they wanted to check the product out first, so they smoked a spliff while they were all gathered around the bird cage.

Dally was inside the cage, it was feeding time, he threw strips of fish in Cain's direction, the bird was catching them in midair.

Cain wasn't afraid of Dally anymore, at times it looked as if they were kindred spirits.

The weed quickly took effect, the twins were more than happy with the product, they left with six pounds,... the Dredd man got two,...nine more sales were made that day equaling a total of twenty seven pounds.

Rudy called Emmitt Smith.

I'll set up a meeting in the morning, said Emmitt. Rudy met with the lawyer the next morning... Avery

Brooks, he was strictly a drug case lawyer, he had gotten

drug dealers off, that were facing ridiculous sentences, criminals that were caught red handed, with tons of hard drugs, Heroin, Cocaine, Meth, you name it,... he guaranteed results, and Emmitt Smith was confident in his ability.

Mr. Brooks took the twenty seven thousand as a down payment, the fee was fifty thousand.

We can get started as soon as you get the rest of the money.

Rudy went back to work,... looks like today is gonna be a long one.

Most of the stops he was scheduled to make today were first time buyers, at least, it would be the first time they bought from him.

Rudy had grown up around countless weed salesmen' but had never been one himself, now he was getting a taste of what they go through,...growing the weed had proven to be an exciting venture, you would think that the sale of the weed would be even more exhilarating, was that why his heart was beating like a drum.

The fact is, drug dealers should be on the most endangered species list.

Drug dealers put themselves in a very volatile situation,... the drug users usually get caught with their stash, then turn around and point out the dealer, the Cops are constantly on the lookout for dealers, even the general do-gooder, (Joe Public) will turn you in.

Stick to the plan Rudy! sometimes his thoughts get the better of him.

The first seven sales went smoothly, he aborted the eighth sale, he had a bad feeling about it, there were two guys outside next to the drop.

One was working on a car, an older model Chevy with a coat of primer as a temporary paint job, the other guy was playing with his dog in the opposite yard of the drop point.

Rudy wasn't taking any chances.

After the tenth drop was done, the phone rang,... it was Pealo, the guy from the drop he'd aborted.

Hey, where you at man, I'm still waiting for you, is everything alright.

Yeah, said Rudy, "I'll be there in an hour.

Hurry up, partner, I've been waiting all day for this.

Rudy still had that uneasy feeling about this dude, he told him he'd be there in an hour, that gave him time enough to pick up a scout.

Rudy picked up a guy from the neighborhood named Rick, he was to help check out the area, and the house, for any signs of Police activity.

When Rudy reached the location, he circled the block.

No one was outside now, Rudy parked around the corner and had Rick walk back to the house...Rick kept his eyes open,.. on the lookout for anything odd.

Pealo greeted Rick at the door, once inside, Rick stood perfectly still in the front room.

Where's Rudy, Pealo asked.

Rudy's having some issues, said Rick, he wants to make sure everything's as it should be, Rick leaned in close,.. we were told that the Police were here.

Man, ain't no damn Police nowhere round here. I'll feel better if we check it out,... you here alone?

No, my boy's are in the back room, they waitin on the weed too, they ain't got nothing to do with the business end,... their cool.

Rick had already heard the movement coming from the room.

Yeah, said Rick,... well how bout this, we're gonna drop the weed off at your brother's spot, over on 29th & Lake, he'll call you when he gets the package,...you pay him.

Rick turned to leave, a man stepped out of the room and stood directly in his path,... pistol at his side, locked and loaded,.. he pointed the gun at Rick's head.

Where's the weed, he asked.

Do I look like I have the weed, said Rick. Holding his arms out.

The man hit him on the side of the head with the weapon.

Rick hit the floor hard,... again, the man put the gun to his head.

Where is it, he yelled.

Rick didn't know how far these guys would go, but he sensed they were ready to go all the way, now he was in fear for his life.

Rudy's parked around the corner, the weed's in the car. Let's go, said the man.

When Rudy saw Rick and the man come around the corner, he knew it was trouble.

The money from the last sale was in his pocket, the rest, in a bag inside the glove box.

He quickly took the money from his pocket and put it in the bag, then went under the dash to a rack he'd set up for hiding this type of stuff, it was equipped with a bungee strap, that held it in place, the rack was flush, and couldn't be seen through normal inspection.

The two approached the car' just as he came from under the dash.

He was holding Rick by the neck, from behind, the man put Rick's head in the window, and pointed the gun at Rudy.

"Hands", let me see your hands. Rudy raised his hands.

I saw you go under the seat, what you got under there? Nothing, said Rudy.

Where's the weed?

In the seat, back there.

The weed was wrapped up like a Christmas present.

Thanks for the present, he said, still pointing the gun at Rudy,... "Get Out".

Rudy stepped out of the vehicle; the man got in, and drove off.

Another car fell in behind him, the one with the primer on it,.. Rudy ran to the corner, both cars made a left on twenty sixth street.

Good, I hope they stay on twenty sixth.

The weed, and the money was gone, and he'd lost Cole's gun again, it was under the driver's seat, the rental car was probably going to be trashed,...but he was able to keep his cell phone.

Rudy's cousin, Keith, lived on twenty sixth street, he was at the house earlier when Rudy passed by.

Rudy quickly put in a call to Keith, he answered on the first ring.

Keith this is Rudy,... I need a favor,...run outside right quick and look down twenty sixth street' toward the bottom's, there should be a cream colored S.U.V. and a older model Chevy with primer on it' headed in your direction.

Yeah, I see two cars coming,... looks like them, "what's up".

I just got jacked, my money's in that S.U.V., follow them if you can, I need...

Follow em my ass, said Keith, Cuz, we been here all our lives, that Chevy with the primer on it belongs to Pealo, he's only been in Tampa for a hot minute, relax, I got this.

Keith had been watching the ball game with some of the fella's,... four cars left Keith's house, and fell in behind the robbers.

They overtook them' and stopped them, surrounding the S.U.V.

Keith didn't usually carry a gun, and today he was the only one carrying.

Five guy's emerged from four vehicles and headed for the S.U.V.

The Chevy's tires were heard squealing in reverse about this time, leaving Mr. Car Jacker and weed stealer' all alone.

The man stepped from the S.U.V.... gun in hand,.. he was surrounded.

Keith spotted the gun and took the point position, he stepped forward, making sure the man saw that he was strapped also.

If the man made any attempt to bring that weapon up, Keith was more than ready to "Drop" him.

The man was talking and pointing, he asked, what was the problem,... even said he didn't want no trouble,..

Words that fell on deaf ears, he was careful not to raise the weapon.

Even though the men in front of him, (with the exception of the guy holding the point position) didn't have weapons showing, he took that as a sign that he wasn't to die,... yet.

(at ground level, if a man pulls a gun on you, nine times out of ten,...you're going to get shot.)

Keith kept his eye's on the gun,... the man turned slightly, and Keith noticed,...there wasn't a clip in the gun.

"Oh, Hell No", Keith walked toward the man with his gun leveled off at the man's chest.

Drop that damn gun, said Keith.

The man hesitated for a couple of seconds,... then dropped it.

Keith lowered his weapon, finally able to exhale,... there wasn't a clip in the gun, but there could have been a bullet in the chamber.

You've got to be one of the dumbest mothafucka's alive, said Keith... You rob my people, then challenge me,...with an empty gun, you made me feel bad bout how disrespectful you are.

Philly-C,... come hit this bitch in the face, said Keith.

Philly stood in front of the man' he drew back for a good swing.

The man raised his arms to protect his face.

Put your arms down, said Keith,... if you put them up again, I'm gonna have to shoot you,.. Don't move.

Philly swung hard... the blow landed flush, a cracking sound was heard, the man's head bounced off the S.U.V., blood splattered the vehicle, as the man slid to the ground.

Keith woke the man up, he and Philly held him up in the same spot.

Mike Stone,... see if you can hit him harder than Philly did, said Keith.

By the time the last person got his turn, the man was completely unconscious...they had to lift the man's head up, to make sure he got a nice flush punch.

Once the man regained consciousness, Keith kneeled down beside him.

Leave Tampa,... you need to put some distance between you and us.

If I see you here again, I "will" kill you.

Get up,.. you embarrass my people, so in return,...I embarrass you.

This is for Rudy,... take your clothes off,.. put them in a pile' right there, and get your stupid, no bullet having ass outta here.

The buck naked man staggered slowly down the street, it was obvious his embarrassment was overwhelming, and the fear for his life was still a concern.

He looked back, the pile of clothes was now on fire.

Rudy and Rick had reached twenty sixth and Columbus when Keith picked them up.

The gun was still under the seat, the money was still there, and so was the weed.

He gave Keith two pounds of weed, he had to hold on to the cash for the lawyer.

Cuz, seems like you're always in the right place at the right time, I don't know what I would have done, if you hadn't been there.

We got lucky that time, said Keith.

I'd better get this rental car back before something else happens, hey, I still got a lot of work ya know, I need somebody to ride with me,.. I can't pay you what you're used to, but you won't be disappointed.

Tomorrow then, asked Keith. "Tomorrow then," said Rudy.

Before Rudy turned in the rental, he went to meet with the lawyer, Avery Brooks, at his office.

He gave Avery twenty thousand dollars, Avery sat back in his chair and gazed admiringly at Rudy, then back at the money on his desk' with the same admiration.

I like the way you raise money, he said.

He wasn't surprised,.. almost all of his clients paid him in this manner.

You have a balance of three thousand dollars, which I'm going to waive,.. I'm waiving it because you didn't leave your friends out in the cold, I like it when productive people learn to help one another,... they must be pretty good friends.

Best I've ever had, said Rudy.

They'll be out this week, I'm also going to see if I can get their files sealed,... here's my card' just in case you find yourself in need of a lawyer someday.

Rudy called Keith the next morning, he was there in no time, they went out to Dally's place' they were both

Ready to get started.

Dally came out of the bird cage with cain on his shoulder.

Hey Dally, you know you got a big ass bird on your shoulder, said Keith.

Dally smiled, come out back I want to show you guy's something,... Rudy, get one of those Rabbits out of that cage in the barn, and bring it out back with you.

The Rabbit cage was just inside the barn door' to the right, Rudy stuck his hand in the cage, the Rabbits ran to the farthest corner, he reached for them in the corner and the Rabbits attacked, he got his hand out of there as fast as he could.

For some reason he'd assumed the Rabbits were domesticated... these were wild Rabbits, ole country ass Dally must have went out and trapped these little monsters.

He'll never let it rest if I don't get one of these Rabbits out of this cage.

The door at the other end of the barn opened. "What's taking you so long," asked Dally.

Here I come...here goes nothing,. He reached in quickly, grabbed a Rabbit by the small of his back, and brought it out fast, then he grabbed the hind legs, which were going wild..."Gotcha".

Rudy brought the rabbit out behind the barn, Cain was still on Dally's shoulder, he was looking at the rabbit like a fat boy looking through the candy store window.

Take him about fifteen yards out, and let him go, said Dally.

Rudy took the Rabbit out a lot farther than Dally had requested, then let him go.

The Rabbit took off as soon as he touched ground, Rudy had never seen a Rabbit cover so much ground, so quickly.

The pasture behind the barn was short grassed, for a quarter mile in all directions.

The Rabbit ran straight out for a minute, then headed for the tree line to the left.

Dally pointed at the Rabbit, he really didn't have to, the bird had never taken his eyes off him.

Get him Cain, he shouted.

Cain leaped from his shoulder, gaining altitude, and headed straight for the tree line, he turned in front of it, and headed straight down the line to cut him off.

Somehow, the Rabbit sensed this, and changed directions.

Cain banked off the tree line and started coming in low, directly behind the Rabbit, who in turn' picked up speed, as Cain zeroed in on him' he began the long zig-zag jumps.

He made a nice jump away from the bird, when he touched down again, he immediately jumped in the opposite direction, he could continue this process until he reached the safety of the tree's,.. But an inch before his feet touched ground, he felt the Talons dig into his flesh.

Cain caught the Rabbit in midair, with one foot, he brought the Rabbit back, came to a stop above Dally, and dropped the Rabbit right into the cage.

He brought me all three of those Rabbits in there, Dally said proudly.

Cain lighted on Dally's shoulder again.

You're quite the hunter, huh Cain, Rudy said this talking directly to the bird, the way Dally does, Cain just looked at him, not fidgety at all, Rudy felt the bird was taking to him a little also.

Where the hell did you get that bird from man, said Keith.

Rudy and Cole brought him here, said Dally, taking Cain back to his cage.

Hey, I'm getting ready to move some stuff out of the barn, said Rudy.

Glad to see you've got some help,.. I got you on this end.

Rudy took Keith inside the barn; he went around the back side of a stack of hay, he pulled out one of the bottom bails, crawled inside and came out with a large plastic bag.

The bag was three quarters full, Keith pulled out a bag also.

This the same stuff you gave me? Yeah.

How much you got?

About ninety pounds, I need to move this shit, I'm getting too paranoid sitting on it, I'm getting myself into more and more fucked up situations,..I know you're not in the game anymore, so if you're having second thoughts.

Second thoughts,... no way, I'm all in, this is some good fucking weed, we may be able to move all you got, in just a couple of stops, said Keith.

The car was dangerously packed, if we get stopped, we're gone, there's no way to hide this much weed.

We've got to avoid law enforcement like the plague.

They got on the highway and headed east,.. destination Brandon Fl.

Keith pulled into a gated community, then onto the driveway of a large, very Modern home, it couldn't have been no more than two years old.

Howard Andrews was the name of the man that came out to greet them, he was a thin man, thick mustache, professional, at whatever it was he did.

What's up buddy, come on in.

He led them into the living room,.. the place was huge, the pool was in the living room also.

The ninety-inch television, with the movie theater surround sound system, was sunk into the opposite wall, and set up like a real theater, it could be enjoyed very tastefully from the pool area.

The place was immaculately furnished, everything was in order, in theme, and was obviously, very well taken care of.

Rudy felt different in the presence of Howard Andrews, he was about to tell Keith' not to mention anything about the weed, a guy like this, might freak out.

Right about that time, Keith said,... Howard, I got that weed you been trying to hunt down, top hat,...you're going to be the first one running it.

Howard brought over the drinks he'd fixed,.. still standing, he took a deep drink of Remy Martin, he brought the glass down, completely satisfied with it.

"Let's see what you got," said Howard.

Keith brought in a one-pound bag, Howard took the bag and smelled the contents inside, a pleasant look crossed his face, he reached over and pushed a button beside him at the bar,... a young lady came from upstairs,... he handed her the bag,... she disappeared upstairs,.. five minutes later' she yelled from the top of the stairs,...."Get It".

It must be pretty good, she's turned down the last four sources of weed that came through here.

What kind of weight you working with? I can cover whatever you need.

Then leave me thirty pounds. I got you, said Keith.

Hold on a minute, let me make a call, said Howard.

When he got off the phone, he asked if we had forty more pounds.

Yes, I do, said Keith.

Rudy remained silent, these were different kinds of people, he felt out of place, but Keith was comfortable here.

Keith was once a Giant' in the Cocaine movement, he gave it up once he dodged a forty year sentence, that he only did six years on.

This here wasn't operating at ground level, this was privileged, it almost felt safe,... he couldn't even tell how these people watched their backs,...but he knew their backs were covered.

I'm going to cover my partners order, said Howard,.. what's the damage.

"Seventy grand said Keith.

Howard didn't change words, he disappeared in the back, and returned with the money.

If you have more of this, in about two weeks,... come check me out.

Will do, said Keith.

We got two more places to check, said Keith.

They headed back west, with the last of the weed,.. It was dropped off at a beach house on Madera Beach, in St.

Petersburg' to the same type of people, the privileged.

Rudy enjoyed being off "Ground Level", even if it was' only for a moment.

Rudy gave Keith five grand, that left him with eighty five G's.

He was dropped off at the house that Cole had been talking about, he talked to Mrs. Culpepper, and explained who he was.

You had a deal with Cole, for this place, he asked me to give you the seventy thousand dollars, and pick up the Deeds.

Mrs. Culpepper was happy to get the money, she retrieved the Deeds immediately, Rudy gave her a thousand more dollars to turn on the utilities.

He found some moderately priced furnishings for the place, he cleaned and prepped until it started to come to life, Rudy was surprised at how nice of a place it really was.

He felt good, the next morning,... it was time, no matter what, today was going to be a good day.

He rented a Limo, and set up three bottles of Crystal Champagne, in the back.

The whole world seems to be cooperating, there were no snags, the weather was perfect.

He had the Limo Park at the end of the walkway, at the front door of the Orient Road Jail.

It was after four o'clock in the afternoon, when the newly released inmates finally made it out of custody, and out of the front door.

Cole was one of the first, he walked to the center of the platform and stopped, he turned around and looked over the twenty or so people that were filing out of the exit door behind him.

The last person to come out was Felicia, she looked relieved, she met Cole at the center of the platform, they gave each other a hug, then chatted for awhile.

Rudy just watched' from behind the tinted windows of the Limo.

Felicia began to look a little anxious, she started fumbling through that big paper bag (Jail house suitcase) and came out with her cell phone, she removed it from the airtight plastic holder, Rudy could tell that it was still charged, she did that little "happy bounce", she dialed a number,.. Rudy's phone rang, he answered.

Hello!

Hey, it's me, Felicia. Felicia who?

Very funny Rudy, me and Cole are out of jail, can you get someone to come pick us up?

Turn around, said Rudy.

She turned, cell phone still in her ear, the Limousine door opened.

Rudy stepped out and bowed at the waist. Your Carriage awaits Madam, and Sir.

All the newly released inmates watched as Cole and Felicia made their way to the Limo.

They seemed impressed at the way some people leave a bad situation.

Rudy took them for a night on the town, they ate at the Colonnade Room, on the waterfront, after eating jailhouse grub, one learns to appreciate real food.

They partied in the streets of Ybor, and drank Champagne all the way back to the house.

Rudy dangled the keys to the house in front of Cole, you now have a Permanant residence.

In the following months, Marcus Whites plan was in full effect, although Orlan Petrini had been labeled, dangerous, on a world wide level.

Marcus White declined the witness protection program,.. he'd long ago found a spot in a foreign Country, where he'd never be found.

Mrs. Petrini was placed in charge of Orlan Petrini's estate, she and Marcus Cleaned... Him... out.

They took everything he owned, she sold the house in Carolina, the summer home in California, and the vacation home in the Virgin Islands.

They left the Country with over eight hundred Million dollars, and got away "Scott" free.

Orlan Petrini's trial, was the next event.

Petrini had four lawyers working around the clock on his behalf, Petrini was their Firm's number one client.

Petrini made it clear that he would never plead guilty to these charges, simply because they weren't true, his lawyers tried and tried, to turn the prosecutors in the direction of Marcus White.

But the law of the land, in most cases, will follow the money.

It wasn't long before his lawyers caught wind of Petrini's wife, she had taken all of his money, and was leaving the Country.

The Firm handling his case lost interest almost immediately, the four lawyers assigned to him, suddenly came up with far more important cases, and his case was no longer, priority one.

Petrini's legal defense had come to a halt, he had forgotten how quickly one can find himself, all alone.

All of his associates had turned their backs on him, they didn't seem to care if he was guilty or not.

This fight was going to be far more difficult than he ever imagined.

It wasn't until he revealed the fact that he had other accounts, that his wife had no knowledge of, that the lawyers came back' like a flock of seagulls.

He'd been able to hide quite a bit of money in other accounts, the first two accounts he opened were twenty Million strong "each".

Petrini's first wife had left him broke,...and like his current wife, didn't seem to have any consideration what- so-ever, for his well being, the money in those other accounts were "Just in Case" money.

Just in case my wife leaves me, and steals all the money on her way out, accounts.

He had no idea that Marcus White and his wife, were lovers, the news made him feel small, and stupid.

They've probably been seeing each other for years, he thought to himself.

Marcus had betrayed his friendship, violated his home, and was now setting him up to take the fall' for a bumbled job that he couldn't have possibly fucked up any worse.

The sleeping with his wife part hurt, but the fact that, together, they had robbed him blind, and left him for dead, really hit home.

Orlans rage caused him to scream out loud in his cell, opening new channels of thought,...he wanted revenge so bad' he could taste it.

He funneled money into every nook and cranny of the Penile system in order to gain favor,... the trial will be coming up soon.

The money from the weed didn't hang around long, Rudy still hadn't found a job, he was working out of a day

labor joint, doing hot, hard, good for nothing work, he was working way too hard for the small amount of pay he was getting, he was averaging two to three days of work per week, at minimum wage.

Cole was building Pallets for a free lancer, and Felicia was working at a fast food restaurant.

They were barely making ends meet, they were more than willing to work together to keep the house, Felicia loved the place, they discussed plans for another weed crop in the spring.

Emmitt Smith stopped by the house, he'd come to prep Rudy for the trial, they went over all of the more sensitive aspects of the case, the "what to say", and "what not to say", on the stand,...after they'd finally reached the point where they knew they were on the same page, Rudy took that time to bring up something he'd been working on.

Rudy had been asking around for quite some time, he was trying to locate "Big Moe",... Moses Herman, he knew Moses was in prison, he just didn't know where.

He finally found that Big Moe was in an Amarillo Texas, prison, Rudy pulled him up on the computer, and found out that he had an appeal in the system, that would require him to return to Florida, for sixty days or so.

Rudy asked Emmitt to check on that appeal and see if he could push it through.

Emmitt agreed to check on it, he got on it right away, and it wasn't a problem pushing it through.

Not very long after, Big Moe was on his way to the Orient Road jail, in Tampa.

Big Moe had been in prison sixteen years, he was doing a life sentence, he killed three white boys at a bar one night, they had mistaken him for something to play with,...the last one' he had to chase three blocks to catch, the fact that this was done with his bare hands, brought up serious anger issues that had him labeled a "Menace To Society".

The appeal that he was coming to Tampa for, wasn't important,... what was important was the letter he had received from Rudolph Clayton.

The letter contained a photo of a young girl, who had been Tortured, raped, beaten,... and Murdered.

The name under the photo read, "Chantell Harris".

Her Mother, Linda Harris, was Big Moe's sister, and Chantell,.. his very first Niece.

Chantell was two years old when Big Moe went to prison, and in the years to follow, had turned into his most reliable pen-pal,... she kept him updated on everything going on with his friends, the City, and herself, she was his one connection to the outside.

He had over a hundred pictures, sent by Chantell, he watched her grow up, through the pictures she'd sent.

The picture he was looking at now, was almost unrecognizable as Chantell,... the kindred spirit, that had loved her uncle so much, had been ripped from her body, and discarded like trash.

There was a second picture, one of two men in a newspaper clipping.

The names were James Dawson, (Alias) J.D., and Emanuel Menendez, (Alias) Manny,... the one called

Manny, had been Murdered in Orient Road Jail a few months earlier, the other inmate was still awaiting trial in that facility for the brutal rape and murder of a young Tampa Teen.

Big Moe concentrated on the photo of the man' until it was etched into his memory.

On arrival to the Orient Road Jail, Big Moe was placed in Delta West, a compound for those charged with violent crimes, from first degree murder, to Manslaughter, all armed robbers were there also.

He hadn't settled in till well past midnight,.. the next morning at breakfast. He surveyed the entire compound,... the man in the picture wasn't there.

A couple days later, he began asking for J.D. as if he knew him,... no one did!

J.D. in fact, was denying anything to do with the death of the teen, he dropped the J.D. nick name, and was now simply called "James.

Big Moe would have to check the next compound over, after sixteen years in the system, he knew how this was done.

An infraction, or D.R. (Disciplinary Report) would get him moved to another compound.

The infraction shouldn't be a major one, or he'd end up skipping the minor infraction compounds on his way to the worst.

He spotted the inmate across from him peeking around the corner, keeping an eye on the guard station, he would disappear, and clouds of smoke would come into view.

Big Moe went over, give me a cigarette, said Moe.

The man gave him a cigarette without changing words, no one knew Big Moe's reputation, but his size' and demeanor alone, demanded respect and cooperation.

There's a no smoking policy at the Orient Road Jail, and if caught, it would only be a minor infraction.

Big Moe smoked the cigarette on the basketball court, in plain view of the guard; who finally saw him, after Moe was starting to turn green,... he hated cigarettes.

He was written up, and asked to pack his belongings, he was transferred to "Charlie West", if the man wasn't here' he would have to do whatever's necessary to get to "Bravo West", he would check there, then on to "Alpha West", where the worst of the worst reside.

After he'd gotten settled into his new compound, he took a look around from the second floor balcony.

His eye's locked on a man that was laughing and having a good time' playing cards, Big Moe studied the man for quite some time,... it was him!...it was indeed the man from the picture.

Big Moe headed back to his cell; he kneeled down beside his bunk, and prayed,...he prayed all day, the session lasted so long' the compound Bible thumpers came into his cell and began praying also,...some prayed out loud, some silently, they were happy to have such a devout man of God in their midst.

And Big Moe knew he would need every ounce of prayer that was going up' on his behalf.

He was praying for forgiveness, for what he was about to do.

He didn't get off his knees till that night, only a half hour before lights out.

He started downstairs, his walk was callous and set, he stopped short of the table that held the endless card game.

The men at the table could feel the tension in the air,... one by one, the men left the table,... J.D. also got up to leave.

"You", said Big Moe,... don't go nowhere,...I need to see you!

What you need to see me for?

Moe stepped in close' in a non threatening way, and spoke calmly,... that was my Niece you killed,...I need to see you about that.

J.D. stepped in even closer, man, I ain't killed nobody, ain't have nothing to do with that shit, an I don't appreciate you spreading that kind of shit round here, now step off, before shit get ugly up in here.

I'm not here trying to find out who killed my Niece, I know who killed her, I'm not here by mistake, or because I've been misinformed...you can deny it all you want, it don't change nothing...it was you.

J.D.,... not being a punk and all, attacked Big Moe.

He hit Moe with two solid blows to the gut, then went to the head with a third, the fourth blow was caught in mid- air,...Moe pulled him close enough to get a big hand around his throat, he was squeezing, and forcing the man to the floor at the same time, once on the floor he continued to apply pressure to the throat' until he was unconscious.

Not much noise came from this encounter, the other inmates watched from a distance, no one attempted to alert the guard,... the officer on duty, hadn't heard a thing.

Big Moe drug the man up the far stairwell and into his cell' and locked the door.

The inmates that crept closer to the cell to listen' had to break into a song in order to drown out the noises that were coming from the small cell.

It sounded like ten fighters were locked into a death match in there.

There were desperate screams, that were silenced by mind jarring blows, bones were being broken, it wasn't long before blood was running from under the door.

J.D.'s life had come to a very bitter end, by a man that was not yet satisfied with his death,.. the man was still beating J.D.'s skull in, thirty minutes after he was dead.

Earlier, the officer on duty had to put in ear plugs,.. the sound of a man being beaten to death is almost unbearable.

But the officer was aware of what J.D. had done,.. he had baby girls also, and to know that J.D. would never get his hands on them' was a relief,...and yeah, the earplugs worked just fine.

At "Ground Level" there's a saying (what goes around, comes around).

If you take advantage of someone because you're bigger, and stronger than they are,... you "will" be taken advantage of by someone bigger and stronger than you are.

(They say, it is impossible to reap anything other than what you yourself, have sewn)

The news of J.D.'s death spread fast, when it reached Rudy and the others' they put together a small party to celebrate.

It was finally done; Chantell's killers had finally been brought to justice.

Now that everything had been made right by Chantell, the case was closed, and a new found peace came over the group.

As the celebration was going on, Rudy left the group and went out on the balcony alone.

Old memories of the little girl that had befriended him at the age of five, held his mind captive, he'd provided so much to Mrs. Harris's efforts to care for her daughter properly over the years, Chantell was having a hard time coping with the trials of the lower class teenager, but he knew she would end up being one of the most beautiful people, anyone would ever want to meet.

I'm sorry you had to die' to point out some of the problems among us, I just wanted you to know that we kept searching until we found a couple of the problems.... and fixed them.

I will never forget you.

The expectations of the trial, seemed to be gaining momentum, Rudy overheard people of almost every walk of life, talking about it, the upper classes were talking of the Pheasant man, trying to swindle money from a hard working pillar of society.

The poorer classes spoke of the David verses Goliath story, of how the big wigs with all the money' take advantage of the have nots.

Orlan Petrini stepped into the Courtroom' full of confidence, a small herd of lawyers trailed him.

A capacity crowd had gathered for the trial.

Emmitt Smith was in his element, he met Rudy at the Courthouse steps, Rudy had been going over Courthouse etiquette for weeks, he was trying to wrap his mind around this Country's legal system.

It had been proven, time and time again, that the American Courtroom, is the worst place on earth for a Black Man, things can turn bad quickly, if the Court senses something that you don't fully understand.

You can be taken advantage of by Courtroom Rhetoric, and fast talking, silver tongued liars; with law degrees, using terms that sound like witchcraft' being thrown back and forth, from prosecutor's to judges, from judges to lawyers, from lawyers to states attorneys and so on.

Rudy was nervous to even walk in on this group,... he knew he'd have to be strong, confident, and very attentive.

Rudy and Emmitt walked through the Courtroom doors together,. And down the center aisle, Emmitt opened the little swinging gate to the plaintiff's table.

Rudy turned at the table, and locked eyes with Orlan Petrini, at the Defendants table.

This was the first time he had been in the man's presence... he was stuck, he couldn't move, he couldn't break eye contact, he felt his blood temperature rising, as his heartbeat pounded like a drum, everything he'd been preparing for, just vanished.

He began to feel faint, then saw himself in the dark, running in full retreat, he saw the muzzle flashes of a gun, repeatedly light up in the darkness, no sound, just the flashing,... he saw his Father, stumbling downward, his body being riddled with bullets.

He saw himself turn and run, shielding his mother as the muzzle flashes erupted once more.

He saw himself looking up from the ground as his mother fell alongside the house, the muzzle flashes were coming from the front of the house now, another shooter was up front.

He felt someone repeatedly slapping him in the face, soon he heard his name being called,... he opened his eye's.

He was lying on the Courtroom floor, Emmitt Smith and a couple of others helped him up' and out of the Courtroom,...Rudy couldn't stop shaking, Emmitt Smith called it an anxiety attack, someone else said it was a nervous breakdown, Rudy didn't understand the fear that gripped him, nothing anyone said' could get him to reenter the Courtroom.

Emmitt called for a recess.

The Judge recessed the Court proceedings for two hours,... Rudy's testimony was pertinent to the case, and to reschedule the Court date, would give the Petrini clan, the months it would need to think up new strategies.

You've got to go back in there, said Emmitt.

I don't think I can, said Rudy, I think It'll be better for everyone if I drop this case against him, he doesn't operate anything like I do, he'd rather have me killed' than to go through this trial,...I don't want anyone else' that's close to me, to die' just because their present at the time he sends another army of killers after me, I'm not taking this any further,...I'm out.

I understand your concern, but you've got to take a closer look at what's in front of you.

This situation only looks bad "to you", when in fact, you're the only one that can claim it, this guy has given you everything you need,... you can't lose,...Emmitt was trying to calm Rudy down' and get him to relax.

This kind of reminds me of a story,...about this King that had a son that he loved very much, he had a mansion built for him as a gift' when he reached the age of maturity' and was getting Married, the King dreamed of his son raising his family in the home' that he'd put so much of himself into,...but the son hated the Mansion at first sight, he hated all of the highly colorful stones, his father used in building it, the eight foot' stone wall that surrounded the

Mansion, was made of the same' way too colorful stones.

The son never set foot inside the place.

When he Married, he had another Mansion built on the opposite side of the kingdom.

Years later, the king died, and the son became king,...he decided to bring in revenue through trade, instead of war, like his Father,...ignoring his Military proved to be a bad decision, the neighboring kingdoms sensed his weakness, and his kingdom was attacked.

After three years of battle, he could no longer financially support his dwindling, Army.

He surrendered his kingdom, he and his queen were allowed to leave peacefully, he had no treasure to plunder, and the kingdom's people were all starving.

He and his queen were living very poorly, when rumors of his kingdom began to reach him, the kingdom had grown to twice the size it once was, people were flocking to the kingdom from every part of the world,

It was said that it was the most prosperous place on earth.

Curiosity overcame him, and he sent a message to a council member friend that had stayed with the new order.

The man told him that the Mansion his father had built for him was the treasure of all treasures, the

Mansion was built entirely of precious stones, Diamonds, Rubies, Sapphires, Pearls, every rare and precious stone known to man,...even the eight foot wall that surrounded the Mansion was made of precious stones of all sizes,...thanks to you, this new king is the wealthiest man in the entire region.

All I'm saying Rudy' is take a closer look at this gift that's been placed at your feet, it's yours' and yours alone, you "can" surrender... but you don't have to, you already have everything you need to win this, you can take this killer off the street and make this place safer for everyone.

Don't let him get away with what he did!

Rudy said nothing for a while, as he slowly came back to himself, he stood, straitened up his suit, then he and Emmitt headed for the Courtroom.

Emmitt kept a close eye on him, wondering if he could hold up under this pressure.

When he reached the plaintiff's table, Rudy once again locked eyes with Orlan Petrini.... he wasn't scared anymore.

Rudy took his seat,... and the lawyers went to work.

Emmitt Smith was in rare form; he had the Courtroom in the palm of his hand' as he ran down count after count, on Petrini, he rounded out at 43 counts.

Petrini's defense was to put the blame solely on those that worked under him, and hide behind the fact that he wasn't there, and knew nothing about all that had taken place.

Petrini's lawyers fought hard, and brought about something close to what they needed,... "the reasonable doubt".

That, along with the money that Petrini had placed in the most strategic places of the system, gave their case a formidable boost.

Emmitt Smith fought the Petrini clan back and forth for three days.

The closing arguments from both sides were compelling, no one could tell which way the verdict would fall, the media bustled around outside the Courtroom door, unsure of what to report.

The judge was on pins and needles, this hadn't played out as he had expected, there was chatter among all, as the Jury retreated to their chambers.

Emmitt and Rudy sat in the cafeteria while the jury was deliberating, Emmitt yelled for two Coffee's, he knew this could take some time, Cole and Felicia spotted them and rushed over, they hadn't been able to get in the Courtroom.

How's it going in there, said Cole.

I wish I could answer that question," said Emmitt, "all I can say is, we're still in the game.

Four hours later, a reporter ran into the cafeteria to gather his comrades.

The jury's back in, he said, loud enough for everyone to hear.

After the jury was seated' and the Courtroom brought to order, the judge asked if they had reached a verdict.

The jury Chairman replied...yes, we have your honor.

The count sheets were passed to the judge, the judge eyed them closely, they were passed back to the jury Chairman.

Count one, said the judge,... Conspiracy to commit Murder,.. what say you.

Not guilty' your Honor, said the Chairman.

All 43 counts were brought forth, and a verdict reached on all; out of 43 counts, Petrini was only found guilty on 11.

Petrini and his lawyers were happy with the results, the money that he'd been pumping into the system was finally paying off, and by him pleading, "not guilty", to all charges, means the system must leave the door open for any appeals that he may file in the future,...plus, the inner workings of the system' contains places where "time" can be paid for, with Cash.

Things weren't looking so bad after all,... there was a good chance he could finish his sentence, and still have enough life left for a brand-new start,.. his worst fear at this point had been, to die in prison and never get the chance to have a face to face with his wife, and Marcus White.

He would never get over being left holding the bag, for Marcus's misdeeds, and with the help of his wife, his fortune stolen by this man,...yes,...he will be found, there would be no place on earth for him to hide,.. his wife would also be facing the same fate.

Marcus likes to kill people huh,... I'll show him how it's done.

Emmitt Smith was happy with the outcome also; they had won on six counts of Discrimination' from the Restaurant chain,... Criminal Conspiracy, from planned attacks on innocent U.S. Citizens, for exposing their unlawful Discrimination practices.

They had also won, three counts of "Involuntary Manslaughter", for the deaths of Rudy's Parents, plus the death of one of his own men, in yet another planned attack.

These were the main counts that Emmitt was after, the rest would have just been icing on the cake.

Emmitt knew these charges wouldn't carry a lot of jail time' for those who are considered the pillars of society, but the time he'd get, plus the retribution he'd have to pay,...would surely swing a knockout blow.

Sentencing was set for the following week, and all Civil matters, within thirty days.

When Rudy got home from work the following day, he was feeling pretty good, he set up the Bar-B-

Q grill in the front yard, and brought the speakers outside,...by the time Felicia and Cole got home, there were a couple of other people there, they expounded on this good idea by calling a few more of their friends over.

Before long, they had a pretty nice little get together going, they had spareribs, shrimp kabob's, and chicken on the grill, beer and wine flowing, and best of all, a lot of good friends around, even Dally and his wife Sandra showed up.

Dally very seldom spent time in the inner city, he liked country living, his place in Seffner had lots of open spaces for raising animals and growing his own food.

Rudy stayed close to him, trying to make sure he was comfortable during his visit.

This was the first chance he'd gotten, to see the place that Rudy and Cole had purchased with the money from the weed crop.

You guy's really made out on this deal, said Dally' after he'd gotten a tour of the place.

It's the only good thing we were able to get out of that whole crop, said Rudy.

Dally actually seemed to be having a good time, he had a nice buzz going and talked on end.

How's Cain doing, asked Rudy.

Cain's good, replied Dally, I let him go, been about a week now, it's mating season' and Cain was showing signs of agitation,...I couldn't keep him locked up like that, he's one of the freest creatures on the planet, I had to let him go,...but guess what?

What, asked Rudy.

Watch this,... he pulled a piece of chicken from the bone on his plate and threw it in the air toward the trees that lined the driveway.

Rudy's mouth fell open when Cain darted from the tree' and caught it in his beak before it hit the ground, then perched on a low branch of a tree on the opposite side of the drive, to eat.

The whole gathering seemed to be in awe of this majestic creature, sitting in the tree, in plain view, who seemed to be part of this get together.

You brought him here in the truck? asked Rudy.

No, said Dally, I've noticed sometimes he follows me around.

Cole was making his way over to where they were standing, Dally and Rudy were snickering at his unsteady walk, he was getting pretty drunk.

"Hey, you guys," said Cole, his words a little slurred,.. look here, my girl's birthday's tomorrow, I want you to come help me pick out something nice' for thirty bucks.

Dally tried to contain his laughter; but couldn't... Rudy was next, then they all started to laugh, they had too, their financial situation hurt too bad sometimes' to do anything but laugh.

Come on, said Dally, we'll find something nice for her. I'll drive, said Cole.

"No", said dally and Rudy at the same time!

They left the gathering and headed for Channelside Drive, this is the Luxury Cruise ship district, buildings and shops of the latest designs, lined the waterfront, the high tourist rate' makes shopping expensive in this area...but with so many shops competing for business,.. Bargains can be found.

They were hitting one shop after another; when this one shop caught Cole's eye, the process had been moving slower than expected' due to the intoxication factor.

The name of the shop was "Crystal's", the entire front of the shop, was glass, the sun would shine through the window, and get divided up into millions of beams of light' as it went from Crystal to Crystal,..it was awesome to watch from outside, Cole seemed to be drawn to it, he staggered inside, he was completely focused on this one particular Crystal ornament.

That one piece happened to be at the top of a twelve tier' display setting, that started from the floor, and went up Pyramid style,... he stumbled just as he touched the piece he was after, he lost his balance into the display,...as it was falling, Cole tried his best to stop it, but ended up running into the next display that was set up behind the first,...Rudy and Dally watched in horror as the Domino effect was happening in real time.

From outside, for a moment it looked as if the whole shop was caving in,... when it was over, Cole was standing in a disaster area, holding the one Crystal Elephant, that held his fascination throughout the whole ordeal.

The little Oriental woman that ran the shop, stood between him and the front door, baseball bat in hand.

You go nowhere, she yelled, police come now.

Cole was ticketed' and given a bill for every item that was broken, forty-six hundred dollars' worth.

Rudy and Dally purchased the Crystal Elephant for him, as his thirty bucks were pretty much tied up.

We all knew this was one that Cole would never live down.

Rudy and Dally laughed so hard; tears were flowing.

They loaded Cole into the truck and started through the Channel-side District.

I don't feel too good, said Cole,... I think you'd better pull over.

You'll be ok, said Dally, just relax baby boy.

No, I'm serious, pull over, I think I'm gonna hurl.

Pull in over there, said Rudy, pointing at an available parking space, which is uncommon in this part of town.

Cole bolted from the truck, and headed across the finely manicured grass, around the big fountain, and out to the Channel wall.

Rudy and Dally got there just as he'd finished barfing his guts out,... his face was beet red, his eye's redder,.. he really looked sick.

They each took an arm, and walked him back and forth along the waterfront until the effects of the alcohol began to subside.

They spent a little time leaning on the wall, admiring the view across the Channel, the Penthouses were stacked atop one another, the color schemes and architecture was immaculate, all the Penthouses had Piers with Gazebos at the end,.. they even had mid-sized luxury boats that were electronically hoisted from the water, and hung in their own private slips, they hung in mid-air, what a beautiful way to live.

It was no secret that Rudy and the others were jealous of the upper classes that resided on the Islands of Tampa Bay.

This one was known as Harbour Island, a little farther down the Channel, was Davis Island, one just as immaculate as the first.

Cole's jealous anger exploded within him without warning...what are we going to do man, he said, more frustrated than Rudy or Dally had seem him in quite some time.

What are we gonna do?

He was too frustrated to be approached, Rudy just kept quiet and let him blow off steam.

Every time we turn around, we're knee deep in shit, and everything I do' turns on me,... everything,...I had just got promoted to kitchen manager at the Two Cronies Restaurant,.. then thirty days later, I'm throwing Molotov Cocktails through the windows of the fucking joint,..

Wait,.. wait,... are you telling me, you're the one that burned that place down, asked Rudy.

You damn right I did it, that's what they did to us!

I always thought you had something to do with that, said Rudy (showing Admiration), but I wasn't gonna question you about it.

My job went up in those flames, everything I do turns out the same way,...it throws me backward,... I go and take back some weed that was stolen from us, and the little prick that stole the weed,... calls the fucking Cops,... and again, we're in a downward spiral, even something as simple as getting a present for my girl ends up with me nearly tearing down everything in the store.

And once again, we're in a downward spiral,.. if things don't change, we're not going to make it, we're gonna go under.

Cole was drunk, but what he said was right, the ground was slipping from under our feet; and it was because of our own stupid mistakes.

This forced Rudy to take a realistic glance into their future, they had no truly marketable skills, and qualifying for school grants wouldn't be happening,.. all of a sudden, the future looked pretty dim.

We'll be ok, said Rudy, look,...we may get some money from this law suit I'm working on, if we do, we're gonna hold on to it until we find out how we can go into business with it, all legal like,..that way we'll have less to worry about' if something goes wrong, lets face it, there's no way we're gonna stop making stupid mistakes, but if we stay legal, our mistakes may not cost us as much.

When they got back to the house, there were only a couple of people still hanging out.

Cole waited till everyone had left to give My ra her birthday present, her response to the present was unexpected, mostly because no one, not even Cole, had paid much attention to her fetish for Elephant related items,...she couldn't have been happier with her gift, she placed the Elephant on a shelf on the wall over her computer, no one hardly ever went into the room, this was where she spent a lot of her private time.

It was her own little sanctuary, there were already two Elephants on the shelf, and they were remarkably similar to the one that Cole had just bought her, since the one that Cole got her was the largest, she put that one in the middle...it looked like a Mother Elephant with her two baby Elephants, out for a stroll,.. there were other Elephants on the second shelf, and still others on the wing shelves.

There were Elephants of different types on shelves all over the room, some were carved wood, some porcelain, some were made of stone, she even had Elephants that were like Bronze or something.

There were paintings on the wall,.. all Elephant related, the Kool-Aid pitcher in the fridge an Elephant trunk spout, the more they looked, the more they found.

I knew she liked Elephants, said Cole,... I just didn't know how much.

You don't think she's crazy do you, asked Rudy. She likes Elephants, what's wrong with that?

Cole,.. how could you "Not" notice, all these Elephants.

You're down here every day yourself, Cole argued, how come you've never seen them.

Myra was standing there listening to the whole conversation, she acted as if she'd heard that conversation a few times before, she just gave Rudy and Cole that "Very Funny" little smirk.

Felicia finished what she was doing outside and came through heading upstairs to wash up.

Come check out my birthday present, said Myra. I'll be right back, she replied.

She was in a good mood, but Cole noticed she gave Rudy a funny look as she passed him.

Whoa, what was that, asked Cole. You saw that, right?

Yeah, that was kind'a cold.

When I was in the Hospital she had mentioned that she didn't like Nurse Miranda,.. she obviously thought I shouldn't like her either, but I do, Miranda's as strait as they come, I went to see her the other day to thank her for helping us out the way she did, she ended up treating me to dinner, when she dropped me off, Felicia was chillin on the balcony, she started talking trash the instant she saw her, I don't see why she hates Miranda so much.

Felicia wasn't mad at that girl, said Myra, she was mad at "you", I know you two aren't an item, but she definately has feelings for you.

Yeah, I know,.. she's pretty protective,.. she's my favorite person in the world, but we don't work well as a couple, I've just got to work my way through this little hissy-fit that she' milking the hell out of,...and if she keeps cutting her eyes at me, I'm gonna back hand her ass, "pimp style".

Who you getting ready to pimp slap, asked Felicia, as she came downstairs, she'd heard the conversation' but was playing it off.

We were just Kickin the Bobo, that's all, said Rudy, nobody slappin nobody round here.

That's what I thought, said Felicia,.. cutting her eye's at Rudy once more.

The guy's took the hint and retreated to the front room and claimed the Tv area.

Marcus White's Reign as one in complete control of his own destiny, was in full effect.

He understood that his new "Rich Life" would have to be kept low key,.. the fortune he now possessed was stolen from Orlan Petrini' who is now penniless and more than likely doing a life sentence, but just because Orlan would be in prison for the rest of his life doesn't mean that he wouldn't be hunted,..he manufactured a false trail that would take the cleverest of trackers half way around the world and back, without the slightest bit of progress.

He changed his name, and the name of his mistress (Petrini's wife).

He was surprised at how easy it was to get her to put all the money under his new name,.. Vernon Mathews, Petrini's wife was now, Mrs. Patricia Mathews.

The power grew fast within him, they hadn't run far, just across the Border a little south of the mainland of South America.

But the hiding place was perfect, he'd purchased a small two bedroom block home that a dirt farmer had on the far side of his property, the farmer owned a thousand acres, three hundred of which were undeveloped, he had plans of developing this property but had never gotten around to it.

Marcus paid the man a hefty price for the three hundred acres, it was sold with the promise that he would develop, and farm the land as the farmer had planned to do.

White would get eighty per-cent of the harvest grown on his property, plus he would also be paid for the use of his property, that way, the farmer wouldn't have to worry about his new neighbor turning into another competitor.

Marcus's dirt farmer cover was actually going to turn a profit,.. even with the elaborate modifications he had made to the small home, the place was going to pay for itself.

The modifications were his own brainchild, the basement area was transformed into their new home.

The basement was now two stories underground, each floor was fifty thousand square feet' with lofty ceilings, Chandeliers, and decorated Victorian style.

It was a complete underground Mansion, a lot of thought went into the design, it even came with an escape route.

The topside small home was simple looking, the paint was peeling in places, the furniture was cheap' and gave the appearance of a sharecropper's home.

No one would figure a man with his wealth' would be anywhere close to this place...he was safe here,.. this is where he would spend the rest of his life.

Marcus and his lady love didn't have to hide their relationship any longer, she loved the home he had worked so hard to get to her liking, she loved him with all her heart. And he was crazy about her, the man was insatiable, their love making was always hot and heavy, and as close to never ending as you can get, she craved the extra attention the man had brought into her life.

The place was complete in record time, considering the secrecy involved, next was the developing of the land.

There were tree's to be removed and rooted, big boulders that had to be relocated, he purchased a 9 series John Deere tractor, with all the gadgets, he put rust colored paint on it so it wouldn't appear to be an expensive new tractor.

But even so, the landscaping of his new property was brutal, he wasn't used to this level of manual labor, so when he got tired or too hot, he'd quit for the day.

For the first three months' he would work in the fields till he got tired, then run back to his lavish, underground Palace and make love to his beautiful mistress for the rest of the day.

They hardly did anything else,... because he still felt as if he was fucking another man's wife.

This is a major taboo in almost every known community on earth, but the taboo of the relationship was the turn on for Marcus.

After a while, that rush of adrenaline that came from the ever-present possibility of being caught in the act by her husband' was beginning to fade.

He found himself having to pretend; he was fucking another man's wife, and it wasn't working too well...the truth is,.. she's his woman now, and the excitment of having her' was grinding down.

Marcus threw himself fully into the dirt farming trade; he cleared the land tirelessly, not long after, he was planting seeds. The fresh air and sunshine proved to be good for his health, his strength and stamina were at a steady climb, he was in the field day and night.

When the first of the sprouts began breaking ground, he saw the unhealthy appearance of the plants, he went to Victor Vada, the original dirt farmer, out of concern.

Victor could tell' the gringo Vernon Mathews didn't know much about the trade that he had bought into.

Victor taught him how to spot anomalies in the growing plants, taught him how to keep them healthy,.. insects were arch enemy number one, to the dirt farmer.

The language barrier also proved to be a major factor; he hadn't found anyone at this point that spoke legible English.

When it came to his crops, Victor had to physically take Marcus to his storerooms and show him what was growing on his land.

There were 144 acres of coffee beans, and 144 acres of soy beans,... both crops were always in high demand, it was explained to him in broken English, but Marcus got the gist of what he was saying.

He was planning on turning the crop over to Victor anyway and letting him market the product.

In the fields the staking seemed to go on forever, Victor watched the gringo working his field, he smiled to himself as he remembered an ancient named Sisyphus, who continuously rolled a large Boulder up a steep hill, he'd get to a certain point and couldn't force the Boulder up any further, the boulder would knock him down, and they would both tumble all the way back down the hill, this went on for years, he didn't understand that he was trying to do something that was impossible to do, "without help".

This American doesn't know, what he's trying to do is impossible as well, he was going to need help.

It took some convincing...the man was determined to handle this task alone, two factors got his attention,.. the fact that at the rate he was going, he would surely miss the next two harvests, and the second factor was,.. the helpers he needed could be found in a remote campsite quite a distance from town,.. he wouldn't be spotted or putting himself in any type of risk, not many people were aware of the Camp.

Victor showed him where it was, a group of men were brought before him, he was to choose twenty men from the group of fifty or so,.. being no one spoke English, and they were all eager for work, Marcus found himself having to ease backward to keep the mob from swallowing him up.

He wasn't making much progress till he heard someone say..."I speak English".

A young girl had approached, she was weather beaten' her clothes soiled, her English was broken, but understandable.

Marcus pointed at a man' and asked the girl to see if he had any field work experience, the girl asked...Si, senor, Si, said the man.

With the girls help' he got the twenty workers he needed, she explained to them where they were to report to the following morning.

Marcus had already climbed back into the truck with Victor, when the voice was heard again' right outside the window.

I have worked the fields also, and I can talk to the workers for you, said the girl.

She couldn't have been no more than seventeen or eighteen years old, but seemed serious about the request, he believed she would be more than willing to do the work, and he was certain that she needed the money.

If its ok with your Parents, you can report to work in the morning with the others.

His Arian Nation background required him to hate all other races and religions, but his newfound wealth made him feel automatically superior, he didn't have to hate these people...he would just use them.

Victor was surprised at how well the Americans fields had progressed over the next couple of months.

The young girl always fell far behind, but her hands showed she was really working hard, she lived in Victor's storehouse, whereas the rest of the workers pitched tents along the perimeter of Marcus's property.

The girl was said to have no family, no one knew who she was, none of the other workers knew her, she never made phone calls, and no one ever came to see her.

She had been hoarding all of her money for the last couple of months, and went nowhere, but today she went to town with the others.

Marcus didn't recognize her on her return, she was seventeen years old, and today she wore a new dress, it was a little short, and a little snug...she was clean, her dark' full head of hair was done very cleverly, the earrings gave her a new poise.

Today Marcus saw her for the first time,.. today, he saw how sturdy her legs were,... how round her buttocks were, even her breasts had been hidden under those rags she'd been wearing, the girl he saw before him now was sexually appealing.

She showed up for work every morning on time, just like her older field workers.

Only now, Marcus had his eye on her, he hadn't been able to get her out of his mind.

About three hours into the workday, she began to fall behind as usual,.. then six hours into the day, she'd fallen so far behind, she was in a section all alone.

There was no one around when he approached her,.. she saw him heading in her direction' over the shoulder high crop, she stopped and waited for him, he probably had something he wanted translated to the other workers.

But when he approached her, he forced her to the ground,.. she didn't know what to do,.. she didn't put up too much of a fight...she didn't scream for help.

She was seventeen years old, all alone, and had traveled way too far out of her way, she was getting paid every week for working this field and translating for this American.

She couldn't forget, a couple months ago she went two whole days with nothing to eat,.. even the thought of starving was scary,...so she did nothing, she let him have his way with her.

Knowing that the girl was only seventeen years old was the taboo that sparked this encounter, then finding out that she was a virgin, was the next.

This exited him so much, that after he'd left Mica in the field, he hadn't even made it to the house before once again, he had a throbbing hard on.

These people are nothing more than servants, he felt he was superior to them, and what he'd just done' made him feel more powerful than ever, he was the Master of his own little plantation, no one had any say about anything he did.

The young girl would be one of his most prized possessions!

The girl hung the bag that she was working into back over her head, it came to rest on her shoulder, she gathered herself and continued pruning, trying to make up for lost time,...even though her mind was scattered in all directions, she pushed on, she wanted to get as much done today as she possibly could.

All of her belongings had been stolen months ago, she had been saving her money for the last couple of months, the only thing she bought was a dress, and some good walking shoes.

She had been given a name to track; what seemed like an eternity ago,...the name disappeared somewhere in the Embassy district of Brazil, she figured the name had been changed, she knew it could be done there illegally, and without record, there were no traces of it.

She followed three other leads of wealthy Americans that had recently become residents,...they had all turned out to be blank trips, and had taken her farther than she'd ever planned on.

Now this one was also a blank.

This American isn't Wealthy, he lives in a small house that he rents from Victor Vada.

She would have to give up the search for now, she would work long enough to get her I.D. and Passport, along with bus fare back to Belize, her dream of getting to the United States was looking dim.

After she went to bed that night, she reflected back on what had happened in the field...and how she had lost her Virginity,. A tear escaped and ran down her cheek...she could have stopped him, she could have fought him off,.. she could have screamed; and alerted the other workers,...she could have at least said "No".

Her Virginity hadn't been taken from her,...she gave it up without a fight, in America, that would be serious offense, the rape of an under aged child' would make you a marked man for life,...but out here, in a land that lacks a law that's responsive to all, she wouldn't be recognized

as a victim,...she would be recognized as a problem.

She was able to find peace with the loss of her Virginity, she had to, because she realized that it was going to happen again,... and again.

She also knew that she was going to let it happen,... right now, he was her only way out.

The call came early that morning,.. today's the day,...you ready?

Rudy recognized Emmitt Smith's voice, I'm ready, he replied.

Meet me at the Subway shop across from the Courthouse at ten o'clock, said Emmitt.

I'll be there,.. Rudy walked down the hall; wiping the sleep from his eye's, he stopped in front of Felicia's door, and just for the hell of it, put his ear to it,...he knocked lightly,...then a little harder, he heard a rustling sound on the other side, then there were footsteps heading toward the door,... he straightened up,...she opened the door groggily, and leaned against the door jamb, she said nothing.

Come have breakfast with me, said Rudy.

You ain't got no money... and there's nothing "here" to eat.

There's still a couple of eggs left, said Rudy

Felicia sensed something, but couldn't put her finger on it.

Well, I guess I'll have to make you one of my famous' scrambled egg sandwiches, she said, while pushing him in the direction of the kitchen,...did you call the labor hall to see if there's any work today, she asked?

No, I've got to be in Court today, Emmitt called this morning.

You ok, she asked? No, not really.

Felicia was concerned about his answer, this must be what she'd sensed ealier, she knew she'd better make light of the situation.

She started sniffing the air around Rudy,... is that pussy I smell?

Rudy followed suit, and took a long, pleasant sniff in felicia's direction, yeah man, that's what it is,... you going down there with me today.

No, I can't miss any more days from work, come by the restaurant when you get outta there, I'm going to be stuck there for most of the night.

Rudy put his arms around her, pulling her close,.. wish me luck, he said.

She tapped his chest with her open palm, slowly pushing him back.

Good luck, she said.

He met Emmitt at the Subway shop as planned, a man that had been hovering around them' approached their table.

Are you the guy that's challenging the Petrini Clan, he asked.

Are you a reporter, asked Emmitt.

I'd just like to get a comment is all, said the man. There are none, Emmitt replied.

The stern look that Emmitt gave the man made him leave rather hastily...the next time they saw the man, he was in a crowd outside the Courthouse, the man pointed in their direction as they walked toward the crowd.

The crowd turned and started toward them,... the Media was making a big deal about this case,

Microphones were being pointed at them, as the crowd anxiously shot all types of questions in their direction,...Rudy walked closely behind Emmitt, who answered questions while still in full stride.

This trial was by far, the biggest thing that Rudy had ever attempted, he could barely keep his mind focused, he felt as if he was all alone in a dangerous place, he had to fight himself to keep from visibly shaking,...his mom and Dad came into his thoughts, as they usually did when he found himself in tough situations, they would always have just the advice and backing he needed, they knew him better than he knew himself.

He visited their graves often, it seemed to bring him some type of comfort, he could talk to them for hours at a time.

But the fact that they had gotten caught up in an attack that was designed for him,...ate away at his soul,...so did the hatred he had for the man sitting across from him in the Courtroom,... "Orlan Petrini", his thoughts rested on one fact,.. that he would take Petrini's life, like Petrini took his Parents.

The Bailiff walked to the front of the room, silence came across the crowd...All Rise, the Honorable Judge Bennett presiding.

The Judge walked in,... be seated, he said.

We're going to make this short and sweet...we're at the sentencing phase of this case.

The Plaintiff, Mr. Rudolph Clayton,.. Sir, you have won both the Civil, and the Criminal cases that were brought before this Court' through a jury of your peers,... Retribution has been approved, so have the allegations surrounding your lawsuit,...so we'll start there.

Will the Defendant please rise.

Petrini and the four lawyers at their table came to their feet.

Mr. Petrini,... you have been found guilty on six counts of felony Discrimination,...this usually carries the amount that the plaintiff is suing for,.. but this column has been left "Open", well, it'll be my pleasure to fill it in now,.. "there", said the Judge; as he finished filling in the blank areas of the lawsuit.

You will pay two-point five Million dollars per count,.. you have violated every Civil right granted this man by the United States of America... And this Country wants you to pay dearly for that,... that concludes the Civil matters...we're moving on to the restitution, and criminal sentencing.

For your part in the conspiracy to Murder the Plaintiff, the Trespassing, Evidence tampering, the destruction of personal and Sentimental property, the Murder of Mr. and Mrs. Clayton, I can go on, but its clear to this Court, that you have a Callous disrespect for the Law.

You will pay Mr. Clayton an additional Fifteen Million Dollars, and in accordance with the Laws and Statutes of Florida, and these United States.

I sentence you to Twenty Years in a correctional Facility, you will be eligible for parole in twelve years.

I'm being lenient with your sentencing, due to the indirect nature of your crimes,.. personally, I hope you weather this storm, and one day rejoin society; with a healthy respect for its laws...your sentence will start Immediately.

Emmitt Smith sighed as he close his briefcase, the verdict was a relief, and it showed,...he stood, looking as proud as any man ever had, Rudy stood with him, Emmitt gave Rudy a big hug; and the Courtroom came alive, there was clapping, whistles, and shouts from the onlookers.

As they came through the gate, everyone ran in their direction, those that waited outside had Microphones and Camera's, as they tunneled their way out, Emmitt told Rudy that he should give the Media some sort of comment, but at that moment Rudy wasn't able to focus, his mind was reeling, he could barely talk.

Can you do it for me,... as my representative? Sure I can,... it'll be my pleasure.

Emmitt Smith dashed out in front of the Camera's and grand-standed like a Politician, he would be a well sought after lawyer after this day.

They met up later that evening at Woody's Restaurant on twenty ninth street.

They were supposed to meet at Emmitt's office, but there were people all over the place with

Camera's, awaiting their arrival, they'd have to meet somewhere else.

Woody's was one of the last quality Soul Food Restaurants left in the Mid-Tampa area, it looked like a hole in the wall type of joint, but once inside; it was top quality, the atmosphere was very homie, with the Sassy waitresses and all.

I pulled out your files, and the first thing we should do is get your debts taken care of as soon as possible and get your credit beacon in its proper place.

Emmitt was all Lawyer, Rudy was numb,...it didn't seem real, how could he have won?,...those were the same people that have hated his guts, all lawyers, judges, prosecutors, police, everyone in their network of people; have always hated him, and in that place, they have complete power, countless innocent Black men have spent their lives in prison, after being Railroaded through their Court system.

On Halloween, people dress up in their scariest costumes, the Wolfman... Count Dracula...Frankenstein,.. Black people don't pay them much attention, the Costumes that really scare Black people are those dressed up like lawyers,.. judges,.. police officers... Now that's scary!

I see your biggest debt is this Child support, the others are minimal, not posing any threats.

Lets go get the Child support taken care of first, said Emmitt.

At the Department of Children and Families, Emmitt did all the talking,... the first installment of your settlement will be available in two weeks.

This is one of the departments that has to be clear, the

I.R.S. will redirect your funds through here if you owe Child Support.

They will take control of your funds, your money will be unavailable to you; until they've taken way more than their supposed to.

Miss, he said, getting the attention of an irritated looking female employee,... I need to find out how much Mr. Rudolph Clayton owes this Department in Child Support.

The woman looked up the information quickly... Mr. Clayton is Four Thousand Dollars behind in his Child Support payments.

Can you run all three of his Children to the age of twenty-one' and tell me what the total comes to, asked Emmitt.

With what he owes now, through the age of twenty-one, for all three...the total comes to Forty-Eight Thousand Dollars, said the clerk, with an, as a matter of fact; smirk on her face.

He hasn't had an income for quite some time, so if it's alright with you, I'd like to pay the entire tab, and have his case closed.

After going through two more supervisors; and a lot of red tape, Emmitt was finally able to cut a check, and Rudy's name was removed from the Giant Child Support Machine, with paperwork stating that he owes nothing further.

We had to do that swiftly, said Emmitt, because right about now, your hearing is being Broadcasted Nationwide.

A phone rang on Tampa's North side,... Rudy's X-wife picked up the phone.

Girl turn on the television,.. hurry,.. turn it on now.

Her Sister's voice sounded frantic,... she ran over to the set' turning it on as fast as possible... still on the phone,.. she saw Rudy leaving the Courtroom looking spellbound, and the man with him, his lawyer' had "Victory" written all over his face.

She had no Idea what this was about, she knew he'd lost his Parents, but she had no intention of attending the Funeral... she had forbidden the children to attend also, it's as if she was hosting the "hate Rudy" show.

She taught the Kids to hat Rudy, she made it clear that she didn't want him coming around them...while constantly reminding them that their father never cared about them, they were all in their early teens now, they developed behavioral problems and had been forced out of regular public Schools, they were attending Alternative Schools, doing the bare minimum to remain students, two days a week.

Her new man's name is "Killer", she didn't like him, but she let him stay, the sex was great, she called the Police on him every month.

When Rudy's Child Support check arrived, Killer had stolen the check and gotten away with it on several occasions.

Rudy had disappeared in the crowd now,.. the Cameras and Microphones were now in the face of his lawyer.

Mr. Smith, said one reporter,... do you feel that the Thirty Million Dollar Settlement was sufficient for the atrocious crimes Committed by the Defendant.

My Client, Rudy Clayton; was granted a Thirty Million Dollar Settlement,... that shows me that this Court system' made a Valient effort in the direction of justice, he didn't get what he deserved, but he did get his point across, today' his case was heard!

His X-wife's eyes were glued to the screen, as her jaw dropped,... did you hear that, came the voice from the other end of the phone, that nigga just made Thirty Million Dollars,... and Thirty per-cent of that is yours,... that's Ten Million Dollars,

"TEN MILLION"

He ain't gonna give me no Ten Million dollars, I've been trying to ruin his ass in every way I can for years, he hate's me' and I hate him.

He don't have to give it to you, "Dummy", said the sister, you got his ass on Child Support, those

Child Support people will "Take" that money from his ass,...I'll be over there first thing in the morning; so we can go get our Money.

They were at the Child Support Office before the place opened the next morning.

They nearly stumbled over each other as the doors opened for business.

I am the Mother of Mr. Rudolph Clayton's children, his financial status has changed recently' and I'd like to have my payments adjusted to coincide with his new income.

I'll pull up his file, said the social worker.

She went through all of the computer files, and found nothing.

I'm sorry but the person you're looking for is no longer in our files.

He has to be, said the sister, he's been in the system for years, if you can't find him, we need to see your supervisor...this is ridiculous.

Two supervisors later!

Ma'am, I see Mr. Claton's case has been closed, he's been unemployed for quite some time, and a private sponsor has paid his support for him, he owes nothing additional to you, or this institution, your payments will continue without interruption until your children's twenty first birthday.

What,... said the sister, can't you see what he's done, he's trying to cheat the system, he just got a lot of money, and he's trying to keep us from getting our fair share.

The sister as furious,... C'mon sis, we're gonna get us a lawyer' and take his ass to Court,.. he's not getting away with this.

The X-wife called Rudy everything but a child of God, and swore to get her brothers to kick his ass.

It was after dark when Rudy got home,... Cole and Myra were upstairs with Felicia.

"Heyyy", you finally made it, we've been waiting for you, said Cole,... how'd it go.

Rudy held his head down, as if preparing to share some bad news,... when he was sure he had everyone's attention, he broke out dancing, he did the running man, then the slide, he even Crip walked,...we won,... we won,... we won, he made all get up and dance with him,... he ran to the television set and turned it on,... and there he was,... breaking news teams volleyed the story back and forth so much, it had taken on new twists and turns, Rudy thought he was listening to some other case.

Cole,... Felicia,... and Myra's, mouth fell open when they heard the news castor say, Rudy Clayton's Thirty Million Dollar settlement,..... they all looked at Rudy, silent and stunned.

We've got to start making some plans, said Rudy,... you guy's can turn in your resignations at your jobs,...we've gotten ourselves a chance to do something on our own.

Felicia's phone must have been on speed dial,... Hi, Marian, this is Felicia, I won't be coming in tomorrow,... no, I'm not sick or anything, I'm quitting, bye now.

Everybody laughed.

The next few weeks were spent looking for investment opportunities... Rudy and Cole decided not to make any risky investments,... neither of them had ever had any real Capital, so they felt vulnerable trying to invest large sums of money, with the clever and ever so slimy business experts they'd met thus far,... those fuckers are money experts, they'll steal your money, then make you pay penalties on the money they've stolen.

I don't think we should put the money in their hands, said Cole.

You're right, we're no match for them, they'll bleed us dry,... I'll tell you what, said Rudy,... lets invest in ourselves,... we can just do small things that we know how to do,... it may not make much money, but if we get enough small stuff going, it could be lucrative.

They all put their heads together; and it looked as if they would be able to enter the Real Estate Market' with enough natural skills to make a successful venture of it.

By the time the first installment arrived, a deal had already been put together for a one hundred fifty unit Apartment Complex; located right across from an Industrial Business Park,... they were all very pleased with their first purchase,... Myra was put in charge of the Complex, which was a steal, for Seven Million.

They splurged with the money a little, they all bought new vehicles.

Rudy and Cole got new pick-up trucks, the girls got new luxury Compacts.

They made plans to look for more of the smaller types of investments such as this.

Rudy was sitting at a traffic light' when he heard a horn blow, h checked out the car next to him,... it was Pretty Tony, he was driving the S.U.V. right next to him at the light.

Hey, what's-up Rudy, you got a minute? Yeah, said Rudy.

Follow me, he said,... when the traffic started moving Tony moved over into Rudy's lane' in front of him,.. Rudy followed.

Pretty Tony owned a car lot, undoubtedly that's where they were headed.

Tony pulled into the lot, Rudy came in behind him, they exited their vehicles and greeted each other properly.

Tony was known for taking advantage of almost any opportunity that passed his way,... Rudy was well aware of this, he could feel that Tony had something up, he would usually say, whas-up Rudy, and keep it moving, this was the first time he'd ever invited me to his place of business.

And sure as shit, Tony got right to business!

I heard you came into some money, said Tony, they say you've bought four cars in the last couple of weeks,... you could have at least bought one of those cars from me.

Yeah, I came into a little money,.. but I've only had it for a minute, on the other hand, you've been making real good money for a long time, and you've never even offered to give me a good deal on a ride, so lets put all that shit on hold,... what's up?

I wanted to talk a little business,... I've found a way to lower my prices on my high end cars,...I'll be able to move three times as many cars than I'm moving now, but I'm going to need a primary investor to get a State of the Art" shop up and running.

You know my brother's a master mechanic, but he needs a place to work from, and proper equipment to work with.

This is what's supposed to boost your car sales,... a mechanic shop?

Not exactly,... you see that Mercedes over there,... and the Beamer next to it.

Yeah,... "nice".

They've only been on the lot three days' and their both already sold, I can sell a Forty Thousand Dollar car for Twenty Thousand, and still hold a ninety percent profit margin.

Can't see how that's possible, said Rudy.

I'll tell you; cause I know you,.. and you know me,... we got an understanding that I know; won't be broken.

The cars were stolen, said Tony,... they were taken from somewhere down in the South Florida area,... my brother stripped them down,... took everything off of them.

And when I say everything,... I mean everything, he took out the engine, the seats, took the doors off, the windows out, removed the tires, even the side panels were removed, he stripped them down to nothing but studded frames, then he'd take the frames and leave them on a dead end,... or on the side of the road, ya know, somewhere it could be found,... when they find it, the'll trace it back to the owner by the V.I.N. number, the number will match up to the stolen car, the owners will then get in touch with their insurance carrier, after they've investigated, the carrier will label the car a "Total Loss"

And the guy whose car was stolen, gets a new car, compliments of the carrier,..... Meanwhile, the frame will go to the auction,... my brother will follow the frame' and bid on it, after he purchases the frame' it will be registered in his name, he then puts the car back together,... and there they are,... sitting on my lot, clean as a whistle, and selling like hot cakes,...you'll be getting a steady percentage,...you in" ?

That's quite a racket, said Rudy, but the money I've come into isn't mine alone... I'll have to run this by the others... I'll get back at you as soon as possible.

Rudy left in a hurry,... Pretty Tony, and those like him, are who Rudy knew he had to stay away from,... they were ruthless businessmen, almost everything they did' was a set-up.

Rudy never even brought up the meeting with Tony to the others.

The gang stayed on course, and in the following couple of years, their business senses were being fine tuned,... they had made quite a few investments and purchases that were paying off fluidly.

As their wealth grew' so was Rudy's yearning for female companionship,... Cole and Myra were doing great, they were able to look at the good life through each other's eye's.

Rudy and Felicia went almost everywhere together, but they never ventured into what they called the forbidden zone.

They found themselves having to move out of the house in Temple Terrace, due to very frequent, almost back-to- back visits from friends and relatives' that would show up for some type of financial assistance,... at first, they would stop by to say Hi, and visit for awhile.

But as of late, they would show up crying about something that had happened' or hopping on one foot, due to an accident of some sort, they would even show up with lots of paperwork containing various investment opportunities, every visit would eventually turn into a money issue.

So, they quietly moved out to the Riverview area, not too far from Dally's and his wife's place.

It was good to see Cain still hanging out with Dally,... their friendship had grown, Dally could almost talk to Cain now,... it reminded Rudy of his relationship with Ty.

Cain was fond of Rudy, Cole and Felicia,.. he kind of shied away from Myra.

Sometimes they would all go for a ride, and following high above the clouds was their feathered friend, sometimes he could anticipate where they were headed' and he'd be there waiting when they got there.

Their lives were all changing, they were more comfortable, the new place was really nice, a lot larger than the old place,... it sat right on the River.

Not too long ago, Rudy remembered the night that Cole threw up over the Channelside Railing,... that night they were all gazing jealously across the Channel at the rich properties on the other side,... Harbour Island, the homes and Penthouses were Awesome,... they all had docks that ran out over the water, their expensive boats were hoisted out of the water and hung in mid-air.

Now here he was,... with a house on the River,... he even had a dock.

Sometimes, the grass really is greener on the other side of the fence.

Rudy started feeling like,.. Since his money situation was straight now, he felt entitled to have the romance that goes hand in hand with those who have the funds to sponsor it,... he put together a couple of romantic settings for Felicia,... but it didn't take.

The sexual frustration kept nagging at him, he even thought about just taking off, checking into a plush hotel on one of the Tropical Islands somewhere,... a place with never ending beaches, and far too many beautiful, single women,... he day dreamed about living the wild life for awhile, he would have too many women, way too much wine, and all the song he could stand.

He was buying a lot of properties, and was getting them up and running, in these times, anyone with money was able to get unheard of deals in any venue.

On one particular occasion; Rudy was out bided on a home he wanted to purchase, his broker in turn offered him a better deal on another home he was selling, Rudy went to inspect the home, the place was a Gem, he loved it,... it seemed strangely familiar,... it finally hit him, when he was just a kid' his Mom had brought him to this house on several occasions,... this was her Dream House, he was standing in her dream house.

He couldn't wait to show it to her, he drove all the way back to the old house,.. he stopped short when his eye's locked onto that empty lot, his mind reeled,.. he just sat there as the reality set in,... Mom's not here anymore.

Rudy felt as if he had slipped, and was hanging on to the very edge of a cliff, trying with everything he had to keep from falling, he didn't feel sane, or safe, when he got out of the truck, he didn't even feel like he was standing on solid ground.

A "For Sale" sign was on the property where they used to live,... I'm losing it, he thought to himself.

He figured it may have something to do with the change in his financial status that was causing him to slip like this, this lifestyle was causing him to miss things, this made him nervous.

Felicia said that this happened because he hadn't taken the proper time out period to Mourn the people he had lost.

It wasn't long after that, when Rudy parked the new truck,... and unless he was working, he rode his bike, it kept him connected to his past, he was always a little sharper at "Ground Level".

Jeff was Rudy's banker, a young, stylish, yuppie type, he has that gift of gab, and can make anyone feel comfortable in his presence, he was very ambitious and had a hand in everything, one of his more lucrative endeavors was monitoring all cash accounts,... he was being paid on the side by certain Companies, and individuals, to inform them of accounts with substantial holdings, or rapid growth.

Rudy's gang had done a lot of spending early on,... but in four short years, the cash was rolling back in,... they now owned one hundred twenty pieces of Real Estate,.. and twelve businesses, he had over a hundred employee's,... Ninety of them were Felon's, he hired the Black men that had been unjustly accused, and are now listed as Felon's, and are shunned by Corporate America.

When the account reached the original Thirty Million again, Jeff, the Banker made his usual contact calls.

In Tallahassee Florida,... Sophia was sitting at her computer when the incoming message signal came on,..it read, "This one's for you".

She opened it,... Single, Black, Male,... wins Discrimination Lawsuit,... Thirty Million in holdings,... then a complete profile pops up,... everything accept a picture.

Hey, Michelle, shouted Sophia,... check this out.

Michelle came in, still working on her hair, both ladies were going out tonight.

She looked over Sophia's shoulder at the screen,... looks like this guy has hit the lottery.

That's what I'm talking about, he's never had money before, he's been holding on to this money for a couple of years, and he's still listed as single,... he's a sure Mark if I've ever seen one, feel like taking a trip to Tampa?

Wouldn't miss it for the world.

There's no way he'll be able to resist us, said Sophia,... there's no point in looking this good and not getting paid for it.

Sophia could catch any guy's eye, even if she was standing in a room full of Models, she was gorgeous,. Michèle was two inches taller, and just as beautiful.

I can't find any close relatives to this guy either, said Sophia, this may be easier than I thought, no family in the way.

Keep searching, said Michelle, see if you can come up with a picture.

With this kind of money, I don't give a shit what he looks like.

C'mon girl, it's about time you started getting dressed, we can't miss this guy Wilson tonight.

Wilson was the overseer of one of the largest construction firms in Orlando, they had run into a couple of snags on this project they were heading up, Wilson was to pick up Two Hundred Thousand Dollars from the main office that had been approved' in order to push a few permits through' that were holding up progress.

Sophia and Michelle found out through a big mouthed Executive that worked at the head office, they got him drunk and clipped him for five hundred dollars, he even told them what time the man was to pick the money up.

Now, Wilson was Marked.

He walked into the main ballroom of the Embassy Suites Hotel about nine thirty that evening,.. and just by sheer coincidence, sat at the bar between two very stunning young ladies,... a few drinks later, the three were getting along like old friends, Michelle was fascinating to him, he told her so, the girls were showing him such a good time, he didn't want the night to end.

So, he invited the girls up to his Suite' so that they could enjoy each other's company even more, in a private atmosphere... he was aware of the dynamics that usually comes with these types of encounters, so he was being extra cautious about what he was doing,.. his infatuation with Michelle grew stronger by the minute.

He asked Michelle if it would be possible for her to come to Orlando with him, he would show her the sites in that Magical City,.. his treat.

Michelle knew that wasn't the plan, but she kind of liked the guy, both girls had sensed he was being very cautious, even though he was a little tipsy, they found no opportunity to remove the briefcase that lay under the front of the bed in the opposite room,... he would short stop any attempt to enter that room,... Sophia had to say good night as Michelle agreed to go to Orlando with Wilson,.. Sophia wasn't far behind.

He felt Michelle's interest in him was genuine, there were gold diggers everywhere, but if you pay attention,.. they all have a point where they must start digging, this girl wouldn't know where to start, she doesn't know me from Adam, she hasn't shown any interest in the briefcase, because she doesn't know what's in it, who in this day and age, walks around with a briefcase full of money.

No, this girl is just out having a good time, she may even be looking for a husband, I'll just spoil her for awhile, then I'll have to get rid of her before my wife begins to suspect something's going on.

The one thing Sophia didn't like about Michelle, she was susceptible to falling in love.

When they got to Orlando, Wilson put her up in a four star hotel, the Suite was paid up for the month,... their encounter had gotten sexual the night before, and she had been open with him to the point that if he didn't throw

the briefcase at her, she had abandoned her plans to take it from him,... but now she was getting a glimpse of who he was, she knew he was well off enough to have a home, but he put her in a hotel, why?... because he has a wife at home, and with that sex drive of his, he has kids there also.

This knowledge got her back on track,..Wilson took her out to explore the City, they spent all day frolicking in the Magic Kingdom,... then they went Clubbing, they danced into the wee hour of the night, picked up a late supper, and came back to the Hotel and crashed, Wilson climbed into bed with her, snuggling up close.

Not tonight baby, said Michelle, I'm plum worn out.

Well, you just lay back and relax, he whispered, as he began kissing her in that special place,... What a night, she thought to herself' as her toes were curling.

They woke up late the next day, and had brunch at a classy little restaurant on International Drive.

You know that little thing you did for me last night,... that was really nice.

I knew you were tired, I just wanted to make sure you were able to relax.

Well, I really appreciated it, and I'm good now, so today,... you're all mine, I'm going to the ladies room, and I'll be right back.

She had been with Wilson since Friday evening, it was Sunday now, whatever he picked up that money for was probably going down on Monday, and if he is Married, his wife will be expecting him tonight,... Michelle was running out of time, she called Sophia, who was in a Hotel right down the street.

Sophia, its me,... I'm going to put the briefcase behind the bedroom door, be there in an hour.

Wilson was anxious when they got back to the hotel room.

Hold on a minute, she said, I want to surprise you, I'm going to make myself a little more presentable.

She went into the bedroom and shut the door, she'd paid attention to where he put the briefcase, in the top of the closet' behind his travel bag,... she grabbed the case and sat it behind the door, when she got herself ready, she swung the door wide open, and stood in the doorway in a seductive pose,... her sheer;

see through top fit her like a stocking, the G-string made itself known.

Wilson could hardly believe his eye's,... she looked like something you'd find in a Master Sculptors Dream.

She took Wilson to bed, treated him like a king, she knows how to completely and totally satisfy a man.

Sophia opened the unlocked door' and came in on tip- toe,... the bedroom door was still wide open, she entered the room; reached behind the door and got the briefcase, she turned to leave... and froze, she couldn't take her eye's off of her friend, her sexual skills were off the charts,... she stood there and watched this man who was dangling somewhere between heaven and earth, she could tell that his whole world was somewhere inside a blinding white light, Sophia's pussy twitched and began to moisten, she had to tear herself away.

Michelle and Wilson fell asleep in each other's arms.

The White Jag pulled out of the parking lot and started down International Drive, Michelle opened the briefcase, it was full of cash.

Nice work said Sophia.

That's a lot of money, said Michelle, trying to come to terms with what they'd done.

Sophia stepped on the gas, drawing Michelle's attention back to the road.

What's going on, asked Michelle?

Sophia said nothing until she had cut off a Greyhound Bus that was about to pull out of the station.

Sophia grabbed a bundle of cash from the briefcase and shoved it in her purse.

I'm going to catch this bus, said Sophia,... you take this money home and put it in the bank,... that sign said that Tampa is only ninety miles from here, I'm going to Tampa to catch our boy, I'll call you when I make contact.

When Wilson woke up, Michelle wasn't in bed,... he called her name but there was no answer, she wasn't in the kitchen or living area either, he got a drink from the fridge, as he passed back by the open bedroom door, he happened to glance toward the spot where Michelle kept her overnight bag,... it was gone.

He ran to the closet and searched up top, he threw everything out of the closet, his heart ached as he sank to the floor,... he jumped up in a fit of rage, he tore the room to pieces, then jumped in his car to try to find her.

Sophia had Rudy's last known address, which was the Temple Terrace House... .she had the cabbie drop her off at the house, there were small children playing on the front porch area... their clothes were not expensive,... neither were the two cars in the driveway,.. this can't be the right place, thought Sophia.

The woman that answered the door introduced herself as Annette.

These people seem pretty docile,...when she asked about Rudy Clayton, Annette gave her his new address.

These people act as if they are personal friends of this Rudy, thought Sophia,... and if these were the type of people that he calls friends,... I'd better lose some of this glamour, and tone it down a bit.

When she got to New River Drive in Riverview, she had the cabbie drop her off there, it was obvious that anyone who ventured up New River Drive,... didn't do so by accident, she would have to have a reason for heading up this street.

There were only four houses that were visible through the trees along the river, the properties were so large, the neighbors probably didn't even know each other.

Still there were no signs of anyone with "New Money", no parties, no cookouts, no over priced, or show off type vehicles, there was no movement on this street.

I'm going to have to play, the Damsel in distress,... she just stood out on the main road' and waited.

It wasn't long before she spotted someone leaving from behind the third house on a bike,... and he was headed her way, she pretended to be studying a piece of paper with directions on it.

She put together a confused look, that should have worked, but the man didn't seem to have any intention of stopping, even though her jeans were hugging her hips perfectly,... and although she had dressed down, she had still been turning heads all day.

"Hey, Sir," she yelled, as he went past her. This is New River Drive right, she asked? Yes, it is," said Rudy.

I was looking for a guy named Rudy Clayton, does he live on this street, she asked, adjusting her vocabulary accordingly.

Yes, he does, Rudy replied, Rudy replied, trying to get an angle on this person.

I really need to talk to him; do you know if he's at home? No, he's not... not at the moment.

Any idea when he'll be back?

Well, can you do me a big favor and tell him that I came by; and I really need to talk to him, I'll be doing dinner at a Restaurant called Woody's, it's in Tampa, I'll be there at five O'clock tomorrow evening, let him know that I'd like to meet up, my treat.

Who are you, asked Rudy?

Tell him I'm a friend of Annette's. I can do that.

Thanks a lot, said Sophia, she gave him a wholehearted smile, then turned and left.

Rudy hadn't moved,... so she figured, from experience,... he's checking me out.

She was right,... Rudy was captivated by her beauty, he just stood there and watched her, she had that youthful glow, she was in the prime of her life, in full bloom, a woman like that is simply irresistible.

She said she was a friend of Annette's,... that's the lady that's renting the house that they'd moved out of in Temple Terrace, she probably wants to talk about something related to her housing situation.

Sophia was glad that she had remembered the lady's name that had given her the address and directions to Rudy Claytons new location, at least that'll give him a little air of familiarity.

Rudy rode his bike all the way to Dally's place,... Dally had been working on a project, that Rudy was sponsoring,... Dally's not dumb by a long shot, but the project that he was working on was, for the most part,... way over his head.

He found it necessary to go scouting at the University of South Florida; for a couple of overachievers that could help.

He found a couple of guys that were anxious to put their talents to work on the project, their endeavor had been progressing smoothly ever since.

They were getting in on the ground floor of the battery powered car, since he knew the big Auto Industry would soon Monopolize this business, he was going to concentrate on just changing gas engines; to battery powered.

After the fourth draft of the modified battery engine, he now had one that would run at peak for 26 hours, and it peaked out at 80 miles per hour,

The plan at this point was to keep tweaking the engine until it peaked at 90 miles per hour.

Although the prototype was already inside the perimeter of all the other competitors, raising the bar on their own work' kept them motivated.

Rudy could hardly believe they had accomplished this dream, he had thought of this as a long shot,... and now, it was a reality, Rudy couldn't remember ever being so proud to be a part of anything before.

Dally pulled out beer's from somewhere and passed them around.

Here's to our Environmentally safe transportation alternative, said Dally,... the website will go up in just under a month.

The beer went down easy,... and even with this monumental milestone swimming throughout his being, Rudy's mind kept wandering back to the lady on the corner,... he had to tell Dally about her.

She was that beautiful huh, asked Dally. Rudy just nodded his head, yeah.

And sporting the body of a Goddess,..that's what I'm hearing right.

Yeah,... I wouldn't mind seeing her again, said Rudy, I should show up at Woody's tomorrow.

Dally listened to him,... he recognized the reckless abandon,.. and being as fond of Felicia as he was, he felt compelled to say something; in fear of the outcome of this turn of events,... but he also knew that they hadn't been referring to themselves as a couple,... so he remained quiet while Rudy went on about this new girl.

His description of her,... where they met,... even her invitation, brought only one thing to Dally's mind,... "trouble".

This new girl even showed up in Rudy's dream that night, the dream was intense, and seemed so real,... he was with her all night, the excitement of his dream went all the way to it's "Climax". He woke up shuddering, at first he couldn't believe she wasn't there,... as reality set in, he couldn't believe what had happened, he rushed to the shower.

Man, it's been too long.

He was sitting on the top step of an abandoned Church that was across the street from Woody's,... he saw her when she got off the City Bus, she walked past him on the opposite side of the street,..and into the Restaurant.

He stepped into the place just as she was ordering, she glanced over and saw him standing there.

She continued to order as she motioned him over, and as soon as her order was taken, she turned to him.

Well, did you deliver my message?

The waitress that had taken her order, now turned to him,.. a big smile came across her face.

Hi, what's up Rudy, you gonna eat? Yeah, said Rudy.

The usual, she asked. Yeah, he replied.

She scribbled the order on her pad as she headed toward the kitchen.

When he looked back at the young lady, her mouth was hung open, and her expression was blank.

You... you're Rudy Claton? Yeah, said Rudy.

How could you do that to me? she said angrily, "Why would you pretend to be someone else?

You just assumed I was someone else, I just answered your questions the best I could, while I was freaking out, see I had just approached a person that seemed to be looking for directions, then finding out that person was looking for me,... for reasons unknown to me, so excuse me for being a little cautious.

Rudy, she said, while offering him her hand, my name is Sophia, I mean you no harm,... I lost my job recently and Annette told me that you've been pretty busy lately, and you may need some help.

What do you do, asked Rudy.

I'm not in a position to be choosey right now, if there's anything I can do to help you out,...I'll do it.

By the time the food arrived, Sophia had begun leading the conversation to a more expanded platform,... more personal, trying to get a peek inside the man,.. she deducted that Rudy wasn't a womanizer, he had a hard time expressing his inner feelings with women,.. and the good part was ,... this man needed satisfying, she could see the hunger bound up inside him, a woman's touch is all that would be needed to set him free, this is going to be easier than I thought!

She tuned on the innocence,... and throughout dinner; she hung on his every word,.. she practically bowed down before him as they made plans to meet again.

Chico was on a role, down in Miami, the painting contracts were flooding in, and work would be steady for quite some time,... he'd kept the same work crew, minus Manny and J.D.,... when word of Manny's death reached him, it brought on mixed emotions' he was sad for him, then he was furious, because he knew his death had something to do with him running his mouth.

Not long after, came word of J.D.'s death, Chico knew, if given the right deal, J.D. would spill the beans, instead he was viciously murdered... this had Chico nervous,... J.D. was hard as nails, he should have been able to take care of himself in any situation, he knew better than to run his mouth,... that was a revenge murder.

Both men had been killed in jail.

If it wasn't for that damn dog, they'd still be here.

The police got a lucky break that time,... a dog tracked us down, it's still hard to believe.

Chico hated to admit the relief he felt, now that his two best friends were dead, there was no one left to implicate him in the murder of Chantell Harris,... no more clues to his involvement,... he was free.

There was one thing for sure, no matter what,... he was "Not" going to jail, that would be a sure death sentence.

Many and J.D. were murdered for a crime that he himself had committed. He often dreamed of that night, when he did,.. it would always end in over stimulation, the wet dreams he was experiencing every night' were followed by cold sweats,.. that night was by far; the most exiting night of his life.

He knew he would always cherish the memory,... deep down inside, he longed to do it again.

Marci, the girl he was with now, was into the gothic movement, Chico wasn't interested in the Cult.

He didn't even ask questions about it, he figured they were some type of devil worshippers,.. she always wore black, black eye liner and lipstick, she even dyed her hair black, all of her clothes were black, all the way down to her panties.

He was able to trust her with his deepest secrets, the worse the secrets were, the more they turned her on. He told her about the girl in Tampa, and what they had done to her, he tried to explain how exciting and exhilarating the actual execution had turned out to be.

Marci mentioned something about the girl being a gift from Satan,... about her being some sort of ritualistic sacrifice or something... she also said something about these types of sacrifices having a cleansing effect.

Marci drank heavily, and drugged in the same manner, when she was sober, she bitched and complained way too much,.. Often, Chico contemplated her being his next victim.

None the less, Chico kept his craft and livelihood surprisingly straight, due to the growth of his business, he could no longer fit all of his painting eqiupment in his tool shed, he rented a building in Liberty City,... and in his own painting genius,.. he put the name,.. J.D. and Manny's Painting Company, on the front of the building, in honor of his two friends who had given their lives, and never told who the real murderer was.

Marci wanted to get to the Club early, as always, they went out three or four times a week.

Chico always took his time getting dressed, making sure his appearance was perfect, this drew Marci into a frenzy, she hated it.

She needed Alcohol, and her body was already anticipating that need,.. what's taking you so long, she shouted,.. you're as bad as a female when it comes to getting dressed, get the lead out of your ass man, "Let's Go".

At last, everything was in place, the baggie jeans were hanging down just under his buttocks, he tucked his oversized T-shirt into the front of his pants, just enough to expose the large belt buckle, his white sneaks and crop socks were perfect,.. his gold chain hung to his stomach, he pulled his hair back and put the baseball cap on.

All that was missing, were earrings,... he picked up an earring that would go perfectly with his blue Tee, and he blue and white cap, they were his favorites, the Diamond Studs,... inside the Diamond' there was an awesome depiction of a blue water fountain, it appears to be gushing upward, if you look at it closely, kind of umbrella like.

Chico had lost the mate to this earring somewhere,.. it was probably in that house in Tampa.

They had to pack up and leave so quickly, it must have fallen somewhere between the house and that moving truck.

So once again, tonight he'll just wear the one earring,.. it looked good with his outfit.

Although all of Marci's earrings were black, she had also worn that earring on occasion,.. she would look at it sometimes in wonder... how did they do that.

That night, Chico was introduced to a man called Gus, after talking for awhile, Chico found out that Gus owned a car dealership,... Chico in turn told the man about his Painting Company.

I've been looking for a good Painter, said Gus, maybe we can work something out.

By the end of the night,... Chico had another Painting Contract.

The rental car Dealership wasn't super big, it was only three buildings,... the main building was the car check out building, the second building was the car return building,... the third was the clean-up and repair building,... non the less, it was a welcomed Contract.

The man's name was Augustus Kline.

It's a pleasure doing business with you' Mr. Kline, said Chico.

Mica was saving her money more desperately now.

Marcus White's heightened lust for her itched at him uncontrollably, he caught her in one place or another in the fields; on a daily basis, as time passed, he felt like she was his own personal property.

He had to replace several of his hired hands' over time, for interfering in his exploits with the girl, they would come running when they heard the screams, some even made threats, now anyone that responded to the screams were fired on the spot.

The workers would go about their business sadly, as the child's screams rang out in the distance.

She had been working the fields since she was seventeen years old, she was going on twenty now,.. she had long stopped crying out for help, steady work was hard to come by, and she didn't want to keep getting those who were concerned about her' fired from their jobs,... she didn't fight it anymore.

As time passed, the novelty of screwing an under-aged child began wearing off as she aged, every now and then he would lose his erection,... this day, out of frustration of losing his hard on, he slapped her hard.

So hard, Mica saw stars, she was disoriented as the pain of the attack burned into her soul, she was so frightened for her life, her whole body trembled violently.

The smell of fear coming from her, the pain and agony that showed on her face, brought his erection back like new.

The slapping led to outright beatings,... the other workers would hide and watch, but did nothing.

Marcus began having the girl watched, he feared she may try and get away from him, he knew she was terrified at this new turn of events, she was no longer allowed to go to town with the other workers.

One day, the man that had been chosen to watch her, saw her hiding a small device in a secret hiding place' the girl had found near her private bunking area.

This was brought to Marcus's attention,... he had the man take him to the secret place,.. inside he found what looked like a cell phone, it was fully charged, but there were no numbers or names, or even a listing, there was nothing to suggest there had been any calls made or received, he tried to make a call,.. There was nothing,.. the little device didn't seem important; but he kept it anyway, just to be on the safe side.

It was early the next morning when she discovered it missing, that was the first morning that she wasn't the first one to work.

When she didn't show up for work, Marcus was the first to notice, she's usually in the fields alone,.. when he steps out of the front door in the morning, he would look out across the fields; and he would always see her out there already getting started.

Marcus worked harder than any three of the workers that he employed.

He wanted to set the example for the others, he had completely transformed the place from the way it was when this venture first started, his crop and property looked better than Victor Vada's, a man who was a third generation farmer.

He was surprised at how empty this place seemed when he didn't see Mica.

He rushed over to the bunk house that he and Victor had put together for the workers,... when he walked through the door, he stopped short,.. the place was trashed,.. bunks were overturned, all of the workers personal items were scattered throughout the place, Mica's living space was separate from the other workers, when he opened her door, she was sitting on the side of the bed, her legs crossed at the ankles, her fingers intertwined lay in her lap, the tears were flowing freely.

She was truly afraid now,.. she was trapped,.. all hope had disappeared.

You sick or something, asked Marcus,.. why aren't you out there with the others.

They're stealing my stuff, said Mica.

What's missing, asked Marcus, acting as if he had no idea what she was talking about.

Whatever's missing shouldn't be too hard to find, what am I supposed to be looking for?

Mica didn't want to tell him what was missing, her point- to-point locator looked just like a cell phone, and cell phones were forbidden on this property.

My phone is missing, said Mica, finding it necessary to hide the device's true nature,... I've been using the calculator, and it was a game on it that I like to play,.. and it belongs to me,.. it's mine' and someone's taken it.

Although it sounded like she was telling the truth, Marcus had never seen her get this upset about anything, he knew she couldn't make, or receive a call on that thing, yet, his cautious nature kicked in,..he didn't want her to have it.

I'll see if I can locate your little toy, he said.

Marcus needed a little time to think,.. he told Mica to take the day off, and he had a man to stay with her.

He returned two hours later,.. I found out who stole your phone, said Marcus, it was one of the workers, he still had the damn thing in his pocket, I had to let him go,... stealing won't be tolerated around here. But you know the rules,... no cell phones,..I'm going to hang on to this.

It took everything that Mica had in her, to keep from flat out begging for the device, but she had to act as if it wasn't as important to her as it was.

Marcus thought about how he felt when he didn't see Mica in the fields earlier that morning, he knew he'd rather not feel that way again.

Mica, I'm taking you out of the fields, come with me.

She followed him to the little house, when she stepped inside, she automatically started looking around for Mrs. Mathews... she sensed no one was there, the place looked as if no one lived here,... Marcus was standing in the doorway of the smallest of the two bedrooms,.. He motioned for her to come in.

She was frozen in place, her whole body stiffened, she balled her fists tight and forced herself to face whatever was about to happen.

She walked inside the small room,.. there was no bed,.. no windows,.. only a sofa and a coffee table, the floor was carpeted, and there were a couple of pictures on the walls, the pictures showed no personal connection to anything.

Marcus closed the sliding door behind her, he went to the light switch and pulled it down,... the lights didn't go off,.. instead, the whole room went into motion.

Mica almost panicked when the room started downward, Marcus watched her closely.

The room came to a stop; and Marcus slid the door open, they stepped outside the dim little room, and into a well laid out; glistening Palace.

She stepped out of the elevator room, and stood there as if her eyes were playing tricks on her, she could hardly believe what she was seeing.

The little house that was topside' was just a smoke screen,.. this guy's got loads of money.

As Marcus led her through the Palace, the highly polished hardwood flooring ran off into an expensive skid resistant Marble, the pictures on the walls now, were nothing less than works of art, they were elegantly displayed and made her feel as she always had,... "poor", and out of place,.. no wonder he treats me like I'm nothing, she thought to herself.

She followed him to an open area of the Mansion that was Mrs. Mathews pride and joy, the open circular area displayed five large stone pillars, colorful drapery hung between them from the ceiling to the floor, material so sheer you could see right through it.

Her plush lounging chair sat on the upper platform, she could walk down the ten long crescent moon shaped steps from the platform, and into an

Olympic sized pool, complete with decks and greenery.

She was sitting in her lounger, a drink in one hand, and checking out a Magazine that seemed to have her full attention, the movie sized big screen television was more than forty feet away.

She looked up from the Magazine to see Marcus and Mica standing before her.

What's this, she asked calmly.

You're going to need some help around here,.. this is your new housekeeper.

He looked the shapely girl up and down, then looked back at Marcus.

Patricia Mathews was pushing forty years old now, she was in good shape for a woman her age, but she knew she was no match for this young, firm, child that stood before her.

Are you saying, she's going to be "Living" here.

Marcus knew this tone, it was trouble, he could see the wheels spinning in her head,... it was coming back to him, all the nights he was unable to have sexual relations with her, because he had already spent all his energy out in the fields with Mica,..he saw the suspicion in her eye's, she would never allow this girl whom she was now suspicious of, to live here.

But he was not about to take a chance on Mica getting away from him.

She can work as your housekeeper till the end of the day, when she's finished you can send her back to the bunkhouse at Victor's.

This explanation seemed to put her mind at ease. He left Mica there and returned to the fields.

That evening when Mica was finished with the housework, instead of escorting her out to the bunkhouse with the other workers.

He took her deep into the Mansion, he put her in a large remote bedroom that Patricia Mathews knew nothing about.

The room was nice, but to Mica; it was nothing more than a dungeon, she knew,.. if she wasn't trapped before, she sure as hell was now.

She did the housework by day, and was sodomized regularly by night, right under Patricia's nose, and she detected nothing.

Mica roamed the Mansion freely as she did the housework, it gave her time to think... all this time, and she had no idea that there was a mansion below that little crop house.

Who was this guy?

She remembered back to the day she turned seventeen, her friend Carlos was there, he was eighteen and was considered an exceptional student, he went to a school for the gifted, they had been friends for years, Carlos was chosen for a Mission that required a lot of foot work, but even the thought of physical exertion, and weather exposure, made him physically sick.

He could have cared less about the finder's-Fee, 80 young people of the same age group were chosen for this Mission, the younger they were, the less conspicuous they were to those who someone may be trying to find.

The finder's-Fee was Ten Thousand Dollars, this got Mica's adventurous spirit peaked.

She suggested to Carlos that she do the Mission, and they split the Finders-Fee if she was successful,... he agreed, but insisted she keep the money, he showed her how he would go about finding someone who didn't want to be found, he told her where to look, and what to look for, he told her of the dangers she might encounter along the way,... he told her not to let anyone know what she was doing.

She took all this information with her, and set out to find either one, or both of the wealthy Americans listed.

One of the listed names was a Mr. Marcus White, the other was a female, Mrs. Petrini.

She had just turned seventeen when she started the Mission, she was twenty now,.. this American she had been working for all this time, his name was Vernon Mathews, the Woman, Patricia Mathews... wealthy American's... just the wrong ones.

Mrs. Mathews was on the computer in the library, when Mica came in to clean, there was a safe in the rear of the Library, today, the safe's door was ajar,.. Mrs. Mathews had never left the safe open before, and certainly not unattended.

Mica cleaned as she usually did, paying no attention to the open safe.

Mrs. Mathews paid her no attention as she plucked away at the computer,.. as Mica's cleaning duties brought her closer to the open safe, she told herself to just keep cleaning and ignore it.

But she knew that was senseless,... she glanced through the open door, her heart sped up, there it was,... her locator, the silver' cell phone looking device was just inside the door.

She glanced up at Mrs. Mathews, she was still busy on the computer.

Mica saw her chance and went for it,... as she removed the locator from the safe, she happened to glance upon a document with names on it, it was from the Brazilian Government.

She slipped the locator into her pocket and continued cleaning,... the Document kept flashing across her mind as she cleaned, she made up her mind to take another look at it, if she got the chance.

It was like Mrs. Mathews was in another world, Mica had no problem getting another peek inside the safe.

The first two Documents were in fact from the Brazilian Government, they were their Documented Citizenship papers,.. the second two were

Documented name changes, her heart skipped a beat as she scrolled down the Document to the name,... her hands began to tremble as she gazed upon the name that had been tossed out by Vernon Mathews,... the name was "Marcus White",... the other tossed out name was "Petrini".

She had to cover her mouth with her hands to keep quiet,... she had been held hostage, and forced to be the Concubine of the person she was sent to find.

She dropped the Documents like they were hot coals, and hurried away from the safe, continuing her cleaning on the oposite side of the room.

The trembling stopped,... she felt strength flowing through her body; and a clarity of mind... for the first time in three years, she felt good about herself, she had unknowingly completed her Mission.

By the time Vernon Mathews came to get her that evening' to sneak her into the remote bedroom,.. she had already put together a plan to activate the locator and get it topside.

She would be locked in this bedroom by night,.. and Mrs. Mathews kept a pretty close eye on her as she cleaned by day,... she would have to gain their confidence, if they trusted her' they wouldn't watch her so closely,... from now on, she would put up with her state of captivity willingly,.. until she get her chance.

Rudy's children were around a lot now,... his two son's both of whom had pretty much given up on school, while in their mother's care, were now going on a regular basis.in his attempt to keep from spoiling his children, he let it be known; that they were not to come to him asking for money, he thought it would be best if he helped them develop a work ethic.

Any money you guy's need,.. you can work for, said Rudy,.. and I've got plenty of work.

They sneered and cut their eyes at him frequently,.. talking about him behind his back, and reluctantly doing the small jobs they were being paid to do.

They had never known Rudy, their Mom let them talk to him on the phone, when she needed extra money, but he was never allowed to visit them,.. this was their first time being exposed to their father, they were just getting to know him, and were cautiously waiting for all the terrible things they had heard about him over the years to show up.

So far, they hadn't seen the dope addict, the drunkard, or the sorry good for nothing whore monger,... nor had they seen the dumb selfish looser' that wanted nothing to do with his children,... the man that walked off and left them to fend for themselves, who never gave their Mother a dime, nor did they see the other hundred or so names that their Mother had insured them were the reasons that they should stay away from him.

But he seemed happier when they were around, and was genuinely concerned about everything they did.

And no matter how rude they were, or how hard they tried to push him away,.. it never changed the way he felt about them,.. on quite a few occasions, they knew they had hurt his feekings,.. but he never tried to hurt theirs in return,.. he never tried to explain himself, nor did he ever say anything bad about their Mother.

It wasn't long before they stopped calling him Rudy, and started calling him Dad.

Felicia had been spending a lot of time putting together a Soul Food Restaurant,.. to her, getting this chance was like a dream come true, it was what she always wanted to do, she found a promising location' in the North Tampa area, that area was nicknamed "Suitcase City", due to the multitudes of Apartment Complexes that surrounded the University of South Florida,.. College students were constantly moving in, and they were constantly moving out,.. so the name Suitcase City came about kind of naturally.

She was putting the place together the way she wanted it, she was using a lot of her own recipes,.. she worked at length on the Menu and the restaurant personnel.

They were all trying to come up with a name that would bring about curiosity.

Rudy would stop by from time to time and pull her away from her pet project, just to make sure she didn't work herself to death.

He and Sophia had been seeing more and more of each other, he loved the attention she was showing him, it seemed as if she got more beautiful day by day.

Even though she was dressing down, in jeans, and little Polo outfits, she turned heads, both male and female' wherever they went.

She never talked about money, or asked for any, Rudy felt this woman would love him with or without money.

It wasn't until he went to the men's room of the Studio where they were hanging out one night with friends, that reality hit him, as usual, when he returned, she was surrounded by a lot of the male patrons of the Club,... most men, no matter who, were fascinated by her beauty.

Deep down inside, Rudy knew that if he was that broke man of not long ago' and came upon this woman while riding his bike,.. she wouldn't give him the time of day,.. but there he was, with this fascinating creature who wanted to spend every spare moment she had with him.

Two months had passed before he invited her to his house, it was through a long lustful night that she insured Rudy that with him is where she belonged.

Felicia usually got home late,... she'd wake Rudy for breakfast, and they would spend the first part of the day together, catching each other up on the events from the day before, and plans for the day ahead,... sometimes she would get him up so early in the morning, it would still be dark outside, they would launch out in the Jon-boat' into the peacefulness of the River, and catch their breakfast, she loved freshwater Catfish,.. she preferred Fish-n-Grits to any other breakfast.

This morning when she knocked on Rudy's door,..he yelled back,... I'm gonna sleep in this morning.

Aw,... Come on, said Felicia,... what are you doing in there, playing with yourself.

Yeah, said Rudy.

Can I watch, she replied, giggling outside the door.

We'd rather not be disturbed right now, yelled Sophia.

Felicia drew back from the door and just stared at it,... she turned to leave, but hadn't taken two steps before she turned again, and headed back to the door,..

She knocked on the door with a little more force than necessary,. And yelled.

Rudy,... come here for a minute,.. I need to talk to you.

Rudy stepped out into the hallway, closing the door behind him,... he pulled Felicia down the hall and into the living room, out of Sophia's earshot.

Felicia paced back and forth in front of him,.. you just wanted to get your rock off right,.. if that's what you're doing, I,.. I ain't got nothing to say about that,... but you can't keep her,.. don't bring her back here again.

Sophia came up behind Rudy, putting her arms around him, she was wearing a white teddy.

Felicia's a pretty woman... but Sophia made her look like a rag doll.

"I'm so excited about the project that you're putting me in charge of," said Sophia.

I've always loved working with the homeless,... now I'll be able to make a career of it,.. Thank you,... Thank you,...

Thank you, she said as she kissed him on the neck, then there was one on the jaw, then there was the one on the lips,... can you come back to bed now,... so I can thank you some more.

Flames could be seen in Felicia's eyes.

Miss,... you just walked in on a private conversation,.. please leave,... and don't "Ever" do that again!

If what you've got to talk to "my man" about is so important,.. then maybe I "should" be here.

Felicia crossed the room and opened the center drawer of the Mantle' she came out with the little .380 caliber pistol; she came back across the room to her original position before she pointed the gun at Sophia's head.

Sophia put her hands up as if they could be used to stop a bullet, she cautiously backed away.

I'm going,.. I'm going, she pleaded.

She sprinted the last fifteen fee to the room, slamming the door behind her.

She called you "her man",... is that your woman,..Felicia asked calmly.

I've been seeing her for awhile,.. she's ok.

And you're bringing her in?

She's got this little idea about helping the homeless,..its actually a good idea.

Well, I'm not gonna rain on your parade or try to talk some sense into you,.. not while your dick is still hard,.. she was patting him on the crotch as she said this.

She turned and slowly headed for her room,.. pistol still in hand, she opened her bedroom door, stopped and looked back.

Bringing her here was not a good idea,... for now, all I'm going to say is, don't bring her here again, I understand you're not thinking clearly right now,... that's where "I" come in,... she gazed down the hall at the closed door... yeah, I got my eye on you Bitch, she said under her breath.

Rudy's children's mother, and her sister were at the Lawyers Office trying to put together a lawsuit against Rudy... by Child Support standards set by the Government, they were entitled to one third of Rudy's gross income.

It looks as if Mr. Clayton's obligation of support has been taken care of, said the third lawyer they encountered.

Can't you see what he's done, said the angry woman,... he paid it all off so he wouldn't have to give me my half.

Yeah, said the sister, she bore, and raised this man's Children, alone, and now when he gets some money, he tricks her, and deprives his Children of their share... that's a shame, he has all that money, and won't give his Children what's rightfully theirs.

He's not going to get away with that,... half of that money belongs to us.

So, you want to sue him for paying his child support off early, said the lawyer.

"Whatever", said the woman,... as long as I get my half.

From what I see, said the lawyer,.. I "can" prove that by paying his child support off early, he did in fact, deny you' your share of his money, the ladies were pleased to hear this,.. they put him to work on a case of "trickery", they were ecstatic when they left the lawyers office.

Didn't I tell you girl, said the Sister,... all you have to do is point the money out to those Shark ass lawyers; and it's like blood in the water,... they'll go get it.

You were right too,.. he said he can prove what was done, I'm glad I listened to you.

We're going to Sue for half, said the Sister, but if we only get the Ten Million that we were originally supposed to get, I guess we'll just have to make do with that,... they laughed whole heatedly.

The Sister was in a hurry to set up an appointment with a realtor, she had always wanted a home in the suburbs, she would give her Buick Skylark to one of her friends,... there was a Cadilac Escalade waiting for her just over the horizon.

The Childrens mother had visions of herself on a grand scale, she would have a Condo on the top floor of the Skypoint Towers, she would play the field, one man would never do,... hell, she would have two or three man servants, everything in her closet will be thrown out; and replaced with fashions from the worlds top designers, she would have more Diamonds than the Zimmerman's,... and a Limousine for Club night, she imagined herself drinking the most expensive drinks,... everyone is going to want to be her friend,... she's going to be the most popular Deva Tampa has ever known.

Rudy's Children were growing on him now, their relationship was getting better all the time, Rudy kept them busy on small projects and also allowed them a lot of free time, they all moved in with him, and pretty much just visited their mother every now and then.

He never brought Sophia back to the house,... instead, he put her up in one of his Apartments and set up a splinter Office there also,... in case he ended up spending too much time there, which was often the case.

Her project had gotten off the ground nicely, she had managed to get a donation stream together, various Companies throughout the City promised to help out, Rudy was surprised to see Starbucks on the donation list,... there was McDonalds, Verizon, just to name a few.

But Rudy was her main source.

The first time Rudy had gotten an uneasy feeling about Sophia,... was when she found out that he had set up Trust Funds for each of his Children,... they each had two Million in a Trust Fund, that would be available to them on their twenty ninth Birthday.

Sophia knew Rudy had been spreading around a lot of money,... she had to find out how much he still had in cash,.. she would have to speed up this operation before all the cash was turned into investment capital.

Her partner Michelle called her cell phone. Why haven't you called, she asked?

I've made contact, and I'm in, but this is going to take a little time.

I'll come down and help you.

No, said Sophia,... it ain't that kind of party,... I'll have to handle this one alone, if everything goes as planned, I should be able to move at least four Million Dollars, but it's going to take a few more weeks.

Four Million,... you sure I won't be able to help? I'm sure,.. just keep in touch.

OK.

Sophia never had any intention of sharing this Major hit with Michelle, after this one,... she would bid her friend, farewell.

One of the smaller rooms of the four bedroom Apartment that Rudy had put Sophia up in, was used as an Office,... it was off limits, a personal station for Rudy only, the door was kept dead bolted shut, he didn't permit anyone inside, not even sophia.

The time for action had begun to draw near, Sophia turned on the special treatment, she served him graciously, and shamelessly,.. Rudy hated leaving, even to go to work.

Then one night while they were enjoying each other's company, she brought out a bottle of Hennessey... they had a great time that night, they laughed and talked half the night away,.. they made love like there was no tomorrow and fell asleep in each other's arms.

Sophia made sure Rudy drank more than he should have.

She was able to get the key to his private Office from his key chain, while he lay in a deep, Alcohol induced sleep,... she called a locksmith, and was at his place within the hour,... she had a duplicate key made' then rushed back to replace the original,.. all went well.

She was logging on to his computer as early as the very next evening,.. using his Access codes that were written on the front of the notepad beside the computer.

She began lining up accounts that were now at her disposal, she checked balances on a large number of accounts,... she was thrilled at what she saw.

She changed her mind about the four Million, and decided eight Million would be just as easy,... being, she had at least ten different companies doing restoration work on her homeless facilities, the plumming, electrical,.. they were even looking at Blueprints for additions.

What she would do is' make up a Phantom Company, and reroute the money through the homeless projects building fund, and into the Phantom Company.

That way, it would take some time to trace, and the paper trail would also end at that point,... not too sophisticated, a quick hit-n-run, it wouldn't take long for them to find out what happened,.. or who the culprit was, so travel plans were made early,... a flight was already booked and waiting,... "First Class".

The kids Mother's intentions of Sueing him for Ten Million Dollars came by Messenger, he was to make an appearance in Court in Ten Days.

Rudy shared this information with Emmitt Smith,.. who in turn, acted as if this was something he had already anticipated.

We're ready, he said,.. all you have to do is be present on the Court date.

Rudy breathed a sigh of relief, to have Emmitt Smith looking after his legal affairs.

Emmitt wasn't moved by the treachery of the Courtroom,... Rudy found that odd, a Black Man' thats cool, calm, and collected, in an American Courtroom, Rudy looked up to him in every way.

Rudy still hated everything about the Court Systems, everytime he pictured himself entering a Courtroom, he was always kicking and screaming.

It took Sophia a few days to get everything set,... when she was set up' she did a test run with one of Rudy's accounts out of Texas,... she transferred the funds from that account' to an account she'd set up in Switzerland.

She logged off the computer, then went back in using various search regiments to see if she could find the funds she'd hidden, she did this as if she was someone else who may be trying to find out where the money was sent.

After she had exhausted every avenue, she was familiar with,... she was finally satisfied,... the money was as good as gone.

It was so well hidden; the account couldn't possibly be found by anyone who didn't know exactly how to find it.

A blind search would always lead to a dead end,... it was perfect.

Michelle made the decision on her own, to go to Tampa and help her friend.

This was way too big a hit for her to try and do alone, Michelle knew Sophia would need her help, if it was only to keep her focused.

But once Michelle got to Tampa, she found herself dead in the water, because at this point Sophia wasn't answering her calls anymore,... she had no idea where to start looking for her,... she hadn't received any information on the guy Sophia had come here to find, and she didn't remember enough about him to search him out through cyber space.

Not answering the phone was not like the friend she'd known all these years,... it was the unanswered calls that got her mind reeling,.. what was going on, was Sophia in trouble,.. no, that's not possible, Sophia knows if things get too hot, she'd just cut her losses and leave quietly.

Was Sophia cutting her out,.. the thought kept eating at her, she'd have to force those type of thoughts out of her head,... she knew Sophia would never betray her, but she also knew that money had always brought out the worst in Sophia.

Once Michelle made a hit for Two Hundred Thousand Dollars, although she made the hit alone, and had to live with the Mark for four Months before she was able to get the money transferred into her account.

Sophia still felt like she was supposed to get half,... she threw the Fifty Thousand Michelle had given her; back in her face, that was the first physical fight they'd ever gotten into.

Michelle ended up giving her half the money, and ever since' they've been splitting everything down the middle.

Now they've come up on the biggest hit of their career,... and Michelle has to wonder if Sophia was actually trying to cut her out.

The deadline Sophia had told her about was coming up in a few days, and Michelle didn't have a clue.

She struck up a conversation with a guy that worked ay the Courthouse, he was familiar with the case that won a young Tampa man Thirty Million Dollars,... her plan was to seduce him' and get him to look up the information she needed, she thought about what she was doing, before asking any more questions, she knew it was a bad idea, she was just desperate, they would surely get caught if she started asking questions about someone, then soon after,... that someone gets robbed.

And once again,.. she was back to square one.

Michelle thought of where Sophia might go' if she wasn't able to catch up with her before the deadline, she had been everywhere that she'd dreamed of going, they had spent a lot of time in California,... Hawaii,.. The Florida Key's and even Jamaica, she had enjoyed those places, but never showed any interest of settling or living in any of them,..the only place she'd always dreamed of living; but never got the chance,... was Paris, France.

And with the kind of money involved here,... that dream is finally within her grasp.

Michelle started spending most of each day at the Tampa International Airport.

There were two flights per day, leaving for Paris, by the way of New York,... Michelle kept track of those flights,... she watched the borders from a distance,.. praying she wouldn't see her friend.

A few days went by, and the money Sophia had moved to the secret account went unnoticed.

She made plans to move the rest; on Rudy's Court Date,.. he would be more than half a day in Court, that would give her plenty of time to transfer the money, catch her plane... and disappear.

Felicia ran from the filing cabinet; back to the computer, when she first noticed an account was missing a Million Dollars, she figured it was an error on her part,.. but everything she did to correct the problem failed.

Was there actually a Million Dollars missing?

The next few days were spent trying to find the mistake,.. she had put together a fool proof method of keeping up with all the accounts, she knew these accounts backward and forward, she was the only one that uses their financial systems,.. Rudy never went near the money,.. if he wanted money for something, he'd ask her to pull it up.

She stayed in contact with the banker until he had confirmed her suspicions... a transfer had been made, but he was unable to track it down.

After exhausting all of her straregies, the results were clear,... this was not a mistake.

She couldn't waste any more time, she'd have to tell Rudy.

She made call after call on her cell phone, she would get everyone together' and try to get to the bottom of this.

Rudy's daughter Rudesha, was downstairs watching television and talking on the phone at the same time.

Felicia's mind was so scattered, she had completely forgotten that Rudy was in Court,... she thought he had cut his phone off because he didn't want to be disturbed,.. and that meant only one thing,... he was with that "Skeeser".

Rudesha, she yelled.

Rudesha told the person on the phone to hold on a minute.

Rudesha, will you please go over to Sophia's place and tell your Dad to get over here quick,..we got a problem.

Hurry baby,... "hurry".

When Rudesha got to the Apartment, the door was unlocked, she walked right in.

She found Sophia in the back room on the computer. Hi Miss Sophia, she said.

Hi, Rudesha, said Sophia,... how you doing sweetie, the child had startled her silly, but she fought to keep her composure.

I'm okay, said Rudesha,.. is my dad here," she asked? No sweetie, he was scheduled to be in Court today.

Rudesha made no attempt to see what was on the computer screen, but Sophia turned her chair around' and made sure she blocked the screen, so it couldn't be seen.

She talked playfully with Rudesha all the way to the front door, she was almost certain the child hadn't seen anything.

Rudesha got back to the house and relayed the message from Sophia to Felicia.

He's not over there, said Rudesha,... she said he was supposed to be in Court today.

"Oh yeah, that's right," said Felicia,.. no wonder he didn't answer his cell phone, all cell phones have to be turned off in Courtroom settings.

You know, you and my dad would be a better match than him and Miss Sophia,... I don't like her, I don't see what

it is he sees in her,... she don't like me either, I was trying to be friendly and talk to her, but she just rushed me right out the front door,... like she couldn't wait to get back there to her precious computer.

Her computers in the front room right, asked Felicia

There's a computer in the front room, but she was on the one in the back room.

Felicia's eyes narrowed.

What, she asked?

She has a whole computer room set up in the back room of the Apartment, said Rudesha.

Felicia knew that Rudy worked out of that Apartment at times, but he had assured her that the work station he had set up in that Apartment was completely secure,.. it was supposed to be under lock and key,.. she had told Rudy time and time again, not to let Sophia have access to that work station.

Felicia had never trusted her,.. now everything was ringing crystal clear.

Felicia picked up the phone and called Cole.

Cole,... meet me at the Apartment that Sophia's in,.. "Now".

She hung up the phone, grabbed her purse and ran out to the car.

When she reached the Apartment, she tried the door,.. it was locked now,.. she noticed the front windows were open half way,.. she pulled the bug screen from the window and stepped inside.

In the off limits room in the rear of the Apartment, Sophia was busy typing away on the computer; completely pleased with herself.

Felicia walked up behind her, close enough to see what she had on the screen.

Felicia recognized it immediately... she pulled her hand from her purse,... the gun was already locked and loaded.

Sophia finally felt the presence behind her, she turned around just in time to catch the butt of the pistol on her forehead.

She was struck with such force, it knocked her completely out of the chair and onto the floor, she lay still on the floor, the dizziness' was overwhelming,. She opened her eyes,. The pistol was pointing directly into her face, while Felicia tapped away at the computer with her free hand.

Sophia wouldn't dare to move and startle the woman,... there was no way she would miss.

Felicia found fifteen transfers that had been made from this computer, the accounts that the money was being sent to were still in the first stages of approval,.. both control numbers were still at the original transfer points,... so all she really had to do was cancel the transfers and check the Account balances along the way.

She retrieved Ten Million Dollars from transferred Accounts,.. when everything seemed to be back in place, that was moved from this station, she still came up short,.. One Million Dollars was still missing,... she scrolled through Cyber space relentlessly,... the screen took her full concentration.

Sophia noticed this as she lay motionless on the floor,.. she had a headache that made her feel as if she had been nailed to the floor,.. as the dizziness subsided, she knew she was going to have to make a break for it, she pretended to slip in and out of consciousness, in hope that the woman would relax a little.

Now,.. the woman's full attention was on the computer,.. this was her chance.

She sprung from the floor as fast as possible, catching Felicia off guard,.. she grabbed her gun hand thrusting it upward, she put her full weight on the woman forcing her from the chair, to the floor.

Felicia turned her body as she went to the floor, cradling the gun under her body as she lay on her stomach,.. Sophia sat on her back, but couldn't get the gun from under her,.. she knew the first break that Felicia got, she was going to come up shooting,.. as quickly as possible, Sophia reached up and grabbed the porcelain desktop lamp' and brought it down on the back of Felicia's head,.. on the second blow' the lamp broke, and Felicia lay still.

Sophia gathered up a few things quickly,.. and ran out of the Apartment.

Once outside, she saw three vehicles speeding into the complex heading in her direction,... she recognized the first truck,... it was Cole.

They hadn't spotted her yet, so she crouched down out of sight, and ran around to the rear of the building and climbed the fence,.. she made her way around to the front in time to see the last of the gang go inside the Apartment.

Quickly, she ran to her car and sped off.

Felicia still lay motionless on the floor when Cole reached her' there was a gash behind her right ear,.. and a soft hickey still rising on the back of her head.

Cole scooped her up and headed for the truck,.. He left two men there on guard.

Do not let anyone in here, he said,.. I mean "No One".

This place is locked down Boss, said one of the ex-felons that was now the majority of Cole's crew,.. and the most effective.

Sophia's plan was still good to go,.. she knew Felicia would never find the money she had transferred a few days ago,... that Million Dollar deposit would finance her life in Paris for quite some time.

She would have to be careful now,... she was an hour and a half early for her flight.

It wouldn't be safe, sitting in the boarding area of the Airport for so much time,... someone may come looking for her,... she would wait until the last minute, then walk straight through to the plane.

The plane was scheduled to leave a 3:45 pm,... she sat in the car on the upper deck of the parking garage until 3:35,.. then made her way to the terminal.

She was incognito,.. she wore a long trench coat,.. a big floppy hat, and sunglasses.

Michelle had been present at each out going flight that had a Paris connection.

Today, a figure emerged from the upper deck elevator,... it was impossible to get a good look at the person,... she was completely covered, her sex appeal somehow dominated the disguise,... she walked just like her partner Sophia.

The woman kept her head down as she made her way to the boarding area of the Paris flight.

Michelle got up and went in her direction' to get a closer look,... still uncertain, she called out.

"Sophia".

The woman's head turned in her direction,.. Then snapped back to its forward position,.. the woman pulled the hat down a little further over her head' and sped up.

Michelle tried to cut her off before she reached the security barrier,.. but Sophia ran through,.. slipping away from Michelle's grasp.

Michelle screamed!

No,.. Sophia,.. no, please,... don't do this,... Sophia please don't leave me.

Sophia was now running toward the portable chute that leads to the Aircraft door.

Michelle bolted through the security barrier,... alarms went off all over that entire wing of the

Airport,.. the loud alarms startled the people almost as bad as the herd of Security Officers that had dropped what they were doing to give chase.

She's got a gun, one officer shouted.

Michelle started firing as soon as Sophia entered the chute,.. and continued firing through the side of the canvas chute, until Homeland Security's muzzle blasts rang throughout the east wing,... they had gotten the go ahead to use deadly force to apprehend the gun wielding woman who was putting so many lives at risk.

Michelle's bullets had found their target,... Sophia lay motionless in the doorway of the Aircraft, she had been struck several times,... the force of the assault on Michelle by Homeland Security' propelled her body through the canvas, where she lay at her friend's feet,... she was riddled with bullets.

The incident was, Breaking News; a couple of hours later.

Rudy and Felicia watched the drama unfold from her hospital bed,... she was under medication,.. but she could see the sorrow in his eye's, as he realized,... he had never been; something special, he was just another "Mark", that had been taken for a ride.

She wanted to say, "I told you so", so bad she could taste it,... but she would spare him the anguish,... this time.

Rudy's children's Mother and her Sister; sat on either side of their Lawyer,.. they were both talking into his ear at the same time.

Neither of them had seen the Children in the last few Months, but they were in Court fighting for their Childrens needs.

Their lawyer laid down the facts.

The Defendant had under-supported his Children their whole life, and owed them dearly.

He has received a large sum of money which should be used to properly compensate these neglected Children.

In fact,... he is now trying to keep from giving them what is owed them, by disabling the system that was meant to ensure proper distribution of funds from a "No Good" or "Dead Beat", Parent.

Then he wanted the Court to hear from the Childrens Mother,... who began crying as soon as she took the stand.

She told the Court of how badly she had been treated by this man,.. and how he was never there for her,... never helped with anything,... and now was denying his Children what is rightfully theirs.

She went on and on ,... by the time she finished, there was a puddle on the floor.

Then they heard from her Sister,... who broke out in tears also,.. no one could care for someone else's Children more,.. it hurt her heart that those Children had been treated so badly by that Monster.

She almost went into convulsions before she finally sat down.

When they were finished, the Court asked to hear from the Defendant.

Emmitt Smith stood, he brought out the paperwork that showed completion of all Monetary obligations to the Agency, then report cards from the Children's School reflected significant improvement over the last few Months.

Pictures of school activities... personal projects, and work ethics were shown,.. shopping spree's and leisure time, fishing, bike riding,.. walks in the park were shown,.. then the fact that each child had a Two Million Dollar Trust Fund that would be available to them at age 29.

The Judge cut Emmitt short.

I don't need to hear anything further, he said,.. if the Plaintiffs have nothing more to add,... this case is dismissed.

Both women jumped up as the Judges gavel came down,... they were outraged.

I object, shouted the Sister.

The Courtroom paused.

And what are you objecting to, asked the Judge calmly.

I object to the fact that these Children can't get their money until they are 29 years old,.. I should have access to these accounts now.

Thats right, shouted the Childrens Mother, the Children need their money now,... why should they have to wait.

The gavel came down again,... a little firmer this time. "Case Dismissed", said the Judge.

Rudy didn't leave the house for the next couple of weeks,... he felt stupid and vulnerable,... he missed Sophia, and hated himself for missing her, he tried to sound enthusiastic when the gang had brought his son in, proud as ever because he had found the Account that Sophia had hidden,... he was getting pretty good on the computer, but all Rudy could muster up was.

Good going kid.

He was lying on the couch watching Soap Opera's when the phone rang.

Hello.

Hi, I'm trying to reach Rudy Clayton.

Speaking.

Mr. Clayton,... this is Orlan Petrini,... I..

Orlan Petrini, Rudy shouted,.. you fucking piece of shit,.don't you "Ever" call this number again.

Rudy slammed the phone down with all his might.

I don't believe this shit,... he couldn't sit down any longer,... his blood pumped wildly, visions ran through his mind of how this man destroyed everything dear to him, he and his closest friends were lucky to be alive right now,... and now he knows where I am.

Rudy struggled to find a way to reach this man,... to somehow manipulate his demise,... there had to be someone in the prison system that can get to him.

He thinks he can't be touched,... but just like the Murderer J.D.,... he too, can be touched by an Angel.

Rudy was determined to bring the fight to him this time.

Rudy was still hyped up when Felicia got home, he told her about the phone call, and pleaded with her to be careful at all times.

Her attempts to calm him down failed,... he was too worked up,... Felicia cooked a hefty Soul Food Dinner, with Ice Cream for dessert, then she brought out a bottle of Wine,... they sat on the floor of Rudy's room, like old times, where they poured glass after glass.

The wine had the calming effect he needed,... he and Felicia were able to talk like they used to,... he hadn't realized how much he missed their quiet time together.

Can we talk seriously for a minute, asked Felicia,... she didn't wait for a response.

You remember back when we were together,... you caught me cheating on you,.. you know,.. I've never gotten over that day, it's been playing over and over again in my head for quite some time,... but what you didn't know is,... that wasn't the first time I'd done that,.. I had done it several times before you caught me,.. I don't know why,... just sex crazed I guess,.. it wasn't because I didn't love you, and I didn't do it to hurt you.

I'll never forget; the look on your face, when you walked in on us.

I saw the sadness in your eye's,.. But what I saw more clearly, was the utter disgust,... I could actually feel, how you felt about me at that moment, just by looking in your eye's,... that's why I haven't been involved with anyone sexually in the last five years.

I wanted to be sure; that whatever it was that made me think that I can do what I did,... is completely out of me, and gone forever.

What I'm trying to say is,... if you're finished, clowning around with these "Juice Head" Zero's,... I'd like my spot back,... you know I never liked Sophia,.. but I couldn't help but notice how happy she made you,... that's the only reason I didn't blow her damn head off when I walked up on her thieving ass, she said playfully,... I was beginning to think I was wrong about her,.. and that scared me worse, because I knew you would never leave her if I was,... I can't take any more chances like that.

Well, I sure need you now, said Rudy. Right now, asked Felicia?

"Right now," said Rudy.

A Month later, Rudy received another phone call from Orlan Petrini.

If this is Rudy Clayton,... please don't hang up,... I have a proposition for you.

Rudy had been unsuccessful in trying to get to Petrini since he'd been in Prison, but was still certain it could be done.

He didn't hang up the phone in anger' like he had the first time,... he was hoping Petrini might slip up; and reveal a way he can be reached.

I'm here, said Rudy.

Going on what you know about me,... you should hate my guts, said Petrini, if you could put your feelings aside for a moment, I'd like to talk business with you.

Rudy said nothing.

I have depleted all of my funds now, and all of my Associates are long gone,... the only thing I have left to bargain with; is Twelve Office Buildings,... with the smallest of them being Ten stories, the thing is they are all now in Bankruptcy, and are about to be lost also, they are very profitable and are all I have left to bargain with.

The person that has your anger at the height that it now rests, has my anger almost at that same level,.. to get a chance to see him again,... I'll give anything.

You are my very last hope,... to you, I give everything that I have left.

I am going to be transferred to my home State,... North Carolina, I have been granted a reprieve there by the Governor, for early release' under monitored conditions.

The Governor is asking' Three Million Dollars for this reprieve,... this is what I'm going to need from you.

I've been keeping up with you, you've been doing pretty good with your money, your business investments are doing well and you're making money,.. but the offer I'm placing before you now' will make you a very wealthy man.

If you do this, I will work directly for you,.. free of charge, until I get all Twelve properties up and running, for this requires expertise, and a lot of experience.

After the buildings are up and running, I will require a meager salary,.. and your Three Million Dollar investment will be paid back in full, in fifteen months, I will also pass on to you, the knowledge it takes to run such an operation, if you accept this offer,... I will be forever in your dept.

Rudy smiled inside,... the man that caused so much pain and heartache to him, was now asking for his help,.. not only did this guy cheat the justice system, and the people who rely on it, by paying his way out of jail,.. but this Bitch actually thinks; that my getting him out of jail is going to be what he may call,.. a joyous occasion.

The man had offered him just what he wanted,.. killing this man may now be a possibility.

I'll pay for the reprieve approval, said Rudy,.. the Governor will have the paperwork done by the time you get there.

I'll have a Limo waiting for your release,... see you soon! Pssst,..... Pssst.

Orlan Petrini opened his eye's,... there was a figure standing outside his cell door.

The door was opened half way and the figure was motioning him to come,.. Petrini got up quickly and quietly, it was well after midnight and all the other inmates were sleeping,.. with the exception of the Claustrophobic's and the insomniac's, who would go for days without sleep, they just collapse when their bodies give out on them.

Petrini was being led through the corridor's at a brisk pace, they were soon entering the Warden's office.

The Warden stood as they entered,.. the guard that brought him in left abruptly.

It seems the Governor of our fine State is granting you a reprieve, said the Warden, all the paperwork is in order, and I have been ordered to release you.

The Warden walked over and picked up the brand new suit that hung on the coat rack,.. complete with shoe's and hat, he handed them to Petrini with a smile on his face.

Don't slip up again, he said,... the price tag on a second reprieve, is Astronomical.

Petrini changed into the new suit and was led through the Courtyard and out to the front gate.

The Warden handed him a hand rolled Cigar as the gate was opened, Petrini took the Cigar and stepped out into the night.

The fresh air was invigorating, the freedom enveloped him and made him smile inside, it gave him hope, hope that he would soon come face to face with Marcus White.

It wasn't long before the Limo pulled up.

Cole was driving, Felicia riding shotgun,... Rudy rode in the back with Petrini.

Conversation was sparse, and polite.

Cole exited the main Highway and headed down into what was known as the Warehouse district.

Cole pressed a button on the remote, and the doors of the Warehouse ahead of them began to open automatically,... once inside, the doors closed behind them.

They all exited the Limo, everyone but Pertrini.

Rudy went around to Petrini's side and opened the door, Rudy stood there and watched him as he just sat there.

We're going to need you out here Sir, said Rudy.

Petrini looked straight ahead as he let out a deep breath, he ran his hand across his face, from his forehead to his chin, he held his head up, gathered himself, and stepped out of the vehicle.

He was led to a chair that sat on a clear plastic Tarp.

Rudy straddled a chair that sat in front of Petrini's, it was turned backward so he could lean forward on the backrest.

Felicia and Cole stood on either side of Rudy's chair,. Guns in hand.

Petrini sat before them with perfect posture, legs crossed,... he dropped his head in the deep regret of not being able to get the revenge on those who betrayed him, there was a hole about the size of a grave, dug into the floor of the Warehouse' close to the wall behind him.

Rudy had never given a second thought to the monetary offer Petrini had used as a bargaining tool,... all Rudy wanted,.. was to kill Petrini.

They said,... if you give me some money,.. and relax in a correctional facility for a few years,... that should pay for the outright war that you've waged against me, my family, and my friends.

But here you are,.. already out,.. and as free as a bird, I think the justice system fell a little short.

We both know that this is far too personal a matter to be judged by a Court's justice, and a non-personal jury of your peer's,... neither of whom has ever experienced such an attack,... this is something we have to work out on our own.

Ground Level is extremely personal, it's almost a religious experience,.... the shedding of a bad habit, a bad influence, getting out of a bad situation, it all leads back to the first law of nature... coming face to face with any threats to your wellbeing.

I've been keeping up with you, said Petrini,.. actually, you're kind of interesting,.. I understand you helped the police solve a brutal Murder.

Yeah, that's right, I did,.. that was a very dear friend of mine, she just happened to cross paths with a couple of Goons that ended up taking her through something that she couldn't have produced in her worst nightmare,

Those two Bastards tortured and killed her' then threw her out like trash,.. on her Birthday,... she had just turned eighteen,.. and you must also know that both of those Murdering Bastards are dead now.

I know I haven't been in jail very long, but when I was locked up in that jail called Orient Road,... I had a young roomy,.. he called himself Manny,... he was a talkative young fellow,.. I found out something that you probably don't know,.. Manny wasn't the one that actually killed Chantell,.. neither was the one they called J.D.,... the girl was alive when J.D., and Manny went back to the house, to bind their wounds due to a dog attack,.. the killer was a guy he called Chico.

There were three rapists, there were three torturers,... but only one Murderer.

I was able to find out that this Chico character is still running the Painting Company they'd started, they are in Miami now, somewhere near liberty city,... Manny and J.D., were bitten in the dog attack, but the dog never got to Chico, therefore leaving him unidentified,.. he let his friends take the fall for what "He" had done.

Rudy sat there thinking about what the man had said, deep down inside, he knew it was true,.. there had to be someone else.

He'd found a Diamond Stud in the house that these guys lived in, yet neither Manny, nor J.D. had a pierced ear.

At first, he figured the earring belonged to a female, but the earring he found was still tagged to its display support.

Whoever the earring belonged to only wears one earring at a time.

Rudy came out of his thoughts and met Petrini's gaze.

This is a pretty interesting fellow, he thought.. the information the man had given him, wasn't something that would save his life, this information wasn't asked for, if Millions of Dollars wouldn't save his life, he certainly knew that this wouldn't,... the man had told him this simply because it was true.

He wasn't trying to save his life.

This man is capable of telling the truth, to me.

A Racist Bigot that lives among the Elite, just spoke the truth to a man that's working with a "Ground Level" intellect.

Rudy had always been able to spot phonies when dealing with Men, those who say what they say, to get what they want,... this wasn't the case, what if I was wrong, what if he had been telling the truth; and there actually was a man named Marcus White' that was responsible for all the mayhem that was directed at my family, and Petrini himself.

The thought of killing this man began to fade into the back of his mind.

As did the hatred he'd been harboring toward him, his hatred had blinded him to the point where he could have easily done something that he would have damaging regrets about later.

Rudy got up and walked away, he sat on the hood of the Limo as he went over what had just transpired.

Felicia and Cole joined him,.. not quite understanding what was going on.

We can't just hang around here, said Felicia, let's do this and get the hell out of here.

I'm beginning to think he's not the person we should be taking this out on.

YES IT IS, shouted Felicia, this man is "Never" leaving this building, she said' as she headed back toward Petrini.

Rudy and Cole had to cut her off before she reached him,.. you sure as hell better know what you're doing, this man is going to be back on his feet in no time, and the next time he comes after us,... we may not be so lucky.

They all climbed back into the Limo in the same seating arrangement as before.

Since you're not going to kill me, said Petrini,... I'll start work tomorrow.

Petrini did most of the talking on the way home, his straight forwardness put Rudy at ease, he had a way of making things clear, even Felicia's trigger finger was at ease.

Rudy began to allow himself to trust him.

Felicia put together a tasty Spaghetti dish that night, the house seemed to be a little overcrowded, Rudy's kids were there' along with friends they brought home.

It was as if Petrini was right at home, he dug into dinner with a vigor, it was obvious that he really enjoyed the meal, Rudy also noticed that he didn't seem to have a Prejudiced bone in his body,.. he enjoyed the antics of the Teenagers, he laughed and teased with them, he even made promises that you can't back out of with Children.

Rudy set him up in a room there at the house, they spoke freely and productively, Rudy was always careful not to underestimate another man,.. especially this one.

They started early the next morning, it was a race against the clock, trying to get all of the building out of Foreclosure.

Petrini started at the Forty story Bank of America building in Downtown Tampa, he made a couple of legal maneuvers that wee probably never heard of before, even the Foreclosure Bank representatives were surprised at Petrini's skills.

All Twelve buildings were out of Foreclosure, and new Deeds signed inside of a week, and three weeks later, one building was fully functional, advertisements were in Cyberspace, in newspapers, and on billboards.

You have great locations for office building clients, said Petrini,.. they should start calling right away.

The work had been very complex, Rudy knew he would have never been able to get that building, State and City Legal to operate.

Watching Petrini work was a thing of beauty.

He poured a lot of business knowledge into Rudy.

Petrini only required one Thousand Dollars a week, he'd spend a lot of time sitting out by the river with four or more Cell Phones.

This day he was perplexed about something.

Looks like you finally found something that can kick your ass,.. what's the problem, asked Rudy' as he walked out to join Petrini in the Gazebo at the end of the Pier.

I've had several contacts, with certain instructions and numbers to a service that streamlines contact information... I got a hit by one of the contacts over a month ago,.. this device has to be activated within twenty- four hours after it receives a hit, or the signal will be lost.

If it was important,.. don't you think they'll contact you again.

It's just that these contacts can find themselves in very dangerous situations,... these are the contacts I put out to find the man responsible for my current situation,... I'm sure he's found a faraway place where he thinks I'll never find him,,, but I have some good trackers,.. as a matter of fact, I'll bet, that the hit I had received last month' was to let me know that Marcus White, has been found.

If he has, said Rudy,.. then that's the man I need to get my hands on.

Your hands are full as it is, replied Petrini, you concentrate on that ass hole they call Chico, down in Miami,.. Marcus White is Mine.

Rudy looked at him, he could tell that, this was the first time that this man had a mission in life that wasn't for profit.

This one was about right and wrong,.. some wrong's cut deep enough; where they must be dealt with, and of these, betrayal is at the top of the list,... the only way he'll cleanse his spirit, is man to man,.. Ground Level.

Rudy began to realize, that no matter who you are,.. rich or poor,.. good or bad,.. we'll all at one time or another' have to stand at Ground Level.

That's probably why I couldn't kill him, thought Rudy, we were standing in the same place, Ground Level is where I live.

They were still sitting in the Gazebo when Petrini noticed something.

What just happened, asked Petrini? What do you mean, said Rudy.

Listen, said Petrini.

Rudy listened, but heard nothing, I don't hear anything, said Rudy.

That's what I'm talking about, said Petrini,.. everything just went silent,.. the birds have stopped singing, and all the ducks are gone,.. even the frogs and crickets are quiet.

Rudy listened again as he looked over the area, you're right, he said,... this only happens when there's a dominant predator around.

Rudy knew what to look for now,.. and there he was' directly across the river from them, high up in a Giant oak tree.

There he is right there in that Oak tree, said Rudy, pointing into the tree.

Yeah,..I see him... what a magnificent creature. We call him Cain.

So, you've seen him around here before. I'll be right back, said Rudy.

He returned with a fish from the frig, the kids' fish almost every day, there was always fresh fish available.

Rudy sat back down in the Gazebo, and held the fish up by the tail, he wiggled it a bit to entice Cain.

Cain jumped from the tall Oak and plummeted straight downward as if in stealth mode, he was no more than twenty feet from the River before he opened his wings and rocketed toward the Gazebo, he banked in mid-air and grabbed the fish with one foot, he took it back to the tree and ate.

Petrini was amazed, the bird had come so close, the wind from his wings caused Petrini to recoil,... the comradery between man and nature can sometimes slap you awake.

Rudy ended up telling him how; it was Ty, who actually solved that Murder case, and how a little red fox, saved their lives out in the woods when Marcus White's Goons came after them.

He also told the story of Cain,.. sometimes strong bonds are formed with the most unlikely life forms, as long as we pay attention to each other.

The urge to get to Liberty City wouldn't let Rudy rest, Cole made plans to go also.

I'm gonna need you to watch over everything while I'm gone, said Rudy.

Hell no,... you're not going to try and do this alone.

I'm just going to see if I can locate this guy, I'll know if I can handle it alone,.. if I can't, believe me, I'll call you, and don't let Felicia know what's going on.

What am I supposed to tell her? Just make up something.

Make up something, Cole argued, you trying to get me shot?,.. whatever I tell her' She's going to check on it, and when she don't find "you",.. she's going to shoot "me".

Yeah, said Rudy, you may be right, go ahead and tell her. No, said Cole,.. you tell her.

Tell her what?, asked Felicia, coming down the interior stairs to the carport Garage.

Hi Felicia, said Cole, innocently opening his arms for a hug.

Felicia walked right past him, and straight over to Rudy.

Tell her what, she asked again, her eye's burned into his as she prepared to properly calculate the story she was about to hear.

Rudy knew whatever he told her; it better ring true.

Dalley's crew has finally gotten a prototype car ready for a longer test drive, I'm going to take it out for a few days and monitor its good points' and bad points.

Not heading toward Miami are you?

As a matter of fact, the heat index, and the salt content in the atmosphere are on the list of things that must be checked out.

Rudy thought he sounded pretty convincing.

You are so full of it, her concern was showing,.. don't go down there alone, there's too many things that can go wrong.

In this guy's mind, he's gotten away with Murder, free and clear, he doesn't know me from a can of paint,... I just want to see if I can locate him, I may get a chance to check him out a little, but I won't do anything until I have you and Cole watching my back.

Promise me! I promise.

Go find him, she said, as she turned to go back upstairs.

Dally's attitude left something to be desired after he found out about the test drive, he was down with Rudy going to Miami to find that piece of shit that Murdered Chantell,.. but he wasn't down with the "car" taking the trip.

Rudy you don't know enough about this car to take it out for a test drive, said Dally.

I'll take good care of the car, it's just that this trip is going to be checked on,.. you're going to be getting a call about this,.. trust me.

Dally insisted on going, if not him, one of the technicians should accompany you on the test run.

But no matter how hard he tried, he was unable to get schedules rearranged to have someone make the trip on such short notice,... he reluctantly gave Rudy the rundown on what to look for during the test run.

The car was a 2007 Cadilac Sts,... the internal combustion engine was replaced with the prototype Dyno-Electric Engine.

Although the new engine was equal to, if not better' than any other of it's kind.

Every test run so far had uncovered a bug or two, this longer test run, although the car was already scheduled for it, could be a major setback if something goes wrong.

The Engines take-off was similar to that of a golf cart,.. no chance of burning rubber.

The second gear kicked in quickly, then the third, the speed progression was beautiful.

He put the medal down on the on ramp of I-75 South, the car was at seventy-five miles per hour in less than 15 seconds, this really was a high-performance car.

The ride was so quiet; it was eerie, the car barely made a sound, Rudy put on some riding music to drown out that loud silence.

The speed limit on Interstate 75 was actually 75 miles per hour, and even though traffic was heavy' it was moving at a faster pace, somewhere closer to 85 miles per hour, Rudy was holding it steady a 75.

Traffic sped by him, he wanted to open it up and ride with them, but he could hear Dally's voice in his subconscious over and over,... make sure you take good care of the car, he repeated.

But this was in fact,.. a test run.

Rudy pushed the pedal down, the car didn't respond immediatly,... in a delayed reaction, another gear kicked in, there was no sound to this new power that took over, Rudy weaved through traffic at 100 mph, the engine had more; but the traffic was too congested to open it up more, the speed and maneuverability of the car was a pure adrenaline rush, he would have to give praise to Dally's work when he got back.

In the distance, he noticed the squaw line running across the sky, underneath the line was dark, he would be running into rain within the hour,.. how dark it is under the squaw line, determines how hard it's raining,.. this one was dark enough to be a storm.

The rain came as he reached Alligator Alley.

The swamp lands of the Everglades are frequently buffeted by heavy rains... traffic slowed to 20 miles per hour, vision was reduced to almost zero.

Rudy noticed that the heavier the rains got, the dimmer the lights across the dash got.

The lights continued to dim,.. then blinked out.

The car came to a stop,.. Rudy was soaked as he fought to get the car off to the side of the road.

He called Dally for instructions, but all the instructions that he provided required Rudy to get out of the car and go under the hood, Rudy being a Florida Native, knows first-hand the dangers of rains of this magnitude.

There was no difference in this rain, and that of a Monsoon' and Florida being the lightning capital of the world' also helped with his decision to see if the problem could be rectified from inside the car.

Hey Dally, said Rudy, a guy just stopped to see if I need any help,.. I'm going to catch a ride with...

"No", interrupted Dally,... do not leave that car alone on the side of the Highway for one second, I'm on my way to get you.

That last remark made Rudy feel like a child,.. how could he not realize how important this creation is to his friend, he wanted to kick himself for even thinking of leaving the car.

Rudy put his seat in the reclined position and relaxed as the sound of the rain allowed his mind to wander.

He went back over a conversation that he and Dally had a couple of days before.

Hey, I'm not trying to rush you or nothing, said Dally,.. but when are you going to pop the question?

As soon as the house calms down a little, there's too much going on right now.

Well, on that special night,... dinner's on me, I wouldn't miss this for the world,... let me choose the place, said Dally,... we're gonna make a big deal out of this, we'll invite all our friends and...

No, Dally, No,... lets just have a few people there,.. I'm going to be nervous enough already.

Rudy snapped out of his thoughts,.. I'd better call the house.

Hello, said Felicia.

Hey, it's me, this may take a little longer than I expected,.. I'm stuck.

What do you mean by stuck?

I'm in Alligator Alley on I-75, said Rudy, there's a problem with the car.

We're on our way. Dal,.. click.

Damn, she hung up before I could tell her Dally's on his way out here.

Felicia got the kids in for the night, hurriedly,... everyone had been downstairs in Cole and Myra's place.

Cole was upstairs playing Video in Rudy's game room,.. Orlan Petrini said he'd watch over the place while they were gone.

While Felicia was waiting for Cole to slay the video dragon, there was a knock at the door.

Felicia opened the door and there stood Rudy's children's Mother, and her Sister,.. as Felicia stood in the doorway wondering why these two particular females were here; after all the havok they had caused by taking

Rudy to Court,... she was about to close the door on them, when suddenly out of nowhere came three big Goons,.. they had kept themselves out of sight until the door was opened, they forced their way inside,.. led by the two females.

The Goon's were the brothers of the two women.

They had the presence of those straight out of the Projects,.. Big,.. Burley,.. and easily influenced.

At this point they were at their sister's beckon call,.. the sister spoke up.

Tell Rudy to get his ass down here "Now", she yelled,.. my brother's want to see him,.. and if he don't have my sister's money' they're going to kick his ass to sleep tonight,.... she turned her attention to Felicia.

And miss thang here,.. you think you're big shit now huh, girl you're still stupid as hell,.. your boy Rudy got over Thirty Million Dollars,.. and got you put up in this little place,.. you should be living much larger than this.

Rudy's not here, said Felicia,... he's out of town' taking care of some business.

That means you're in charge, said the sister,... that also means you're responsible for the money he owes,.. he owes my sister Ten Million Dollars,.. start putting it together.

Hit the safe first, then we can start transferring some accounts.

Cole heard the commotion from upstairs; and was heading down, when he saw Felicia waving him back, unnoticed by the intruders.

Cole tiptoed back to the room and got his Pistol, he sat upstairs in the shadows.

There's no money here, said Felicia,.. and Rudy's accounts are his own.

Mack,.. show this little Bitch we ain't playin.

Mack sprung forward and backhanded Felicia, the blow lifted her off her feet and landed her hard on the floor.

As Mack approached her to dish out a second blow,.. a shot rang out.

Mack stumbled backward, holding the bloody wound to his neck,.. Felicia scrambled across the floor trying to get her purse that lay on the chair; on the opposite side of the room, the sister and the other brother saw the purse she was heading for.

The sister reached into her shoulder bag and came out with a handgun.

Felicia was moving across the room too fast for her to get a good aim, she was holding the brother that was shot; trying to stop the bleeding,.. her eyes were like those of a mad woman, her breathing was so heavy, it could have been mistaken for a growl, she was pissed.

She wanted nothing more than to kill Felicia for this, the barrel of her pistol followed Felicia across the room until she was centered in her sights.

The other brother took chase and made a deserate attempt to catch Felicia before she reached her purse, he caught her just before she reached it,... a shot rang out at the same time,.. the man that held Felicia went limp.

The sister couldn't believe she'd just shot her favorite brother, she dropped the gun and screamed; both of her brothers lay on the floor, the two women were hysterical.

Felicia fought her way from under the man that lay limp on top of her, she came up clutching her purse,.. a cold chill ran up her spine,... that bullet was meant for her.

Cole came downstairs' pistol in the ready position, the first shot had come from him.

The kids were peeking through the rail's upstairs' along with Orlan Petrini.

One brother was losing a lot of blood,.. the other was hit in the spine, he would probably be paralyzed for life.

Both sisters and the youngest of the brothers all cried as they frantically set out to drag their brother out to the car, they were going to need medical attention quickly.

Felicia finally got the chance to pull her pistol from her purse.

"EVERYBODY",... stay put, she said' blocking the doorway while dialing 911.

Rudy woke up to the sound of someone knocking on the window of the car.

Dally had shown up with a tow truck, the flatbed type, the car was loaded up and secured.

They proceeded on to Miami's Liberty City.

After Dally assured Rudy that he wouldn't be getting his hands on the car again, they rode around in an attempt to find a rental, once they found one with a lot of nice cars on the lot, he was still a little hesitant because the building was a mess, it appeared to be under construction, it was already after closing time, so Rudy checked into a Hotel that was only four blocks away from the place he would be renting the car from, he would get the rental in the morning.

At the dealership the next morning, Rudy rented a Nisson S.U.V., the building was being painted, it was in fact under construction, as he had thought when he saw the place the day before... but then again,.. the guy he was here looking for, runs a painting outfit,... what are the odds,... the painting crew was already there' they seemed like a well organized group,.. Rudy reminded himself to come back just before knock-off time, to see if he can spot the crew leader.

He went back to the Hotel to wait for Felicia and Cole. They arrived with the story of the night before.

Yeah, the very excited Felicia said, as she began her story,.. your Children's Mother, and her people showed up at the house to jack your ass last night, home invasion style, we were lucky to get out of that shit, they really showed their ass.

But now, her and her people are facing a lot of jail time.

Their facing a multitude of charges' from firing a gun in an occupied dwelling; and home invasion, to armed Robbery,.. one of the brothers is paralyzed, the others in critical condition.

The two sisters were traumatized, they couldn't understand how such a good idea' could end up so badly.

When they were being escorted off by T.P.D.,.. for the first time, they were crying real tears.

It's going to be awhile before we see them again.

Felicia and Cole went back and forth over the story throughout the day, the story seemed to change a little at a time, as it was told over and over,... it was being demonstrated with Cole being the bad guy's at one point, then Felicia the next.

They stayed in the Hotel for the better part of the day, going through the phone book, and newspapers, collecting information on Painting Crews.

Luckily, they only came up with forty Painting Services that were listed,.. twelve large industrial

Painting Companies,.. and twenty-eight smaller crews that solicited work regularly,.. all these can be checked out in the run of a day.

If nothing comes of any of these... Finding the unlisted Painters could turn into a chore, the first one to check was the car rental dealership that was being Painted just four blocks from here.

It wasn't close to knockoff time for the Painting Crew yet, so they decided to walk around for a while and check out Miami, this being a vacation hot spot, one may as well take in a little scenery,.. Liberty City doesn't compare to South Beach; but it does have a certain effect on people, the days are brighter' the people are of all nationalities and all walks of life.

Felicia was happier than her usual self, Rudy could see it in her face, she was enjoying this walk in an unfamiliar City,... Rudy thought to himself,.. I gotta remember to take her out of town more often.

On the way back they came up to the car dealership from the opposite side.

All the Painters had knocked off, they were sitting at the rear of the building; under a tree, they sat on five-gallon Paint containers and whatever else they could make a seat out of, all the tools were being gathered together in one area, they drank beer and goofed off, laughing and talking loud in Spanish as they waited,.. More than likely, they were waiting for the Boss to come and pick them up.

It wasn't long before a van arrived, the driver, a fairly young, fairly handsome fellow got out and greeted the crew.

He walked around the jobsite with one of the other workers; checking out the work that had been accomplished that day.

The guy that came up in the van, said Felicia,... I've seen him before, in Tampa.

You sure, asked Rudy. Yeah.

We're going to have him checked out, said Rudy,... we may be getting a stroke of luck, we're gonna lock in on this guy for a while.

A plan was set up; to keep their newfound friend under surveillance, they needed to find out who he was,... and until they did,..he wouldn,'t be getting out of their sight.

A tragic fire that broke out in the middle of the night' ended up taking the lives of a small family of farmers, they were survived by an elderly Grandfather, that was able to save one child.

Even before the fire, the farm had proven itself unprofitable, he knew he hadn't the strength, or the time left to get the farm back up and running, his Seventy four years were bearing down on him heavily.

He loaded up the Mule,.. packed what he could onto a cart, and he and his Granddaughter set out to start a new life.

The Grandfather would walk the mule in order to keep the cart moving, if not, the Mule would stop and rest, or wander around aimlessly.

The Granddaughter would walk with him in the daytime, but he would make her ride in the cart after nightfall.

They had been moving steady for days when the Granddaughter noticed they had stopped, she checked out front and saw her Grandfather just standing there.

Grampa, she said softly.

He clutched his chest as he went to his knees.

Her, being a farmer's daughter and all, was able to get him into the cart,.. she had no idea where she was, or where she was supposed to be going, she just kept the Mule moving at a steady pace.

Two days later, she came up on the largest, most beautiful farm she had ever laid eyes on.

She left the cart and ran toward the people she saw moving through the fields.

My Grandfather is very sick,.. Please help him, she said to the first field hand that she came upon.

Several of the men followed her back to the cart.

This man is dead, said one of the men; after checking her Grandfathers vitals.

Deep down inside, the girl knew this, but to hear it from someone else was like being stabbed in the heart.

Her Grandfather was the last of her Family,.. she was unaware of the tears that flowed from her eye's as she slowly slipped into a state of shock, the reality of her situation had dawned on her,.. she had; no one!

The American that approached the cart to check out the situation, seemed unconcerned, he actually wanted to know why so many of his workers were not in the field.

When he realized the man in the cart was dead, and this strange child was crying,.. he put two and two together and realized this situation will have to be treated with a little sensitivity.

The American said a few words, to no one specific,.. none of the words could be understood by the child, or the crew for that matter, this was the first contact she'd ever had with an American,.. the last word he said was "Mica".

One man turned and ran toward the house.

Mica emerged from the house and made her way over to the cart.

Find out what happened to her, said Marcus. Mica spoke to the girl in Portuguese.

Hi, my name is Mica,.. what's yours?

Celia,.. my name is Celia, said the girl, between sobs.

Celia, where were you headed, to a relative's house, asked Mica.

My Parents and my two brothers were killed in a fire, my Grandfather and I were going to start a new life somewhere else,.. he was the last of my relatives.

How old are you? Seventeen.

Where will you go now? I have no place to go.

Mica hated what she was about to do,.. this child was standing before her' in a state of shock,.. her whole family had been killed in a fire,.. then her three day' exhausting attempt to save her Grandfather ended in failure,.. and now she was all alone in the world.

The thought of the girls' harshly unlucky plight' made doing what Mica had to do even harder.

She knew she had to detach herself from the situation' or the emotions that were running through her like a whirlwind would be visible, so would her shame.

She turned to Marcus White and spoke in English.

Her name is Celia, her family was killed in a fire, she and her Grandfather were the only survivors, their trip to start a new life is what took the life of her Grandfather,.. he was the last of her family,... she is seventeen years old, and familiar with farm work,... she wanted to know if she could be of service somehow; until she finds someone who might take her in.

Mica glanced up at Marcus White,.. just as I thought, his eye's were burning into the child, he looked her up and down,.. the girl had a sturdier build at seventeen, than Mica had when she first arrived.

Mica felt as if she'd just locked the little piggy in the same cage with the big bad wolf, the lump in her throat almost cut off her windpipe as she saw the lust in Marcus White's eye's.

Tell her she can stay, said Marcus,.. get her set up in the workers quarters, your old room should be just fine,.. and let her know we'll be having her Grandfathers funeral tomorrow.

A whole week had passed, and Marcus White was still in Mica's room every night, and every night he was at full strength.

Mrs. Petrini had been spending time away from the house every so often, being fully aware of her situation, she kept a low profile, she even wore a veil when she was out and about, that concealed her identity.

Even when she was out, Mica did the house work the same as if she was being watched.

She heard the elevator room coming down into its underground lair, she knew it wasn't Mrs. Petrini, she hadn't been gone long enough to have even reached the first Township,... Mica stayed out of sight and watched to see who would come out of the elevator.

Marcus White stepped out of the elevator and headed off in the opposite direction from where Mica was watching from, Mica was surprised to see Celia come out of the elevator and follow him.

The girl looked smaller than she had the first time Mica saw her, she was actually surprised that Marcus had only had minimal contact with the girl,.. her plan was to set Celia up as bait, but Marcus hadn't fallen for it.

Am I this man's main focus, Mica asked herself,.. am I the only one he's ever going to want to torture.

Marcus went into the washroom and was back out again before Celia had reached the door.

He put something in her hand and handed her a glass of water.

Mica's body went numb when she saw this. Oh no,..its happening, she whispered.

That's why he hasn't attacked her yet,.. Marcus White had Religiously brought Mica one birth control pill every day for the last three years.

The girl couldn't be touched until she takes the pill every day for a week, the all too familiar scene aroused her anger.

He watched her as she took the pill,... afterwards Mica saw the girl open her mouth towards Marcus White; who in turn, looked inside her mouth to make sure the pill had been taken.

A weird feeling came over Mica as she watched, she felt as if she was watching someone else playing the role that she herself had played for so long,... she was familiar with his every move,.. she knew what he was about to do.

She could see the dark dominance, and anxiousness take over his features,... he led the girl further into the mansion, Mica followed, staying out of sight.

He led her right past the remote bedroom that Mica was being kept in by night, her heart was beating so hard she could hear it.

Marcus White led the girl with one hand on her neck, by the way she walked, Mica could sense the helplessness the girl was feeling,,, Mica knew just how she felt.

She knows, Mica whispered to herself.

They went into the next room down from Mica's,.. the door to Mica's room wasn't locked, she tip toed into the room and directly behind the door is where she put her ear to the wall,... there was no sound, she readjusted her ear on the wall for clearer reception,.. the first thing she heard was a loud solid slap, followed by a body hitting the wall in the same place that she held her ear, only it was on the opposite side of the wall, the sounds she heard from there, made her back away from the wall, she was frozen in place, watching the wall from one end to the other, her eye's followed the sounds as if she were watching what was happening in the other room.

Oh God,.. what have I done, Mica kept repeating to herself as the tears began to run freely from her eye's.

She ran from the room holding her ears to protect herself from what she was hearing.

She began wandering around the Mansion, pacing back and forth, she was too disturbed to think clearly, too torn up inside to stop crying, she lifted her apron to wipe her eye's; and the cord to her locator fell to the floor.

She stared at it as her senses began to clear, she snapped the cord up from the floor and headed for the elevator; running at full speed.

The locator was still in the same place she'd hidden it, she plugged it into the wall socket; and the locator came to life.

She punched in her Triangulation code and hit send.

A small hole was cut into the thin lining under the sofa, the wall socket was directly behind it, it would probably be able to go unnoticed there for quite some time.

For the first time, Mica fell to her knees and prayed to God for forgiveness.

Orlan Petrini volunteered to watch over the affairs at hand' when Cole and Felicia left town to give Rudy a hand in Miami.

Petrini had been used to overseeing much larger projects,... although Rudy was doing incredibly well, his entire accumulated investments, and properties, couldn't even bring forth a reasonable challenge for Petrini.

Petrini admired Rudy's decision to hire a great number of x-felons.

He was really surprised to see how many African Americans that had been falsely accused of crimes and stamped with Felonies, turning a job search into an unreachable dream.

These x-felons showed more promise,... competence, and loyalty, than any of the so-called, squeaky-clean employees he had become accustomed to hiring.

This was one of his best idea's thought Petrini

A call came in from the manager of a Hotel that Rudy had Purchased, the Hotel had been attracting a bad element for quite some time, the previous owner had been shot to death, right there on the property.

The wife of the owner wanted nothing more to do with the place, so she sold the place dirt cheap.

If nothing else in Rudy's little Empire brought forth a challenge,.. this Hotel did.

He sat back with the x-Felon manager of the Hotel and watched room 610,.. people would come from other rooms and knock on 610's door, people were pulling up in cars, and heading to 610, none of them stayed long, and the traffic was continuous.

Maybe I should go up and say "Hi", said Petrini. I'll go with you, said the manager.

No, you stay here,... if these guy's are hot heads, there's no need for both of us to get caught up in their shit.

Petrini got out of the Elevator on the sixth floor; balcony side,... on the way to 610, he passed lookouts at each corner.

Everyone that came onto the sixth floor was being watched very carefully.

He knocked on the door, which was opened almost immediately, Petrini walked in, there were two guy's going over paperwork at the dining room table, another guy sat in the living area' on the sofa.

At a quick glance, Petrini saw that the place was clean, there were no signs of criminal activity, the lookouts had done their jobs well.

Petrini talked directly to the man on the couch.

My name is Orlan Petrini, I didn't get a chance to welcome you to my Hotel.

The man made an attempt to get up for a proper greeting.

Please, said Petrini, don't get up,... this isn't a social call,..I hope you've enjoyed your time here.

Yes, I have, said the man on the sofa,... the smirk on his face was non-intrusive,... our time here has been very promising,... in a few days I will call this a very promising endeavor.

I'd call it that now, said Petrini, unfortunately certain natural boundaries of respect have been crossed in the process,... you will be leaving at checkout time tomorrow.

The two men that were doing paperwork at the dining room table, looked at Petrini, then at each other, they both got up at the same time and headed in Petrini's direction.

The man on the sofa held up a hand, the Goon's stoppe in their tracks.

The authority in Petrini's voice, and the confidence in his stature, let the man know that one way or another, he was going to be leaving at checkout time tomorrow.

Thank you for your hospitality, said the man, I'll leave a little something to show my appreciation, please forgive the intrusion.

They all watched Petrini's every move until he had completely left the room.

We should have taught him a lesson, said one of the Goon's,... why'd you stop us?

He knows who we are,... he knows what we're doing,.. yet he's not afraid.

A mob boss that looks just like him was on trial a while back, he shouldn't be out of jail yet,... we leave at checkout time tomorrow.

Petrini appeared calm as he left the room, but for a brief moment there, he felt his mortality hanging in the balance,.. he hated this place, they worked hard to get rid of the negative publicity the place had been known for, and were being met with life threatening resistance every step of the way.

Petrini pulled into the driveway back at the house, and just sat there.

This was common place to him, he did it all the time, he'd gather his thoughts before getting out of the car.

While he was sitting there, the phone that had been silent for so long; began to vibrate as it lit up.

Petrini grabbed the phone immediately, he opened the phone; which was itself a locator, one half of the planet showed on the screen, this was a very far off Satellite view.

A small red light pulsed on and off like a beacon, the light pulsed on the Continent of South America.

He pressed a button and a closer view appeared on the screen,... once more, and he could see' the beacon was emulating from somewhere near the northern border of Paraguay,... he hit the button that said... SAVE SATILLITE IMAGE,... then he turned on the locator connection,... "Got Him", said Petrini.

A quiet calm came over him,... he closed his eye's for a moment and leaned back in his seat.

He picked up his cell phone and called Rudy.

Rudy, this is Orlan, I've just received a very important message, one that's going to require my immediate attention,... I'm going to have to leave for a while.

On the other end of the line; Rudy could sense what was going on.

Wait a minute, said Rudy,... don't tell me that funny little cell phone thingy has a contact on the other end.

Yes, it does, said Petrini.

Look, said Rudy, don't go running around by yourself, take Dwayne and Adrian with you, they can get you through anything that may happen to get in your way.

It seems I'm going to be leaving the Country!

In that case,... this one's on me, I'll set up an expense account in your name, you can head for the Airport now,... by the time they finish your passport, the guy's and everything else you'll need will be there,.. I've got just as much beef with this Marcus White character as you do.

I don't know how long I'll be gone, this could turn out to be a false alarm.

Check it out anyway, take all the time you need, there's no time limit on unfinished business,.. I'll shuffle the staff around to make sure everything's covered while you're gone,... get this thing straightened out,.. see ya when you get back.

Dwayne and Adrian met Petrini at the Airport, a flight was booked to Brazil,.. Pantanal City, then the train to Corumba.

This trip was like an adventure to Dwayne and Adrian, they had traveled Florida extensively, but anywhere out of the State was foreign.

They were both clean cut, well dressed guy's' their slim build with their chiseled muscular features gave them that Daring look.

Orlan was happy to have them with him, they were strait forward, they knew where they were going and was very protective of Orlan, he could tell they would thrive gracefully in any high tension situation,... and it was plain to see that they were with him all the way.

The plane touched down in Pantanal, they exited the plane out on the runway' instead of having the plane nose its way up to the terminal like it's done in the States.

The traveled light, they had each packed only one small duffle bag.

Petrini hurried toward a row of Taxi's that waited by the terminal off in the distance.

"Dwayne and Adrian glanced around at the terrain of the Country, you're not in Kansas anymore," said Adrian.

You got "that" right, replied Dwayne

They took the cab to the train station, the Country was so different, the air so fresh, there were so many loud and distinctive smells, the plant and insect life of Florida is rampant,... but nothing compared to this.

Automobile traffic was sparse, a lot more people walked, or rode bikes.

Animals were used to pull a great geal of the concession goods that flowed through' and set up on road sides.

The people seemed a little curious but were eagerly helpful.

They could tell at first glance that they were far from home.

No one spoke English, Petrini spoke Spanish and seemed to put together their Portuguese language good enough to get by.

They boarded the train and made it to Corumba in good time, from there' they were able to rent a car, a jeep wrangler' it proved to be just what they needed for the terrain in this part of the Country.

Petrini set the Cell locator on two-way,.. the original beep was there, and now a new red pulse showed up, the new pulse was their current location, the old pulse is the contact.

The distance scale calculated it to be just under 300 miles, they were closer than he'd thought.

When the two red dots come together, he would be at his destination.

The inconsistency of the roads took its toll on the trio, the roads would turn from paved to gravel, then to dirt, they ran into dead ends time and time again, they found this 300 mile trip to be more than they'd bargained for,... by the time they got to the Paraguay River, they were beat.

They stopped at a Township on the River' where they found a nice Hotel and were able to get a good hot meal, they got washed up, and readily bedded down for the night.

Petrini's two companions fell asleep immediately, but Petrini couldn't sleep.

He was dog tired, but rest would not come to him,..he went over his reason for being here a hundred times, and still couldn't find peace in it.

He picked up the phone and dialed.

Hey,.. I was wondering when I'd hear from you, said Rudy.

I was just calling to see if you've found that Chico character, said Petrini.

I've got a guy I'm tracking now,... I'm pretty sure it's him, but I've got to be absolutely sure before I move on him.

So, your plans for this guy haven't changed.

No, not this guy, my plans for him are Crystal clear.

When you get to be my age, I guess you think things over a little more,... you do understand that killing him, won't bring Chantell back.

How about if I let him live,.. will that bring her back. I guess not, said Petrini.

Then I don't see how I can spare him,... how about you, does that little locator thing work or what?

It's working just fine, I'm less than 200 miles from the location now,... the thing is, I'm dog tired but I can't sleep.

That's because what you're planning to do is bothering you,.. you've got to make a decision,.. its ok to change your mind,.. I've done this before, and whether it's self- defense, justice, or revenge, either way, your soul is damaged.

God "will" forgive all sins, but even though you've been forgiven,... the sins still have to be paid for,.. if you want to change your mind; it's ok you know,.. you know where he is now, we can visit him later if you like,... but whatever you do,... don't go into this undecided,... you'll lose.

It was late in the afternoon when Petrini finally woke from the deep sleep he'd fallen into.

He was fully refreshed; his head was clear as a bell, he felt the vigor of life pushing him forward into the day, his two sidekicks weren't in their rooms, they were already up and out.

Petrini took the jeep and set out to gather supplies,.. he didn't remember making a decision, but his direction seemed clear enough, he hadn't had one thought of turning back.

Dwayne and Adrian were at a little Tavern across the street from the Hotel.

They were being held up in the dimly lit little joint by two Brazilian females, the girls were gorgeous, they seemed to be enjoying their new friends immensely.

Petrini sat at the bar and chatted it up with the Bartender,... this map you have here, it looks as if you can go straight through due west from this point,.. but west from here goes straight into the Mountain range,... the main road through the Mountains has been washed out in several places by the landslides from last year's rainy season and is un-drivable,... only the most seasoned travelers can navigate their way through, there are many dead ends, and there's nothing up there,... no rest stops,

No place to take care of any mechanical failures,... I would suggest you keep heading South along the river, and cross over on the Questor Bridge here, he explained while tracing the route out on the Map with his finger,... it'll add another forty miles to your trip, but it's a lot safer; and it's a very scenic route.

The information received seemed sound enough to take under consideration.

By the looks of things, Dwayne and Adrian were not going to want to hear anything he had to say right now,... they were getting along extremely well with the young ladies, the language barrier didn't seem to be much of a problem, human nature had taken over at this point.

They made plans to stay another night; on behalf of their newfound friends.

Petrini used this time to rest and rearrange their schedule.

The next morning, they bid the girl's farewell, making promises to see them again soon.

Petrini slid the duffle bag between the two men.

I went and picked up some supplies, he said. Dwayne opened the bag.

Damn, he said as he gazed inside.

There were two fully automatic weapons, and four Semi- Automatic handguns inside,... they both grabbed a handgun and inserted the clips, then proceeded to conceal the weapons on their person so they would be unnoticed.

I rearranged our schedule, said Petrini, the bartender suggested we follow the River South to avoid the unmanageable terrain that we would encounter if we headed West like we'd planned.

Dwayne and Adrian looked at each other.

The "Bartender" gave you directions, asked Dwayne? Yes, said Petrini,.. something wrong.

It's just that these people know that we're a long way from home, that makes us easy Mark's, what we have on our side is the fact that we have our own plans,.. we should keep our eyes open, just to be safe.

After they had been stamped with Felonies in the U.S., Dwayne and Adrian were unemployable, they were forced to scratch out a living at Ground Level, that place where man meets man, words and intentions give clues that must be paid attention to, one mistake can be stunning.

One more look at the map and they all agreed,... the man had spoken the truth, the directions he'd given had proven to be the soundest of all.

As they traveled the route, they found it was also scenery friendly, there were plenty of Townships along the River, some big, some small,.. others were as stragglers, small groups that gave the impression they wouldn't be there on the return trip.

They were happy they had taken the longer' but safer route, instead of heading out across the Mountains, they were able to stop at will' in places that provided the basic necessities.

Later on, they ran into the part of the River Route that was uninhabited, the stretch was heavily wooded, the weeds ran rampant on either side of the road.

In the late afternoon,... up ahead in the distance, a barricade had been stretched completely across the road, two men in Uniform; with Rifles strapped across their shoulders manned the Barricade.

Their hands went up in the direction of the Jeep, signaling for them to stop as the Jeep approached them.

They each left one hand on their Rifle strap.

Adrian brought the Jeep to a stop directly in front of them,.. Petrini was in the passenger seat, Dwayne had the back seat.

One of the men removed the Rifle from his shoulder and leveled it out on the Jeep, he had all the passengers of the Jeep covered.

How can I help you, said Petrini, in his best Portuguese- Spanish.

The second man headed toward Petrini, rambling something in Portuguese.

You are not from here, the man was saying. No, said Petrini,.. just passing through.

We're going to have to check you're Travel Certificates. Everyone in the Jeep flashed their Passports.

The man glanced at the Documents' then shook his head.

No, you need Certificate to travel through "South" Brazil.

These are the only Certificates we have, said Petrini.

The man took two steps backward, and removed the Rifle from his shoulder.

Step out of the vehicle please.

They all stepped out of the Jeep,.. they were lined up on the side of the road.

Place your hands on top of your heads.

I take it your Bartender friend didn't happen to mention anything about this, Dwayne whispered to Petrini.

The man then pulled a cloth bag from his back pocket and stepped in front of Petrini.

Remove everything from your pockets and place them in the bag,... car keys too.

As Petrini began stripping himself of all his possessions.

Dwayne and Adrian began to understand what this actually was,... a simple robbery.

As they cast a suspicious eye on the Duo, they noticed the men wore make-shift Uniforms.

They wore different belts, they didn't even carry the same type of weapons, these were the most essential parts of a Uniform,.. there was no guard shack, nowhere to use the restroom.

The Barricade was a regular sawhorse with an extended two by four, as to block off the whole road,.. which was itself in the most desolate area possible, there would never be a checkpoint in such a place.

The man that held the gun on them was far more interested in keeping track of how much loot was being put into the bag,.. by the time he noticed the movement from the corner of his eye, he knew he should have been paying closer attention to his hostages,... he swung the rifle around just in time to hear a shot being fired, his left arm went limp immediately, the Rifle barrel fell onto the road, the other hand still had a finger on the trigger as he stared into nothingness.

Blood rushed from the hole in the man's forehead,.. he was still standing there as two more shots caught the man with the cloth sack.

They both fell to the ground at the same time.

The whole thing happened so fast, Petrini didn't know what was happening,... the commotion startled him so bad he backed into a ditch that ran alongside the road behind him.

He came out of the ditch brushing himself off and in a wild frantic state.

Oh God, what have you done, Petrini yelled,... we'll never get out of here, their whole force is going to be after us!

Relax, said Dwayne, as they were dragging the bodies into the brush along the roadside.

This was just a simple robbery.

The whole check point had disappeared within a matter of seconds, without a trace.

Petrini had found a new respect for his escorts, he even felt safer; after they had assured him that the men weren't part of the Military, or any other Government faction.

These guys 'waiting for us out here in the middle of nowhere, could have been the result of my conversation with that Bartender," said Petrini.

They both looked at him condescendingly... "Ya Think", said Adrian.

They all laughed.

At any rate, said Petrini,... I like the way you guys handled the situation.

Yeah, said Dwayne, normally, being it was just a robbery, I would have let them get away,.. but we're in the middle of nowhere, and weather you know it or not, they "were" going to take the Jeep,.. that's what got them killed,.. sorry, but I'm not gonna be stranded in this place, no fucking way.

Well, just to be on the safe side,.. lets get out of here, said Petrini.

They sped away from the scene, putting as much distance as possible between them and the Robbers.

Continuing South along the River, they reached the Bridge by nightfall, once on the other side, the red pulsing dots of the locator, once again began moving toward each other.

They drove all night, the roads leading toward the unmoving red dot got worse and worse, at no time were they able to move at a speed over 30 miles per hour, the roads were bad, but the darkness was the thing that was giving them so much hell, visibility was too low to navigate this terrain at normal speeds, they became even more paranoid when they almost drove off a cliff.

By morning they came upon a Township,... they decided to bypass the Town and continue heading toward their destination, they didn't see any need to have someone from the Town getting curious.

At their current rate, the dots will be right on top of each other in just a few hours.

At last,... the Jeep came to a stop, the dots had come together,... from a ridge' they looked over a very large Plantation' with fields that stretched for what seemed like miles.

There was a large house way off in the distance, but it was too far away to be where the signal was emanating from.

The signal's coming from that little house right there, said Petrini, pointing.

They looked the place over carefully,.. each worker in the field or any place that the signal may be coming from.

There was an older guy on the front porch of the little house, he was asleep in his chair, a Rifle leaned against

The porch banister.

The man was a native of the Country,... was it possible that he was the owner of the little house, a sharecropper or something, he looked more like a field hand, but he was way too old for such a chore.

He could be a guard, said Petrini.

Do you "actually" think that this Marcus White character, with all the money he's acquired,... would be in that little hovel,... no way, this has to be a mistake of some sort.

You're right,... Marcus White would be living the life of Riley,.. could my Wife live in that little shack,... not in a Million years, he said, answering his own question, not with the luxuries she's gotten used to over the years.

There may be someone at this location who knows where we're supposed to be looking," said Adrian.

"We've got to go down there," said Dwayne,.. this is where the signal's coming from.

There's a lot of people swarming around down there,.. it could be a trap, said Adrian,... you've been out of jail for quite some time, I know he's been informed of this, and he knows that you're gonna be looking for him,.. if he's gotten one of your operators, he could also have a locator,... this could be a set-up.

Just to be on the safe side, said Petrini,... we'll wait till all the field hands knock off for the day, then we'll see if we can find that other locator,... and whoever turned it on.

They stayed out of sight and watched the place through binoculars, checking out the comings and goings of the place, looking out for persons of interest' or anything that would justify them still being here.

"What's that out there in the field," asked Dwayne... I've never seen anything like that on a dirt farm, is it some kind of new irrigation system or something.

Everyone took turns looking over the giant piece of machinery out in the field through the binoculars.

That piece of machinery alone costs over three hundred thousand dollars, said Petrini,.. that's a state-of-the-art Chiller, there's no need for anything like that on this farm,... that machine can aerate, and control the climate in a six story building,.. what's it doing here?

Well, it's running, said Dwayne,.. I can see the water flowing down the front baffles.

I wonder what it's being used for, asked Adrian? Yeah,... I wonder, said Petrini.

Just before nightfall, the field hands all headed towards the workers quarters,... a man with an apron on, was standing in front of the Barn' yelling for them to come in.

The crisp clean air carried the pleasant aromas of the well-seasoned meal all the way up the ridge, reminding the trio that it had been quite a while since they had anything to eat, their mouths watered as they sat back, waiting for nightfall.

By twilight they had made their way around to the Chiller, a closer inspection showed the ventilation chutes running into the ground.

The only reason I can figure for this, said Petrini, would be a large underground Cold Storage, and anything stored underground that needs to be kept cold, is either very dangerous,.. or very illegal.

A six-foot Electrical box was at the other end of the field, Dwayne spotted it' and remembered that a lot of times in odd situations' the Electricians would tag each wire, indicating its purpose.

They walked around the box trying to figure out how to open it, there didn't seem to be a way to get in.

Adrian, out of curiosity' pressed his foot on a cutout at the bottom of the box, it moved inward,.. he pressed it until it clicked.

The door of the box swung open.

Once inside, they realized it wasn't an Electrical box at all,... it looked as if the box was put there just to cover what looked like a storm Cellar entrance.

They opened the storm cellar doors and looked inside,.. a ladder ran down the wall to the deck below.

You do realize, said Petrini,.. if we enter this place, we could be mistaken for robbers or thieves,.. and the language barrier may make it difficult to explain otherwise,... are you ready for this?

Adrian and Dwayne gave him a big smile,... lets go say "Hi".

At the bottom of the ladder, they found themselves in a dark corridor, they proceeded by flashlight, the corridor itself seemed to be going at a decline, they came to a ninety degree turn and proceeded downward' at what was figured to be about fifty feet down, they came upon a door that was locked.

Dwayne fumbled around in his gear, and the door was opened in no time, they went up a small set of steps to another door, this one wasn't locked.

They all stepped through the door,... and stood there,... they were all instantaneously suffering from the Alice in Wonderland Syndrome.

The Palace was an underground Marvel, they looked around the well-lit Chamber with open Mouths.

I think we're in the right place, said Petrini.

Cole, Rudy, and Felicia took turns watching the guy that they suspected of having murdered Chantell.

Tonight, Cole was on watch.

He followed the man like a bloodhound, the man made several stops at different houses, he spent some time at a local Mechanic shop, chatting it up with friends, then he picked up a dark haired female that was standing in front of a Gentlemans Club,... she appeared to be waiting for him, he dropped her off at yet another house, then he was off to a Paint shop, he had the key to the building.

Cole saw the name of the Painting Company printed across the front of the building, and couldn't believe it,... he took pictures of the place and left.

He dropped the photos on the table in front of Rudy and Felicia.

Check out the name of this Painting Company that our boy just happens to have the keys too.

Rudy looked at it, smiled, he read the name out loud,... J.D. & Manny's Painting Company.

That's our guy, said Rudy,... his little Painting Company is also a Memorial to J.D. and Manny,... he must be really choked up about his partners being killed in jail, and leaving him out here running around Scott free,..if anyone wants to back out,... now's the time.

The Little Havana Club was Chico and Marci's favorite hangout, they had become regulars there, it always had a nice crowd; and it was easy to get comfortable there,... Chico had gotten a couple of Painting contracts at the Club by just hanging out and talking to people who frequented the place.

They always sat at the Bar' in order to meet possible prospects for one thing or another.

Everyone in the Club made their way to the Bar at some point,... one conversation was in spanish,... Marci didn't speak Spanish, so she spent that time nursing her drink, and enjoying the music,... the Bracelet she wore, was a silver Black Widow Spider,.. the legs wrapped around her wrist, it was also a Cocaine dispenser, each time the stinger is removed, it comes out with a small spoonful of the product,.. she had gotten so good, she could snort even if she was in close proximity of other people, they'd never even know she was doing it.

She finished her drink after nursing it for what seemed like an eternity.

Chico would get her another drink as soon as he notices she had finished the first one.

He'd gotten tied up in conversation and hadn't been paying much attention, so she sat and waited' in the name of patience.

The lady sitting next to her, finished her drink and ordered another, she looked over and noticed the empty glass in front of the Black Widow girl.

And bring this young lady another round of whatever she's drinking.

Marci accepted the drink as she asked the lady her name. My name is Merda.

They struck up a conversation and before long' they were laughing, talking, and giggling like old friends.

After a few more drinks, they were even out on the dance floor together.

Marci introduced her to her Black Widow Spider Bracelet, in no time at all, Merda was using the stinger like a Pro.

As the night wore on, the frequency of the drinks and drugs increased,.. due to her newfound friend' Marci's Cocaine supply was getting dangerously low.

Chico's conversation had been over for quite some time,... he watched the girls from the Bar.

The Alcohol and Drug mixture caused them to dance very provocatively.

They made their way back to the Bar hand in hand, and very giddy.

Who's your new friend, asked Chico,... he saw the girl was getting wasted, and it didn't look like she was planning on slowing down.

Her name is Merda, said Marci.

He walked over and put his hand out to her.

Hi, Merda,... my name is Chico,... it's a pleasure to have you party with us tonight.

The pleasure is mine, said Merda, I'm having a great time.

Chico looked the woman over; she was a light skinned black female, she wore Micro-braids, Bo-Derek style,... she was pretty' with full lips, her skirt was a wrap-around Mini, it accentuated her legs perfectly, the tummy revealing blouse fit snugly, giving her breasts that extra lift.

Chico whispered in Marci's ear.

Do you think you can get her to leave here with us?

Marci recognized the tone of his voice, he had told her about a lot of the things he had done, mostly Tortures, but her favorite was what he'd done to a young Black girl, the things he told her were frightening' and intriguing at the same time,... sometimes he would whisper these things in her ear while making love,.. it always made her Cum.

She's getting pretty loaded, said Marci,..it should be easy.

Marci noticed the faraway look in his eye's as he watched the girl.

Are you gonna "do" her, asked Marci? You gonna help, he replied.

I can get her there, but,... I just want to watch.

They began to make plans,... Merda was so intoxicated they didn't even bother lowering their voices, he had been anticipating this,... he knew some day, this opportunity would present itself again.

They went back and forth over the plans, tying up all loose ends,... this time it'll be perfect.

His fondest dream was about to come true again,.. this time it will be a clean Torture, Rape, and Murder.

"Marci, let me check that Spider's stinger for any signs of a white powdery substance," said Merda.

We're all out, Marci replied,... here, drink this.

Merda took the drink, but wasn't at all satisfied.

We're gonna need some more Coke guy's,... I can call my dealer, he'll bring it right here to the Club, he's got the best stuff in Town.

Go ahead and give him a call, said Chico,... we're definitely going to need more Coke.

Merda made the call and set up the drop.

He'll be here in ten minutes, she said,... he's supposed to meet us in the parking lot.

I'll get a package from him too, said Chico,... the best in town huh.

Yeah, said Merda,... you're gonna love it.

Petrini knew, as he and his two escorts gawked at the Awesome structure they'd stumbled into, that they were in the right place,... the Butterflies raced around in his stomach when he realized that a place of this Magnitude, considering its purpose,... shouldn't have been that easy to gain entry.

When Marcus White worked for me, said Petrini,.. he did a lot of different jobs,... he was also head of Security, he loved lasers and motion detectors.

Before anyone moved, Adrian scanned the area in front of them with a flaslight,... no signs of a laser showed up,... he turned and checked the area around the door they had just came through,... the flashlight stopped on a red beam that ran across the bottom of the door, he scanned up' to find a row of red beams that ran from the bottom of the door, all the way to the top, at six inch intervals.

He knows we're here, said Petrini, "We need to find him, now.

They split up, Petrini took one corridor, Dwayne and Adrian took the other.

Marcus White heard the Security Alert; he hurriedly went to check it out on the Monitor,... the

Emergency escape Route Alarm is where the signal originated.

Jhe scanned the lower level by Monitor until he saw them, he saw two Black guys' moving slowly and carefully up the corridor in his direction.

Were they thieves or what,... they had to be,... they had somehow found out about his escape Route entrance and had mistakenly stumbled upon his underground Treasure.

At first glance, these guy's appeared to have that Americanized persona, but the thought of someone from the United States finding him,... was impossible,.. they were just looters' that's all.

The precautions he'd taken in building this secret hiding place were too elaborate,.. sure, Petrini would be looking for him, but that won't be for another 25 to 30 years.

Marcus sounded the alarm in the sleeping quarters of the field hands... at this time of year, there were forty men on staff at all times.

That particular alarm was for Emergency situations that required their presence immediately... the men came running.

Marcus informed them about the intruders, and had them arm themselves with knives, clubs, or whatever was handy.

Since he never saw the two Black men with weapons of any sort, his plan was just to outnumber them, and whip their asses,.. Good.

That should teach them not to ever come snooping around here again, Marcus said to himself.

He led the workers inside the small house, they all crowded into one of the rear rooms, which in fact turned out to be an Elevator,... the whole room went downward. The doors opened and the men stepped out into the Great Palace below.

The workers were Awestruck, they had heard rumors about a big plush Basement under the small house that was topside... but this was far beyond anything they had ever heard.

They were pointed in the direction that would lead them to the two intruders.

They ran noisily in that direction, Clubs and knives in hand.

Marcus let them go ahead, he headed for the study, to get his firearm from his desk drawer.

He'd decided, the two intruders weren't only going to get a good ass whipping,... a harsh example will be set today.

Marcus entered the study and headed toward his desk; he stopped in his tracks as the high-backed Chair behind his desk began to turn toward him.

Marcuse's blood ran cold when he saw Petrini sitting before him, Petrini's handgun zeroed in on him.

I'm glad you dropped in, said Petrini,... you've been on my mind a lot lately,... I would have gotten here sooner, but the Warden frowns at the thought of me leaving the Prison area,... for "Any" reason,... this is a nice hiding place you have here, you must be proud.

Marcus knew the game, if you're going to kill someone, go ahead and kill them, it's dangerous to allow someone whose life is on the line, time to think.

The fresh Country air, and hard work had made Marcus physically superior to most men.

He lunged forward and tipped the desk over on top of Petrini, who was caught by surprise, he fired a shot at Marcus as the heavy desk overcame him, the shot went over Marcus's head.

Petrini fell backward as the weight of the desk took him to the floor,... Marcus was on top of him immediately, wrestling the gun from his hand.

Petrini gave up his frantic attempt to free himself from under the desk, when he looked up, and into the barrel of his own gun.

One good thing has come out of this, said Marcus, smiling,... I'll never have to look over my shoulder again,... good bye old man.

Petrini closed his eyes.

Dwayne and Adrian stopped and listened,... something was coming their way, the noise got louder, and louder.

They started easing backward as the mob came into view, they would not be able to get away from them.

The men were armed with knives, Machetes, Clubs, and other harmful tools, and they were coming full speed.

Dwayne and Adrian both pulled out their handguns, and prepared to fight to the end.

As the mob stormed toward them, the duo opened fire into the crowd.

Men from the Mob began to fall,... Everything stopped,... the whole scene went silent.

Members of the Mob were shocked as they looked down on their fallen friends.

The sound of knives, Clubs, and other weapons were heard falling to the floor, as the men called the names of their friends that lay on the floor, and rushed to their sides, doing everything they could to help them.

Dwayne stopped Adrian's forward progression.

Wait, he said,... these people are just field hands,... their not fighters, look at them,... they had no idea of what they were getting into, they've probably never been in a situation like this in their lives,... let them go.

The Duo stepped back' dropping their guns to their sides.

Six men had been wounded, most were superficial, but a couple were life threatening.

The men were gathering their wounded, when they all heard a shot from somewhere else in the Palace.

Petrini held his eye's closed, as he cursed himself for failing his Mission, the man he came here to drag retribution from, now held a gun to his head.

The shot filled the room, it was so loud that all Petrini could hear now was an intense ringing.

Am I dead, Petrini thought to himself.

There was a crash onto the back wall, hen a hard thump on the floor next to Petrini,... he opened his eye's,... it was Marcus White lying there, a pool of blood was gathering around his head.

From sheer reflex, Petrini immediately began pounding on the man's head, cursing him out loud.

A young girl, with a Winchester Rifle stepped into view, the Rifle was now pointing at Petrini.

Don't move, said Mica, she kept the Rifle pointed at him as she went over and retrieved the gun that Marcus White had.

Petrini kept his hands where she could see them,... she was shaking visibly,... it wouldn't take much to scare her into firing again.

I've never seen you around here before, said Mica, where'd you come from.

Her accent was one that was native to this Country, I'll just be honest with her, and hope for the best.

I've been trying to find this man for quite some time, said Petrini, pointing at Marcus,... a comrade of mine summoned me here.

No one knows this place is here,... no one could have possibly told you where it was.

My Comrade is here somewhere, he has a locator, like this one.

He handed her the Cell phone looking device,... I just followed his signal, it led me here.

Mica opened the device,... it was just like her's,... tears ran down her face as she fell to her knees.

Petrini had finally freed himself from the desk, one of his legs was sore, he sat rubbing it,... he looked up into her tear-filled eye's,... she was staring straight at him.

You're the one, she said, as she started hitting him passionately... where have you been, I didn't think you were ever going to come, I thought I was going to die here,... I've sent out a locator signal every three Months for over a year, why didn't you come?

She was bawling her eye's out,... and still hitting him.

He had to grab her hands to stop her from pounding him.

The signal that I recieved Seven days ago, was the only one that I was able to lock onto, said Petrini,... the signal came from you?

She freed herself from his grasp, and wiped her face with her hands, she pulled her hair back, gaining her composure.

I am your Comrade, she said.

Petrini noticed the numerous scars, cuts, and bruises that had healed over recent years, even her wrists and ankles were badly bruised,... he began to understand the hatred that this young girl felt toward the man that lay on the floor.

The lady that came here with Marcus,... does he beat her also, asked Petrini?

No,... he doesn't spend much time with her,... he gets off when he's doing things that are naturally forbidden.

Is she here now? Yes,... I'll take you to her.

Petrini's leg was throbbing with pain,.. Mica put his arm around her neck, and acted as a crutch,... as they left the study they ran into Dwayne and Adrian, who were still running around the place trying to find out where that last shot had come from.

Mrs. Petrini sat at her Vanity in the Master Bedroom' far away from all the goings on in the other side of the Palace, she was slowly brushing her hair,.. her reflection in the mirror showed pure perfection.

One glance at the security monitor earlier' when she heard the alarm, showed signs of trouble, she put her faith in the man of the house.

He had a lot of hired hands at his disposal,... whatever the problem he always came through.

Mica walked into the Master Bedroom' she passed Mrs. Petrini, and stopped in the center of the room.

Mrs. Petrini followed her with her eye's, trying to figure this odd behavior.

Mica glanced at the door,... Mrs. Petrini followed her line of sight, and sensed that someone else was coming in.

Petrini stepped into the room.

Her heartbeat raced out of control' it was all she could do to keep from fainting, she fought to keep her facial expression from showing the Damnation that she knew was hers.

You're hurt, she managed to say.

What,.. this, he said, pointing at his leg,... this is nothing, you should try getting hurt by the people you love and trust more than anything in the world,... that really hurts, and unfortunately,.. it doesn't heal.

Mrs. Petrini got up and slowly walked out of the room,... with Mica's help, Orlan followed her,.. Dwayne and Adrian were standing at either side of the door, they fell in behind Orlan and trailed them from behind.

She walked slowly so Orlan could keep up.

He walked behind her; she was still the sexiest girl he'd ever laid eyes on, the designer dress fit perfectly,... her pumps were custom made.

I take it' you've already talked with Marcus, she said, without turning around or stopping.

Yeah, said Orlan. Where is he?

He won't be joining us.

She went into the library and sat down at the computer,... she didn't have to be coerced into replacing the funds back into Orlan Petrini's account, she did so without concern,... when everything was back in place, it was then that she looked into Orlan's eye's,... her eye's weren't hard, as he had expected they would be.

Nor were they soft.

I'm not going to beg your forgiveness.

Orlan checked the Money transfer to ensure it had been successfully replaced, he gave Adrian the head nod, and left the room with Mica under his wing,... Dwayne stood outside the door.

The woman met eye's with Adrian,.. then glanced toward the door, but Orlan was gone, she was still sitting at the computer.

Adrian walked over and stood behind her,.. she didn't look back or make any attempt to move, she looked straight ahead, one hand lay inside the other in her lap.

Adrian put the gun to her head and cocked the hammer,... she flinched a little at the sound it made.

Adrian sent up a silent prayer for her.

The force of the high Caliber handgun slammed her face violently into the computer keyboard,... her arms lay limp at her sides.

Adrian turned out the lights as he left.

A badly beaten and terrified little girl stood before Orlan. "This is Celia," said Mica.

As he looked at her, he fought to keep his eye's from watering,.. seems there was one emotional trauma after another, his heart felt like it weighed a ton,.. He wondered if he would be the same after this trip.

Hi Celia, said Petrini.

The drug dealer pulled into the parking lot of the Club Havana,... Merda flagged him down as he entered, Chico noticed the White Toyota S.U.V., was a rental.

He was surprised to see the drug dealer was a white guy. Get in, said the dealer.

They all climbed into the vehicle and found a remote parking space to conduct business.

You got the Fifty sack, right, said Merda.

I gotcha, he replied.

And give me an 8 Ball, said Chico.

Who are these people, the dealer asked Merda. Their cool, she replied.

Well, I only brought your Fifty sack,.. we're gonna have to make a run to get that 8 Ball,..I'll have you guy's back in no time.

After ridind for over twenty minutes, they finally pulled onto a remote trail,... their was high brush growing on either side of the dirt road,... only one light shone ahead in the distance.

There was a figure standing in the middle of the road; near the light.

The dealer stopped the car.

We should walk up from here, he said.

The headlights were left on, bringing forth the very much needed light, they stopped in front of the man,.. the dealer pushed Chico and Marci in front of the man.

This is the man you need to see, he said.

Chico reached into his pocket and pulled out a small wad of cash, he peeled off two one Hundred Dollar Bills.

They tell me you've got the best stuff in Town, said Chico,... I want the best 8 Ball you got, I don't want none of that shit that's been stepped on over and over again,... I want the good shit.

Chico held the money out for the man.

The man glanced down at the money, then back up at Chico.

That's not why I had you brought here Chico, said the man.

Merda stepped up to Marci,... she put the barrel of her pistol just above her ear, and pulled the trigger.

The red mist, missed no one, as it sprayed from both sides of her head, her body fell to the ground as if frozen, it appeared to be trying to say something.

"Merda" , screamed Chico,... what the fuck have you done, you shot Marci, you fucking killed her.

He charged toward Merda,... Cole backhanded him with his pistol, he wobbled back and forth, looking confused.

I "killed" her, how can you even say that,.. is that not what you, and that Psycho Bitch had planned for me, said Merda, through clinched teeth, you were planning to do me; just like you did my friend in Tampa,... Merda's not my name,.. "Murder", is why I'm here, said Felicia.

Rudy hadn't moved, he was just waiting till things calmed dow a little,... Chico noticed his candor, that's the dangerous one, he thought to himself, Chico pretended to be incoherent, he staggered and swayed, getting closer to the edge of the path, suddenly he sprang into the brush without warning,.. no one fired a shot because Rudy was right behind him.

Rudy charged into the brush behind him, it was too dark to see anything, he fought his way through using his hands to clear his path, he stopped for a second to listen,.. ahead he could hear branches breaking.

He followed the sound at as fast a pace as possible, before long he was able to see the moonlight shining up ahead.

There was a clearing, it sounded as if Chico was heading in that direction.

Rudy cleared the last row of trees before entering the open ground,.. he caught a glimpse of the limb that was coming at him, but it was too late,.. the limb hit him on the side of the head, "hard".

Rudy fought to stay conscious, he fell to the ground, everything was whirling, he couldn't find his balance' his vision was playing tricks on him, his eyes were producing spots that were moving in all directions' he knew he had to get up as soon as possible,.. he could see a figure moving through the spots that his vision was producing.

The figure wasn't coming toward him, then the figure bent down and picked up an object,... it was a gun.

It was then that Rudy realized he didn't have his gun, it must have fallen from his hand on impact from the limb, now Chico had it.

Rudy's movements were unsteady as he tried to get back into the dark brush.

Chico was taking aim in his direction as Rudy ducked behind a tree and picked up a rock, this was his last line of defense.

He could see Chico coming in his direction from around the tree, he was poised to throw,... suddenly a Shadow came over Chico, he was fighting it off with all his might.

It was too dark to see what was happening, Chico was screaming and fought viscously to free himself from the Shadow that moved violently across his upper body,... he was being attacked by some sort of animal,.. what was it?, a Badger,.. a Bobcat.

Chico finally freed himself and ran screaming in the direction that he had entered the thick brush.

Rudy saw the gun when he threw it while trying to get his attacker off his face.

Rudy hurried and got the gun' then went after Chico once more.

When Rudy stepped back onto the road, Felicia and Cole held Chico in their gun sights,.. he stood there with his hands up, the deep cuts and Lacerations on his face and neck, his shirt was soaked in blood,.. when he saw Rudy, he fell to his knees.

Hey, look here, said Chico,... that girl in Tampa,... she was a whore, that's all she was, a dirty stinking whore, she didn't mean nothing to no one,... she wasn't shit.

Her name is Chantell, said Rudy, she's been a part of my life since the day she was born, she was one of the most precious things that God has ever created,... that's why I find what you just said about her,... very,... very, offensive.

Rudy's gun went off,.. Chico clutched his midsection,.. Felicia's gun went off, Chico fell to his side,.. Cole's gun went off.

From a distance, all that could be seen was three small flashes of light,... those three flashes went off. Over, and over, and over.

Petrini had managed to get in and out of South America pretty much unnoticed, the same was true for Rudy, they both had managed to return unscathed.

They all met at Dally's place on their return,... they were to stay there for a few day's to go oner anything that may come up concerning their whereabouts during certain periods of time.

The first night there, the gathering that started out as a meeting of the minds, turned into an Engagement Party, when Felicia accepted Rudy's proposal of Marriage.

One would have thought that Dally was the proud Father of both the Bride and the Groom.

Petrini announced the fact that he was going into retirement, he put Dwayne and Adrian in charge of his future financial endeavors,... and he was legally adopting both Mica and Celia,... they would both be starting on their Ivy League Educations in a private facility in the fall,..Petrini could barely take two steps without Mica, she stayed just as close to him as his Shadow, she takes care of him like he's the only person in the world that she can always count on.

The evening was more Spiritual than Festive,.. the scars were too fresh, too deep.

They touched everyone in the room, it was shared by all.

Rudy was up early the next morning; Dally was in the kitchen cutting a fish into bite sized portions.

Fish this morning, asked Rudy?

This is for Cain,.. He's been gone for over a week,.. he just showed up here yesterday, boy was he hungry,... he seemed to be favoring his foot,... if it's hurt bad, he's not gonna be up for hunting.

They walked outside and had barely reached the stoop when they saw Cain heading their way' he was waiting at the tree line at the edge of the property.

He landed lightly on one foot and dug into the fresh fish breakfast.

Something "is" wrong with that foot, said Rudy.

We'll check it out in a minute, said Dally,... he gets kinda testy if you bother him while he's eating.

On closer inspection, they saw something protruding from the middle toe, just above the Talon,.. a pin of some sort.

He should have been able to pull that out himself, said Dally.

"I know he's tried," Rudy replied.

That things going straight through the middle of the toe, that means it went straight through the bone,... no wonder he couldn't get it out.

Okay, you hold him, and I'll pull it out,.. We gotta do this fast, or he'll panic.

The pin was removed quickly, but obviously, still painfully,.. Cain flew back to the tree line.

The pin had a big back end, Rudy rubbed the dirt and blood from one spot,.. it was shiny underneath, he went to the faucet and washed it off,... it was a Diamond Stud earring,.. he looked closer' and inside the Diamond, he could see a working Fountain,... this earring belongs,.. this is Chico's earring, he was wearing it when,.. how the hell,.. the animal that attacked Chico when he was about to shoot me,... "CAIN" .

www.ingramcontent.com/pod-product-compliance
Lightning Source LLC
LaVergne TN
LVHW021756060526
838201LV00058B/3114